ACCLAIM FOR THE NOVELS OF CHARLENE TEGLIA

"This is great erotic fiction! . . . Fresh, sexy, and humorous."
—*Romantic Times BOOKreviews*

"Action-packed and ferociously seductive."
—*Romance Reviews Today*

"If you haven't heard of Charlene Teglia, you soon will. . . . An absolute winner."
—*Romance Divas*

"A great book full of action and adventure . . . Charlene Teglia has a knack for creating wonderful stories with characters that will keep readers coming back for more."
—*Romance Junkies*

"Don't miss out on this incredible new talent."
—*Love Romances*

"A must read."
—*The Road to Romance*

"A gem of a tale."
—*Fallen Angel Reviews*

"Ms. Teglia is a terrific writer who has penned a story of love and magic that left me sighing at the end."
—*Just Erotic Romance Reviews*

"As usual, Ms. Teglia's sex scenes were small doses of TNT and the tension was perfect."
—*Ecataromance*

"I laughed, then I sighed and had tears in my eyes at the end . . . a book I intend to read again and again!"
—*Joyfully Reviewed*

Also by Charlene Teglia

Wild Wild West

Satisfaction GUARANTEED

CHARLENE TEGLIA

St. Martin's Griffin ❧ New York

This is a work of fiction. All of the characters, organizations, and events portrayed in this novel are either products of the author's imagination or are used fictitiously.

www.stmartins.com

Book design by Spring Hoteling

Library of Congress Cataloging-in-Publication Data

Teglia, Charlene.
    Satisfaction guaranteed / Charlene Teglia.—1st ed.
      p. cm
    ISBN-13: 978-0-312-36945-3
    ISBN-10: 0-312-36945-X
  1. Dating services—Fiction. 2. Seattle (Wash.)—Fiction. I. Title.

PS3620.E4357S28 2008
813'.6—dc22

                                2007042122

First Edition: March 2008

10 9 8 7 6 5 4 3 2 1

Dedicated to my own hero of a thousand faces,
who helps me get guy stuff right

Acknowledgments

Thanks to the Wicked Writers, to Jordan and Sam for speed-reading and giving feedback in a crunch, and to the husband for technical support and emotional support and rigging up endless workarounds during all the power outages that happened during the writing of this book. A big thank-you also to Rose for patience and encouragement!

Satisfaction
GUARANTEED

Hard
MATCH

One

"You've been staring out the window for ten minutes," said Sabrina. "Since the view isn't that exciting, you must be taking a mental trip. Where'd you go? Tahiti? I'd go to Tahiti. I bet it's not raining in Tahiti."

"I think it rains in Tahiti, too," Rachel Law answered, but in an absent tone. She continued to stare blindly out the window at the drizzle that was characteristic of Seattle's winter weather.

"Winter's getting to you," Sabrina said. "And it's worse for you than it is for me, because you're a blonde. Blondes are supposed to have more fun. You are not having fun. You work all the time because you wanted that promotion, and you got it, and now you're just staring out the window wondering if it rains in Tahiti. You need to do something fun."

"Fun." Rachel wondered if Sabrina had a point. When was the last time she'd done something just for fun? Lately she'd had the nagging sense that something was missing.

The promotion hadn't cured it. Maybe what she was missing was fun.

Dark-haired Sabrina Daniels wasn't heading for early burnout, and she was always taking off to either ski or sail on weekends, depending on the season. She also liked to skydive. And lately she'd been mentioning cruises a lot.

Skiing and sailing weren't really Rachel's ideas of fun, and the very thought of skydiving nauseated her, but a cruise had potential. Seattle was a popular place for cruises to start and stop. It'd be convenient and easy to book a short cruise. Rachel considered the possibility. "Maybe I should do that three-day Baja cruise you were talking about."

"Excuse me. Are you Rachel? Rachel Law? Or have aliens taken over your body and left a strange being in place who wants to experience planet Earth outside of this office?"

"Ha ha," said Rachel. She stopped staring out the window and turned to look at Sabrina. "I like having a corner office. I worked hard for this office. I sold a lot of insurance to get this office."

"Yes, you are the golden girl, and the home office loves you." Sabrina picked a random award off the top of Rachel's bookcase and buffed it with her sleeve. "You're number one. You are now the regional sales manager, and you left three of the top men in this company choking on your dust. I'd envy you, since I'm destined to remain forever number two and in your shadow, but I'm not the one who says 'fun' in a voice that sounds like you've forgotten what it is."

Sabrina probably had a lot of fun, Rachel thought wistfully. Fun that included the opposite sex. There had been a man involved on more than a few of her ski trips, and Rachel suspected they hadn't spent much time on the slopes. And there was another man Rachel was pretty sure hadn't just liked to take Sabrina sailing.

Although now that she thought about it, over the five years she'd known the outgoing brunette, a couple of men didn't seem like very many. And how long had it been since Sabrina had mentioned the most recent man?

"What happened to Richard?" Rachel asked, wondering when he'd faded out of the picture and why she hadn't noticed. Of course she'd been busy, but—too busy to notice who her closest friend was dating?

"The truth?" Sabrina put the sales award back down and threw herself into the comfortable leather chair on the opposite side of Rachel's desk so that they faced each other over the gleaming cherry expanse. "I asked him to play pirate and Spanish prisoner with me. I should have known better. Richard was not adventurous or creative in bed. Of course he wouldn't be interested in role-playing."

"I thought he was interested in *you*," said Rachel.

"Well, I thought so, too, but not interested enough. My fantasy of playing captive while he played pirate on his boat went down like the *Titanic*. Richard couldn't get rid of me fast enough. He suddenly remembered a presentation he had to make on Monday and never called again. I called once, and he was too busy to talk. Said he'd call back. That was in September."

Sabrina swung one leg back and forth, pausing to admire her shoes midswing. "I don't think he's going to call back. Do you?"

"Forget Richard," said Rachel. "Tell me about the Spanish prisoner thing."

"He's forgotten. And I'm not a deviant or anything." Sabrina pouted, managing not to look like an idiot in the process.

Rachel was pretty sure if she tried to pout, she'd look like a sulky six-year-old. Sabrina just looked sexy as she continued, "But, you know, those pirates had English authority to seize ships, and of course they seized Spanish ships because they had the gold. Suppose an innocent and sheltered Spanish maiden happened to be on board, where she'd fall into the hands of a wicked pirate . . ." Sabrina let the sentence trail off and waggled her eyebrows suggestively.

Rachel sat up, fascinated. "He'd carry her off. She'd be his prisoner. And he'd try to be noble at first, maybe, but she'd have to stay in his cabin because there would be all those unruly, sex-starved crewmen."

"Right." Sabrina grinned at her. "Or maybe he'd just order her to his cabin to strip and tell her she'd better be good in bed, amazing, the best he'd ever had, or he'd give her to the first mate. Who would of course be hot, and hung, but not quite as hot as the captain. Ooh, maybe she'd have to do both of them. At the same time."

Rachel felt her eyebrows shoot up along with her body temperature and her interest level. "Kinky."

"Hot." Sabrina fanned herself with an insurance flyer. "If I keep talking about this, I'm going to need to buy more batteries on my way home."

Sabrina wasn't the only one, Rachel thought. She couldn't remember when she'd last replaced the batteries in the bullet vibrator Sabrina had given her two years ago for Christmas, saying that naughty girls needed something from

Santa, too. After this conversation, she was going to need the bullet operational.

She dragged herself back to the present with an effort. "So you told Richard about this and he ran away?"

That seemed unbelievable. It was one hot fantasy. Why hadn't it gotten Richard's attention? It certainly had hers.

"He ran like an Olympic track star. But it's okay, I'm not bitter. I stole three of his accounts the next week." Sabrina gave her a feline smile outlined with cinnamon lipstick. Rachel found herself grinning back and then laughing out loud.

"Spanish prisoner," said Rachel when she'd stopped giggling. "Now that sounds fun. Too bad I can't book a cruise with that package."

"Well . . ." Sabrina gave her a thoughtful look. "Maybe you can. Look at this." She reached for her slim leather briefcase, pulled out a brochure, and tossed it onto Rachel's desk.

Rachel picked it up. "The Capture Agency? What is that, something to do with image capture technology?"

"Oh, my God." Sabrina rolled her eyes. "You have officially been working too hard for too long. It's a dating agency. Computerized matching. Very accurate, very expensive, and very . . . unusual."

Unusual. Rachel opened the glossy brochure and started reading. She blinked a few times. Then she checked to make sure her jaw wasn't resting on her elegant cherry desk, straightened up, and looked at Sabrina. "This can't be for real."

"Oh, but it is. I picked up the brochure when Richard proved such a disappointment. The thing is, capture and bondage fantasies are very, very popular, but how do you find a partner who's into acting them out? I mean, you can't just bring it up at an office party. And casual dating, you don't want to risk bringing up something like that with someone you don't know well."

Sabrina tapped the brochure with one long polished nail, painted to match her lips. "The Capture Agency is the answer. All clients have to go through rigorous background checks, pass a complete physical, psychological profiling. The computerized matching is top-notch. They have a very high success rate for compatibility."

"You've really checked this out," said Rachel.

"Yep." Sabrina picked up the glossy brochure and used it like a fan, batting her eyelashes at Rachel over it. "I decided I want to experience the fantasy, and I'm not likely to just stumble over a man who wants to play pirate and prisoner with me. I've already paid the agency fee, and I'm going in for my final round of compatibility questionnaires. I'm specifying that I want a man with a boat, too. Might as well go all the way."

Go all the way. Rachel had a sudden, vivid image of going all the way with a fierce pirate. One who would use his dagger to cut her long, flowing dress all the way down the front and then order her to spread her legs. . . . She blinked and wondered when the office temperature had started to climb. It was winter. It shouldn't feel like a sauna inside.

"You want to do it, don't you?" Sabrina stopped playing with the brochure and sat forward, excitement making her brown eyes sparkle. "You don't want to take a cruise. You want to sign up for a trip to Sexual Fantasy Island."

"Maybe." Rachel squeezed her thighs together in an effort to alleviate the aching place between them that had started to throb in a way that told her just how much the capture fantasy interested her. "How do I know I wouldn't get set up with some kind of nut if I did this?"

"The screening," Sabrina answered promptly. "Capture fantasies are about seduction, not violence. Men with criminal records, histories of violence, or showing psychological warning signs of anger problems are screened out. You don't get that in the random dating pool."

"True." Rachel had to admit there were advantages to the agency approach. "Still, if I wanted a man to fulfill my fantasies, he'd have to be able to surprise me. That means he'd have to be smarter than me, or at least as smart. And I'm not average. That's hard to find."

"Yeah, we can't all be Mensa candidates." Sabrina rolled her eyes at Rachel. "Okay, so you want a man who's a few steps above conversations about microbrewed beer and football. A man who could think of ways to surprise you. Makes sense to me; seduction begins between the ears. In the mind. If a man can't engage your mind, it stands to reason he doesn't have much chance of engaging the rest of you."

"Which explains my social life lately," Rachel muttered.

"No, working all hours to get that promotion explains your social life lately," Sabrina countered. "There are plenty of men who are up to your speed. You just haven't been talking to them. Or if you were, you were trying to get their company to give their employees Opal Life Insurance."

"I'm sure it would have looked very professional to break off my presentation to ask if my prospect wanted to date me instead of becoming my new corporate account."

Sabrina gave her an exasperated look. "My point is, you haven't been paying attention to your social life. Until now.

Now you're showing an interest. That's good. You have to start somewhere. Start with a date who will fulfill your fantasies."

Rachel was showing a lot more than interest. She was pretty sure her panty hose was showing a telltale damp patch, and it was a good thing her lined skirt would hide the evidence.

A date who would fulfill her fantasies. Was it really possible? If it was, Rachel admitted to herself, an agency that specialized in matching compatible partners for fantasy fulfillment was her best bet, because Sabrina was right: It wasn't the kind of thing she could bring up at an office party or with somebody she didn't know well. Even if she met a man who wanted to capture her and make her his slave to passion, as the agency brochure worded it, neither of them could admit it in any normal social encounter.

Sabrina must have seen the look on Rachel's face that said she was ready to buy because the brunette leaned in to close the sale. "Come on, Rachel. You want this. You deserve this. What do you have to lose?"

"Five thousand dollars," Rachel answered promptly, quoting the agency fee.

"You can afford it," Sabrina said, dismissing that objection. "But do you know what I think you can't afford? To keep going on the way you have been. Work is wonderful, Rachel, but it won't keep you warm at night. And living out this fantasy would create enough heat to set your bed on fire. I can see how much you want to do it. So, do it. If the agency can't match you with a compatible man, they'll give you a full refund. It's right here in their policy statement."

Rachel read the statement Sabrina pointed to. "Satisfaction guaranteed?" She felt her lips twitch with barely suppressed humor.

"Well, they don't guarantee that you'll have great sex. Besides the fact that it's outside their control, there are legal implications to that. But they do guarantee that they'll provide you with a compatible match."

"Or a full refund?" The question from Rachel's doorway made both women turn. Emma Michaels, their office manager, stood there looking as if the file folders in her hands were the last thing on her mind. The first thing was apparently the brochure Sabrina and Rachel were focused on.

"Um, Emma, I'm not sure—" Rachel broke off and wondered how to avoid telling the woman who'd never slept with any man but her husband and had probably never owned anything battery-powered that wasn't a household appliance that they were talking about a dating agency for people who wanted to have kinky sex. "Thing is, it's a dating agency, Emma."

"For people who want to act out captor and captive fantasies. I heard."

Rachel blinked. "I don't think your husband would approve of you signing up."

"I don't think it's any of his business if I want to date. He lost the right to disapprove when he slept with his assistant," Emma said.

Rachel looked at Sabrina and mouthed, *Did you know about this?*

Sabrina gave an almost invisible negative shake of her head in response.

So Emma's bombshell was a surprise to both of them. It did explain why Emma had become so uncharacteristically tense and silent. Rachel had suspected some trouble at home, but not on that scale.

"I'm sorry," Rachel said, her voice softened with sympathy. "But Em, you don't need to be hasty. You've never been with anybody else, and this might not be the best time for you to jump in at the deep end of the dating pool. You could start smaller, take a baby step."

Emma flinched visibly at the word *baby*. "No, thank you. I'm done waiting. I'm done asking for permission instead of asking for what I want. I may have failed in bed and in my marriage, but I don't have to fail myself. I don't have to repeat my mistakes." She took a deep breath, composing herself. "The fantasy date would be like a practice partner. I can explore what I really want, find out where I went wrong. Then maybe the next time around, if there is a next time, I can get it right."

Sabrina nodded, understanding clear in her expression. "That's not bad thinking. Have a fling under very clear and very safe circumstances. No misunderstandings, no complications."

Emma set her chin in a determined line. "Exactly."

Sabrina had a good point, Rachel decided. If Emma was going to walk on the wild side, at least she'd be doing it in a way that was least likely to get her hurt. And wasn't that what had pushed her own decision over the edge? The opportunity to have an adventure in safe circumstances? Gauging risk was her occupation, and as far as she could see, the risks posed by the Capture Agency were minimal.

"Well, I guess it's unanimous," Rachel said. "Here's to our fantasies, and the men who will fulfill them." She raised an imaginary glass in a toast, and the other two women followed suit.

Two

"You work too hard. You should take more time to play."

Chase Hunter glanced from his monitor's flat-screen panel to the open doorway of his office, currently decorated by Mark Lewis. Mark's flair for men's fashion was accentuated by a pose any male model would envy.

"Don't tell me, let me guess. You want to take me shopping again."

Mark rolled his eyes. "You make it sound like such a bad thing. I'm just trying to save you from your stuck-in-the-nineties look. But I didn't come in here to debate the merits of the latest winter fashions. I came to show you this."

Mark straightened up to wave a computer printout he'd had tucked behind his back. He sashayed across the office and placed it on Chase's desk with a flourish.

Chase knew what it was before he picked it up. He should. He'd designed the client information sheet printouts for the Capture Agency, along with the state-of-the-art compatibility matching software. He just didn't expect to see his name on it.

"Mark." The tone of his voice said it all.

"I know, I know. You don't mix business and pleasure. You run the business, you don't date the clients. But this is a hard match, Chase. We had nobody in our database that came close for compatibility. We were going to lose the sale."

"So we lose a sale. We have plenty of other clients." Chase kept his voice level with an effort.

"Yes, but when in the five years you've owned this place have you ever had a match?" Mark persisted.

"I don't know. I don't check. I don't date clients."

"Well, I check for you. Once a month. Once a week if you're moodier than usual."

"I am not moody." Chase balled up the printout and tossed it into his wastebasket. He'd made a mistake in leaving his information from the software's early development stages in the test database if this was what Mark was doing with it. Chase made a mental note to delete the file. "Leave. Go search the Internet for the perfect sweater. I'll be here doing something radical called working."

"You know what they say." Mark placed his lips closer to Chase's ear and whispered, "All work and no play makes Jack a dull boy."

"So go worry about Jack." Chase focused on his monitor again, ignoring his assistant and right-hand man.

"I'll take care of Jack later, don't you worry. For now, let's talk about you. It's not just your wardrobe that's stuck in the nineties. You need a new interest. A new woman. This woman, for instance. She's a perfect match." Mark produced a second, pristine and uncreased copy of the printout. "The computer says so, and you should know it's never wrong."

In fact, Chase did know the computer was never wrong. His fuzzy logic software was revolutionary and incredibly accurate. Which still didn't mean he was going to date a client.

"Thank you, Mark." Chase took the second copy and folded it into a complex paper airplane before sending it after the first. It landed nose first in the trash. The sight gave him a brief sense of satisfaction. The plane's design was aerodynamically sound, and his aim had been accurate.

"You're just being stubborn." Mark retrieved the paper airplane and smoothed it out. "I signed her up. I took her money. I promised her a compatible date. You're compatible. So if you don't want to date her, you're going to have to tell her yourself."

He dropped the paper onto Chase's keyboard and headed for the door.

"I'm not going to call her," Chase said.

Mark held up a hand behind him. "Talk to the hand."

"That's very mature. I mean it. I don't date clients. I don't care how perfect she is."

Mark's silencing palm answered for him. Then he shut the door, leaving Chase alone with the printout.

He scowled first at the closed door, then at the sheet of paper covering his keyboard. In order to go back to work, he'd have to move it. Mark had left it that way to force him to look at the client sheet. Chase grudgingly admitted the strategy was sound. Annoying, but sound.

Behind the annoyance he felt a vague curiosity. Who was this perfect woman? Since he had to pick it up anyway, Chase took the printout and leaned back in his chair to read it.

Rachel Law. Hotshot sales professional, career woman, single. Smart. Chase looked over the section that showed her IQ and the special notes section that detailed any requirements a client had that didn't come up in standard compatibility testing. It told Chase at least part of why Mark hadn't come up with any other matches in the system. Ms. Law had an IQ of 130, which meant that only 2 percent of the population could meet her special request.

He read the note a second time and entertained himself briefly by calculating the odds that she'd find a compatible man anywhere outside this agency. A man who fit her other personality profile requirements for basic compatibility, shared interests and tastes, and equal or greater intelligence, who had a desire to experiment with dominating sex. The odds were astronomical.

Chase knew he was going to regret it, but he flipped over the page and looked at the photocopied image of her face.

It was her eyes that caught him: hazel, gold-flecked, and direct, with a hint of humor as well as the intelligence he'd expected. Her eyes were set off by a very nice face, with what his mother would call good bone structure. Blond hair worn in a sleek bob, not old-fashioned but not riding the edge of any fashion trends. Which Chase supposed made sense in her line of work.

She looked polished and professional, but not unapproachable. Direct, not the type to waste time or words. She'd probably be impatient with the games most people played in the dating scene.

Judging by her personality profile and her appearance, she'd appreciate being told the straight truth about her lack

of a match, and the sooner the better. She really was a lot
like him, Chase noted, abandoning the photo to read her results again. If he'd decided to sign up for a fantasy date, the
sooner he knew he was following a dead end, the sooner he
could begin to plan an alternative to reach his objective.

He leaned back in his chair and thought about Rachel
Law planning an alternative course. Might she experiment
with one of those BDSM lifestyle clubs? Those attracted
some pretty fringe characters. A woman who was new to
playing around could find herself in a bad situation with a
stranger who might not be trustworthy.

The idea bothered Chase. A lot. So, Mark would win.
He'd deliver the news to her personally that the Capture
Agency couldn't match her, warn her about taking risks
outside of the agency's safety measures, hope she met some
nice man with a high IQ who could surprise her as she'd
requested.

Chase had an IQ of 140. He could surprise her.

The thought was unwelcome, and Chase squelched it. He
was a match, no question. And he could surprise her, but that
didn't mean he should break his policy of not mixing business and his personal life. There were lots of good reasons for
that policy. Reasons that included ethical considerations and a
priority list that didn't allow time for a relationship.

Ms. Rachel Law had gotten along fine without the services of the Capture Agency until now, and she'd manage
without them in the future. Unless she elected to stay in the
system until another match came up. That was an option,
and he'd be sure to point it out to her. Then he could tell
Mark he'd done his best to save the sale.

Although Chase knew Mark's real goal wasn't to keep

the client. Evidently Mark was worried about his personal life. That worried Chase, because Mark was nothing if not persistent.

As if to confirm that realization, his intercom beeped and Mark's voice came over it. "She's waiting in Conference Room B."

Chase blew out a breath but otherwise didn't answer. He might have known Mark would keep her there, using her presence to push him into talking to her.

The office suite included several small conference rooms that could be used for first client meetings. The agency recommended that each matched pair of clients meet for the first time in a neutral public setting to preserve their privacy and give them a chance to decide whether they wanted to pursue a real date. Conference rooms could be scheduled for that purpose, or they could choose to meet for coffee if they preferred to size each other up away from the business atmosphere of the Capture Agency.

There was nothing suspicious about Mark showing a new client to a conference room to meet with a match. It might seem like amazing luck or too-good-to-be-true timing to Ms. Law that her candidate happened to be on hand. Knowing Mark, Chase was sure he'd answered any questions she had about that and left her waiting with the honest expectation that she was about to meet her agency date.

Chase wasn't looking forward to being the one to disappoint her.

Rachel shifted in her chair, toyed with the cup of coffee sitting on the table in front of her, and let her eyes wander around the small room again. Soft beige walls, fluorescent lighting, framed photographs of Mount Rainier capped with snow and the Space Needle lit up at night. The Berber carpet was thick, well padded, and a mix of earth tones that went well with the room's neutral furnishings. She could have been in any office in any business in the Seattle area.

Well, what had she expected, red curtains and velvet wallpaper? Rachel suppressed a grin at the idea of mixing a bordello's decor with an office suite.

The Capture Agency didn't scream "sex" in any way. It looked like any typical office suite, with employees dressed in business casual and computers at every desk. A professional, high-tech environment.

Rachel hadn't felt at all uncomfortable coming in to fulfill all the requirements to become a client. She'd been treated politely and respectfully. The man who'd ushered her into this conference room to await her prospective date had practically bent over backward to make sure she had everything she needed to make the experience positive. And not because he was flirting. She was clearly the wrong gender to appeal to him.

The policy of having clients meet for the first time in one of the agency's conference rooms made perfect sense to Rachel. If she didn't like the look of the man she'd been matched up with, she didn't have to date him. He'd never have any way to contact her outside of the agency, since no personal information like an address or phone number was given out. She'd never have to worry about unwanted pursuit from a rejected candidate.

The closed door gave them privacy, the office setting gave them anonymity, and the office staff on the other side of the door ensured that if the meeting didn't go well, it could be ended quickly, with assistance if need be.

The lengths the agency had gone to to create a safe environment for what could be a risky kind of fantasy to act out impressed Rachel. Whoever had created this business cared about people, or at least cared about avoiding lawsuits and creating positive word of mouth.

This was a good idea, she thought, settling back in her chair. She'd had a few doubts about it, but two things had prodded her to go through with the process. One was that nagging sense of something missing. The other was the realization that the type of man she'd always wanted to meet might remain forever out of reach unless she used some method to look for him other than trusting to random chance and hoping they'd wind up in the same place at the same time.

It struck her as funny that they had, in fact, ended up in the same place at the same time. But then, if a man was looking for the same things she was, this was a logical place for him to try.

The door opened, and she didn't have time to wonder if it had been a mistake to wear the navy blue skirt and sweater set, styles that might have been called classic but could also be called boring, because the man who entered the room made it impossible to think about anything but him.

He had brown hair and brown eyes, a square jaw and a cleft chin that Rachel found herself wanting to touch, broad shoulders, and a general sense of solid masculinity. Rachel thought he'd look equally at home behind an office desk, at the head of a conference table, or sailing a boat. She blamed

Sabrina for planting pirate images in her head, but she could see this man carrying out pretty much any role with capable ease.

He was dressed conservatively, like her, but he didn't seem like the type who considered casual wear to mean not wearing a tie. She could see him wearing jeans and a sweater and looking comfortably at home. In fact, she could picture him sitting outside on her patio drinking coffee and orange juice, reading the paper, having breakfast. The image was so unexpectedly ordinary that she blinked.

"Hello," he said, regarding her with steady eyes. "You must be Rachel Law."

She nodded.

"My name's Chase."

The name suited him, she thought. It was a solid kind of name, but not boring. "Hello, Chase."

He walked over to join her at the small round conference table, pulled out a chair, and sat across from her. "If you don't mind my saying so, you don't look like a woman who has any trouble getting a date."

"No," Rachel agreed. "The trouble is getting one worth the time and effort."

"Sex isn't worth your time and effort?"

The question was asked in a matter-of-fact tone. She didn't get the sense that he was trying to shock her or make her feel uncomfortable, just stating the obvious. Because people became clients of the Capture Agency for a very specific reason.

"It hasn't been," Rachel answered, matching him for directness. "Not bad or anything. It's just that sex was never very exciting. Not fun. No surprises."

She looked down at the tabletop as if the designers at IKEA could help her search for the right words. "The men I dated, the relationships I had, I knew what they were going to do before they did it. Everything was predictable, and it seemed so pointless."

Rachel gave a slight shrug and continued, "I know I could have made an effort. If I wanted something different in bed, I could have shown up with a can of whipped cream. But the problem was on the inside, and I didn't think adding props would change anything. I thought—" She broke off and then looked up at him, meeting his eyes. "I thought if I met somebody who was whipped cream and handcuffs on the inside, then whether we used any props or not, it wouldn't matter. It'd be exciting and different because he'd be different."

"Capable of surprises."

"Yes." She smiled at him. "Exactly."

He studied her as if she'd presented him with a puzzle. Something gave her the idea that he was very good at figuring out puzzles. Finally he said, "Stand up."

"Excuse me?"

"Stand up." He smiled at her, and it reached all the way to his eyes. His expression was warm, reassuring, with a hint of humor. "I want to see if you're really ready to do this."

"What, here?" Rachel felt competing surges of anxiety and anticipation. "Don't we talk first, get to know each other a little?"

"I'm not going to ravish you on the table," he said. The smile widened just a little. "Although that's certainly an interesting idea."

"Oh." She folded her hands primly in her lap and made no move to get up. "Then what?"

"An exercise. Ever been in theater?"

Which had what to do with her sex life? "No," Rachel answered cautiously.

"This is an exercise that casts often do together. Putting on a production means people will be working closely together for some time, playing roles. They have to trust each other to do their part well. It makes for the right environment for creativity and cooperation, for good performances."

She could see how having the right environment could foster the level of comfort needed for the best possible performance and how that could transfer to this kind of sexual role-playing. Rachel nodded her understanding. "I see. And you do this exercise standing up?"

"Yes." Chase stood and extended a hand to her. Rachel slid hers into his grip. His hand felt warm, strong. He helped her to her feet, then let go, not using the contact to try to prolong any kind of physical intimacy.

"How do we do this?" she asked.

"You stand here." He indicated a spot farther away from the table, with more empty space around. Rachel took her position and gave him a questioning look. "Okay, what next?"

"I stand here." He took up a position behind her. "Your job is to relax, let yourself fall backwards, and trust me to catch you."

She felt her whole body tense up at the very idea. "I don't think I can do that."

"You can if you relax. If you trust me. I'm right here behind you, Rachel. I won't let you fall. I won't let you hit your head or get hurt. I'll catch you."

His voice was deep, reassuring. Rachel took a deep breath and tried to relax. "I think you're too far back," she said. "I don't want to fall that far."

"We'll start smaller, then." She heard him move behind her, taking a step forward. "Now I'm just behind you. Only a few inches, less than a foot of distance. Enough that you have to actually let go to fall into my arms, but not too far. Think you can try it now?"

That was okay, Rachel thought. Even if he didn't catch her, at that distance she'd fall into him and then she could right herself. "Yes."

"Close your eyes."

She did and felt her heartbeat accelerate at the thought of falling blind to her surroundings. But she knew he had the right idea. They could talk for hours and it wouldn't help convince her that this would work. That he was the man who could surprise her. Although he was already surprising her with his insight and his practical approach.

If she could do this, if she could fall into him, then she could feel comfortable letting him capture her. She could trust him with her body and her physical safety. This test would prove it to both of them.

Rachel took another deep breath and leaned backward, letting herself go past the point where she could recover her balance, falling into Chase. Her shoulders hit his chest, breaking her fall. His arms closed around her, catching her easily. He held her for a second, then helped her return to her standing position.

"Good," he said. "Now do it again. I'll be farther back, but I'll be right here, Rachel. Just let go. You can do it."

It was both harder and easier the second time. Harder

because she knew he was farther back and if he didn't catch her this time, she really might hurt herself. Easier because they'd already done it once.

Think of it this way, she told herself. *If he doesn't catch you, you'll know within the first fifteen minutes of meeting him that the sex isn't going to work.* As a way to screen potential dates, this technique could be a real time-saver.

The fall seemed to last forever, and she had a panicked moment when she thought she'd fall all the way to the floor, but in reality only a split second passed between the time she went beyond the point of no return and landed in Chase's sure embrace.

The relief made her sag into him. Her pulse was pounding, and she felt very aware of his size and strength behind her, supporting her. His arms held her securely. He didn't let her go immediately as he had the first time, but he also didn't make any attempt to turn his hold into something more. He just held her, waiting for her to signal him that she was fine on her own two feet again.

Her balance was restored on one level. On another it was rocky, so Rachel delayed for a minute and stayed where she was. She liked the feel of his arms around her, his chest supporting her back. There was a level of tension in the air, and all her senses were alert to the man behind her. It was all too easy to imagine his hands sliding up to cup her breasts. She could feel them swelling in anticipation of his touch.

The test was a success. So was the agency's matching, thought Rachel. This man had her attention and her interest, and she didn't know what he would say or do next.

Chase breathed in the mixed scent of light floral perfume

and woman and knew he was going to regret this. But he'd regret it even more if he let her walk away to find satisfaction from some other source.

If she had her fantasy date with him, he wouldn't have to worry about whether or not her curiosity led her to take foolish risks or that some other man simply wouldn't appreciate what she was trusting him with.

His arms tightened around her briefly. "I'm going to capture you," he stated. "I'll contact you through the agency with the time and place. You'll go there, but you won't know what to expect. I'll take you by surprise. Be ready."

She nodded. "It's a date." Her voice was a little less than steady.

Chase let her go and left the room, still wondering what had gotten into him but committed to following through. As far as Rachel knew, he was just another client. He could fulfill her fantasy and she'd never know anything different.

He'd opened the door with every intention of telling her the truth, then sending her on her way. Instead, he'd taken one look at her and hadn't wanted to end the conversation before it even began.

That was where he'd gone wrong, Chase decided. He'd talked to her. The competent, intelligent blonde with the Madonna face sitting there in navy business casual blithely telling him she wanted a man with whipped cream and handcuffs in his soul had flipped some atavistic switch inside him.

He'd had a sudden, overwhelming desire to see her wearing both items and nothing else. Then he'd decided to conduct a little test to see whether or not she meant it, if she trusted him to be the one to play captor and captive games with.

Well, she'd meant it, and now the game was on. He'd caught her, and he wasn't ready to let her go.

Three

"So how'd it go?"

Rachel cradled the cordless phone between her head and shoulder while she searched the freezer for the squat container of Häagen-Dazs chocolate-chip cookie dough ice cream. It was in there somewhere . . . *aha*. She spotted it half-covered by a bag of frozen peas and retrieved it.

"Fine," she told Sabrina. Spoon in hand, she peeled the lid off the container and dug in. "Better than fine, actually. They found my match right away. I've already met him. He looks like one of those quiet types you have to watch out for."

"She shoots, she scores!" Sabrina cheered.

"Not yet, but I can hope." Rachel smiled at the idea of scoring on her fantasy date and then slid the spoonful of fat and calories into her mouth to melt on her taste buds. Häagen-Dazs ice cream was her favorite source of oral gratification, but she was pretty sure Chase could come up with more interesting things for her to try.

Like licking whipped cream off of him.

The thought rocked her, and it was followed by another. Did she have whipped cream? He'd told her to be ready. Maybe she should pick up a few things. If she had one shot at having the kind of sex she'd always dreamed of but never expected to happen, she'd hate to be caught unprepared when the time came.

"Rachel? You there?" Sabrina's voice interrupted her thoughts. The tone told Rachel she'd missed something.

"Yes, sorry. My mind wandered."

"It wandered off to find your fantasy man, I bet."

"It did." Rachel admitted it cheerfully and spooned up another bite of frozen heaven. "I was also thinking maybe I should do some shopping to get ready for the big date."

"Oh, hey, good idea. Some sexy lingerie, maybe?"

That hadn't even crossed her mind. Rachel paused, spoon suspended in midair, as she mentally rifled through her underwear drawer. She had a black lace bra somewhere, didn't she?

No. She'd tossed the black lace after last year's office holiday party because the elastic was shot, and she'd never replaced it.

"Oh, my God," Rachel said, horrified by the realization. "I have a drawer full of plain white and beige, so nothing shows through my clothes. I have granny underwear, Sabrina. I can't be dragged off for fantasy sex wearing granny panties."

"Don't panic," Sabrina said. "*Veni, vidi,* Visa."

"Right. We'll go, we'll see, we'll shop." And with any luck, she'd be conquered wearing something worth ripping off.

She pictured Chase sending buttons flying as he tore

open her shirt to reveal something naughty underneath. "Maybe I should get one of those push-it-up kind of bras."

"You should get whatever you like," Sabrina said. "Whatever makes you feel sexy. It's all about you, remember?"

All about her. Rachel was riveted by the thought of sex that was all about her and her satisfaction. Being selfish and greedy, letting Chase do the work.

The spoon in her hand stayed forgotten until a melting drip caught her attention. Rachel shook her head to clear it. She put the spoon in her mouth, pushed the lid back on the tub of ice cream, and returned the container to the freezer. Obviously she was too distracted to appreciate Häagen-Dazs.

"Shopping. Tomorrow. This is going to be fun," she told Sabrina.

One week later, Rachel parked her car in a public garage near the bar designated for her capture. The agency encouraged clients to plan and prearrange low-key capture scenarios that wouldn't alarm bystanders and result in embarrassing 911 calls. This struck Rachel as sensible and also relieved the concern that she wouldn't know Chase from a mugger. She'd received instructions to come to this address at 5:30 P.M. Friday, and now the fantasy was about to begin. She took a deep breath to calm the butterflies dancing in her belly as she went over her mental checklist for fun.

She'd gone with navy blue lingerie instead of black, because the lace-trimmed satin bra and matching panties were so pretty, she'd had to have them. She thought the dark color looked good against her winter-pale skin. She had two cans of whipped cream. Condoms in a rainbow of colors and flavors, because they appealed to her more than the plain type. They'd looked like the right thing to have for fantasy sex.

"Fun," Rachel said out loud to her reflection in the rearview mirror as she did a final check of her makeup. Her lips curved in a smile, and her eyes were sparkling. She had fun underwear, fun condoms, and best of all, she didn't have to worry about whether her date would think she was a slut for being prepared to do the wild thing. He was there for fantasy sex, too. And Rachel was pretty sure he had some ideas about how to make it wild.

Since she was as ready as she was ever going to be, Rachel grabbed her oversize purse with whipped cream and flavored condoms safely inside and got out of her car. She locked it and kept her keys in her hand, an ingrained habit of city safety. The purse's straps went over her shoulder, and one arm secured it against her body. They were meeting at an upscale sushi bar, not a back-alley dive, but it never hurt to be cautious.

Once inside, Rachel stood blinking at the crowd and felt a twinge of nerves. What if he stood her up? *Don't be dumb,* she scolded herself. What man would stand up a Friday night date for sex? Besides, even if he did, she could still have sushi.

Rachel picked a seat that made her clearly visible from the door and studied the menu in case she had time to order. Chase might already be there waiting for her, or he might make her wait. If he made her wait, she wanted something to do with her hands and her mouth besides biting her nails.

She didn't have to wait. Before she'd even read through the menu options, a man's arms closed around her, his body pressing against her back as he engulfed her. "Stand up, nice and slow, and come with me."

Chase. She recognized his voice and the way he fit against her from behind. The capture was on. Her heart stumbled sideways in her chest, and she forgot to breathe.

"Rachel." His voice was low, reassuring. "It's me. It's time."

"I knew it was you." She sounded almost normal to her own ears and felt relieved that she wasn't stuttering.

"Then stand up. Unless you've changed your mind?"

"No!" Rachel blurted out the word and shot up off her bar stool, banging the top of her head into his chin in the process. She winced. *Way to go, smooth operator.* "Sorry."

His arms tightened around her, trapping her in his embrace. "I was just giving you a chance to be sure, not ditching you."

"Oh. Good."

Chase rubbed his chin lightly against the top of her hair. "I'm glad you're sure, Rachel. I have plans for you."

That sounded promising.

"Oh," she said again, her voice and her legs distinctly unsteady.

"I'm going to ask a lot more of you than a theater exercise this time." His voice was both warning and promise. "Are you ready to leave with me?"

Rachel licked her lips. "Yes."

"Tell me why you want this."

She relaxed into him, enjoying the feel of his arms around her, learning the way his body fit against hers. "I just wanted to do something fun. Before it was too late and completely hopeless." And because something was missing and she suspected it had to do with the opposite sex, although she left that unsaid.

"Hopeless?"

She shrugged. "I'm thirty-two. My fun years are slipping by. I know what I am. I'm serious, I'm responsible. Even when I was twenty-two, I wasn't the kind of person men associated with a good time. So if I wanted fun, if I wanted wild and crazy, where was I going to find it unless I went someplace like the Capture Agency?"

"Maybe you weren't looking for it very hard."

"Maybe not," Rachel agreed. "But it hasn't found me, either."

Chase gave a low laugh. "It's found you now. That's some purse you're holding, by the way. Anything interesting in it?"

For an answer, Rachel pulled it open, exposing the contents to his angle of view as he looked down.

"Whipped cream. That's very interesting." His voice sounded warm, approving, and a little rough. "I have just the thing to go with that."

"Oh? What would that be?" Her voice came out so breathy, she was almost afraid he wouldn't hear her.

"Handcuffs."

Rachel felt her knees go weak and her body go hot and tight.

"Walk with me. We're leaving now."

She obeyed, secretly amazed that she didn't stumble. Chase guided her through the bar and out the door.

An hour and a half later, Chase parked his car, turned off the key, and turned to look at the elegant blonde ensconced in his passenger seat. Her lips were curved in a smile and slightly parted, showing her excitement. Her eyes were bright, her hair slightly mussed from driving the last leg with the sunroof open.

She looked like Grace Kelly, and she was toting whipped cream and a rainbow of condoms. She'd chosen him for experimenting with submissive sex. And she didn't think she was a good time? Chase didn't believe for a minute that this woman didn't know how to have fun. That she hadn't made time for it, he could believe. Which put him in the same class. What did he do for fun? Write new programs. Exchange e-mails with friends at MIT about quantum computers.

No wonder Mark was interfering with his personal life.

"Where are we?" Rachel asked.

He'd told her only that they were taking a short trip to a private place. They'd kept the conversation light and nonspecific as they took the ferry to Bainbridge Island, drove over the bridge onto the Kitsap Peninsula and from there to the Hood Canal Bridge and their destination just on the other side of it. His weekend getaway, a small cabin on the Olympic Peninsula overlooking the Hood Canal.

It had seemed too risky to take Rachel to his house. Chase didn't want her to accidentally discover he was the owner of the Capture Agency and not an anonymous client. His home was bound to contain some betraying clue, no matter how careful he was. The intrusion of reality would shatter the fantasy he'd set out to fulfill for her.

But he hadn't wanted to take her to a hotel, either. He'd considered that while planning Rachel's capture, but the idea hadn't felt right. He'd wanted her on home ground, not neutral territory, while he fulfilled her fantasy of being held in his power. The cabin was the perfect solution. Since he was going to have Rachel Law in bed only once, he'd have her in *his* bed.

And it would be only once. Even if his deliberate deception didn't stand between them, his devotion to work was matched by hers. Neither of them had room in their lives for anything more than a stolen weekend.

"My cabin," Chase answered, deciding it wouldn't matter if she knew he owned it.

"This is yours?" Her eyes widened slightly as she took in the little two-story log structure. "It's wonderful. You must hate going back to the city."

"Business keeps me there, but I get away as often as I can." Chase smiled at her. "Come on, I'll show you around. The view alone is worth the drive."

"I believe it."

They got out of the car and walked up the gravel drive. Moss and grass made thick patches of green on the driveway. Ferns and rhododendrons grew in clumps among the mature evergreens Chase had left standing when he'd had the building site cleared. Buying a wooded lot only to cut down all the trees made no sense to him. He'd left the natural landscaping as undisturbed as possible.

He unlocked the door and pushed it open, gesturing with one arm for Rachel to precede him. He followed her in and closed the door behind him with a sense of finality. They were here, and they were both acutely aware of the reason for it. Rachel had her arms wrapped around her midsection, clutching her oversize bag like a shield.

"Nervous?"

She looked over her shoulder at him and blinked, then lowered her arms as if he'd made her realize how defensive her body language looked. "Yes, I guess I am."

Chase moved closer to her, taking her bag and setting it on the wooden bar counter that served to separate the large, open room from the kitchen area. She let him take it without protest and then let him help her remove her coat.

"The bedroom's the loft above," he told her. "I liked the open concept for downstairs with the sleeping area separated by height."

"It's nice." Rachel tilted her head back to smile at him. "It makes it feel bigger than it is, having it laid out this way."

"Makes it easier to heat with the fireplace, too." The loft design made the bedroom open as well, overlooking the living area below. An overhead ceiling fan pushed the warm air down, and the stone chimney radiated heat once a fire was well established. "Speaking of which, I'd better get a fire going or you'll be cold."

She grinned at him. "That sounds so manly. Making a fire."

"I chop wood, too."

Her eyes widened and she caught her breath, as if picturing him naked to the waist, muscles bunching and moving as he worked. Chase leaned toward her, drawn by her obvious reaction to his words. "I want to kiss you, Rachel."

"Oh." She licked her lips. "I want that, too."

"But first, I'm going to get the fire started."

She frowned in open confusion. "Why?"

"Because once I start kissing you, I'm not going to want to stop. And when I get you naked, I want you shivering with anticipation, not cold."

The winters were mild in this temperate rain forest region, but it was still winter, and the damp could make the temperature feel much lower than it actually was.

"Ah." Rachel licked her lips again and nodded. "Well, make a fire, then. I'll watch."

Since he kept the fireplace ready, kindling laid, it didn't take long to build a fire that would soon make a hot bed of coals. It would keep the cabin comfortably warm as long as he added a new log from time to time. Satisfied, Chase turned to look at Rachel and felt his gut tighten at the sight of her.

He wanted her. He wanted to see all the smooth, bare skin that was covered up by pants and a long-sleeved sweater. He wanted to taste her mouth and then explore the length of her from head to toe, kissing every inch. He wanted to part her thighs and lick between them. And he wanted to fuck her until neither of them could take any more.

Her eyes met his and widened slightly in awareness of his obvious sexual regard. He could see her breath catch, the rise and fall of her chest growing more rapid, the pulse at the base of her throat fluttering.

"Rachel," he said, her name like a brand on his lips. "I have a craving for whipped cream."

She stayed still as he stood upright and moved closer to her, one deliberate step after another, until the last step brought him close enough for their bodies to nearly brush, crowding her, invading her space. She didn't move back. She leaned forward just enough for her nipples to graze his chest.

The contact shot straight to his cock. With a low growl he buried one fist in her hair, gripped her ass with his other hand, and brought her body hard against his as his lips claimed hers.

He took her mouth like an invading conqueror, demanding her surrender, and with a little moan, she gave it. She melted into him, opened her mouth for him, pressed closer as if his hold weren't tight enough to soothe her body's demand for contact with his.

Chase thrust his tongue into her mouth at her invitation, tasting the depths of her. He felt a surge of triumph when her tongue slid along his, tasting him back. Her response confirmed what her body had told him when she'd trusted him enough to relax and fall into him, expecting him to catch her.

Submissive sex required a high degree of honesty and trust, and Rachel was giving him both. Which was good, because he'd never felt more dominant. He'd long since accepted his preference for being in charge in bed, but with Rachel he wanted more. He wanted to claim her, and he wanted her utter and complete surrender.

Chase gentled the kiss, easing back by degrees until his mouth just brushed hers. "Rachel."

"Mmm."

"I'm going to do things to you you've never experienced before. If I push you too far outside your comfort zone, you need to tell me to ease up. If you need to stop, say so. I'll be watching you, paying attention to your body's reactions, your responses, but we haven't played together before, and I don't know your limits. If something feels uncomfortable or you don't like it, say so immediately. If you want more, tell me that."

He felt her shudder in his arms. "I want more right now."

"Greedy." He felt a smile curve his mouth as he nibbled at her lower lip.

"I want to be," she answered on a sigh. "I want to be selfish and greedy and take everything you want to give me."

"I hope you're up to it," he answered. "Because I want to give you everything, Rachel. Everything you want. Everything you need. Everything I'm burning to do to you, because I've captured you, and you belong to me, and I can."

"Chase." She pressed closer to him, and he felt her hook one leg around his hip. *"Yes."*

He brought his hands down to her hips, ground his pelvis into hers until she gasped, then swung her off her feet and cradled her against his chest. "Time to take you upstairs and introduce you to those handcuffs, pretty lady."

Rachel's head fell back against his chest, her eyes wide and dark as they met his. "Goody," she said in a faint voice.

Chase snagged her purse with its stockpile of condoms and cream, ready to use both on her. His hard-on strained against his zipper, and he welcomed the discomfort. He wanted the first time to last as long as he could draw it out, and just kissing this woman, knowing she was his to take, brought him dangerously close to losing control.

Four

"I want to see you naked," Chase said as he set her on her feet, her legs backed up against the four-poster bed. "I want to see all of that creamy skin bare for me, and then I'm going to paint designs on your body with that whipped cream, every place I want to lick it off."

"Works for me," Rachel said, a smile spreading over her face.

"And while I'm doing that, pretty Rachel, I'm going to have you handcuffed to this bed."

"Wow." She gulped as she imagined herself on the bed, naked, helpless, wearing nothing but dots of whipped cream that Chase would swirl his tongue around and lap away until he tasted nothing but her. Her inner muscles tightened, and she felt her sex swelling, a hot rush spreading through her as her body readied itself for him.

She wanted his mouth on her, his tongue teasing her nipples, her clit, plunging inside her . . . A shudder ran through her, and Chase gave a low laugh at her telltale reaction.

"Like that idea, don't you?"

"Uh-huh." She licked her lips, her mouth feeling dry, heart racing as adrenaline shot through her.

He slapped her ass, the sharp sting taking her by surprise. It wasn't unpleasant, just a faint sting followed by a rush of blood that puffed her vulva further. Now that was unexpected. Who knew a light spank could actually feel good and make her sex swell? "Get your pants off. The next time I spank you, I want to see a little rosy flush on your bare ass."

Unbelievably, his words made her react with a liquid rush, her natural lubrication coating her and making her slick for him.

He slid a hand under her thin navy silk sweater, stroking her bare waist beneath it. "I gave you an order, Rachel. Pants off. Or do you need help undressing?"

"Wow." She bunched her hands into his shirt and took a deep breath. "Give me a minute. I'm standing here with a hot man who has handcuffs and knows how to use them, telling me to get naked. The last time I got naked for anybody, I was having a physical."

"Been a while?" Chase kissed the corner of her mouth, light, soft, then nipped at her lower lip with the edge of his teeth. The contrast made her shudder with want.

"It's been so long," she answered. "And it's never been like this. I feel—" She broke off, searching for words.

"What do you feel, Rachel? Tell me." Chase hooked his thumbs into the waistband of her pants and slid them back and forth, caressing the soft skin of her belly.

"Everything. I want to rip my clothes off and rub myself against you. I want anything and everything with you. I feel crazy and needy."

Rachel fumbled at her button and zipper, opening her

pants and sliding them down her hips. The fabric pooled at her feet, and she stepped out, kicking herself free. She grasped the bottom of her sweater and yanked it over her head, pulling out her arms and tossing that aside, too. Her satin panties clung damply between her legs, and her bra felt too constricting. Her breasts felt swollen and achy, and she was pretty sure nothing would give her relief but having his hands and his mouth on them.

"Very nice." He looked down at her new bra, approval plain on his face. "Sexy and classy. Just like you."

Rachel felt a blush burn her cheeks. "Not very classy. I went to an exclusive dating agency looking for kinky sex."

"No." Chase traced the outline of her bra, running his fingers over the curves of her breasts as they rose above the edges of the fabric cups. "You wanted something and you went looking for it. You had needs and you wanted them filled. That doesn't lessen who you are, Rachel. You're a beautiful, desirable, accomplished woman, and you have every right to want a lover to give you pleasure."

She shivered as his fingers sang to her nerve endings, making her feel very aware of her skin as a sensory organ. She wanted to feel his touch everywhere.

"I'm going to give you pleasure, Rachel. And you're going to have to accept it, take it, enjoy it. You don't have a choice. You're my captive, and you have to give in to me."

Chase smoothed his hands up to her shoulders and down her back, where he found the catch to her bra and unfastened it. She pulled her arms through the straps, helping him remove it, and then she was naked except for her panties. Cool air rushed over her heated skin, and her nipples puckered into even tighter buds.

"Look what you had hidden. So pretty." Chase looked down at her breasts, admiring her. "I may make you leave your breasts bare for me until I let you go. Ready for me to touch or lick or pinch." As he spoke, he flicked a finger against one nipple, and Rachel gasped at the sensation. She was so ready for his touch, and to be stimulated so abruptly was like being jolted with low-voltage electricity.

"On the bed, on your knees," Chase told her.

Rachel dropped back onto the bed and rolled onto her stomach, pulling her knees underneath her to kneel on the mattress. She felt the bed dip as Chase joined her, felt his fingers hook into her panties and pull them down. She raised her legs one at a time for him, and he slid off the panties, trailing his hands leisurely down her bare legs in the process.

Working back up, his hands stroked over her calves and then her thighs, kneading lightly at the curve of her buttocks before sliding down to stroke the soft skin of her inner thighs. His fingertips brushed just short of the juncture between, and Rachel let out a low moan, wanting with all her being for him to touch her there.

Chase gave a low chuckle. "Not yet."

Then his palm smacked against the bare skin of her bottom, and she felt it pinking in reaction while her vulva plumped even fuller. A second smack followed, and Rachel felt the inner muscles of her sex clench and a rush of liquid follow. Oh God, she was going to be dripping by the time he finally touched her.

"Pretty in pink." Chase stroked her bare ass, soothing away the slight sting, cupping her cheeks in his hands, and squeezing lightly. It felt good, everything he did felt good, and it all made her want more. She thrust her hips back at him, trying to direct his attention where she wanted it.

"I think it's time to handcuff my pretty naked captive to the bed." Chase gave her bare bottom a final, lingering stroke, followed by a gentle pat. "Crawl up to the headboard, then roll onto your back."

Right. Rachel fought to clear the haze of lust fogging her brain and focus on his words. Simple instructions. She could do that.

It was surprisingly sensual, moving across his bed, naked, knowing he was watching her and that her ass was flushed from the attention he'd given it. Knowing that she was his willing captive and he was going to have her at his mercy. She wanted to pay attention to every detail, memorize every sensation. This was the most erotic experience of her life, and she wanted to savor all of it to replay in her mind and treasure in her memory.

Rachel rolled onto her back, exposing her bare breasts and her sex to him. She held out her arms and waited.

Chase walked around to one side of the bed and snapped a pair of handcuffs onto one wrist, the other cuff to the bed's post. He moved around to the other side and did the same, drawing out the process until Rachel's nerve endings were sizzling with anticipation.

"There." He stroked her arm from cuffed wrist to the sensitive skin of her inner elbow. "Comfortable?"

"Yes." Rachel frowned. "No."

"Which is it?" Chase smiled at her, his hand tracing a light pattern over her arm.

"The handcuffs don't hurt or anything." Rachel swallowed hard. "It's uncomfortable being so, well, turned on."

"Your body wants relief."

"You could say that." Rachel eyed the telltale bulge that strained his pants. "I don't think I'm alone."

"You are very much not alone." Chase leaned over and brushed a kiss just below her belly button. Her hips twitched in reaction, pelvis arching up. Instead of answering her silent invitation and kissing lower, Chase moved away and stripped off his clothes.

Rachel watched, wide-eyed, taking in the breadth of his shoulders, the lean line of his waist, the thick erection that jutted away from his body. She licked her lips, wanting to taste him, to feel that smooth, hard flesh sliding into her mouth before driving between her thighs.

Chase noted her reaction and said, "You'll get your turn later." He retrieved a can of whipped cream, shook it, then joined her on the bed and made soft, white blossoms of her breasts, lines on her belly, a pouf of whipped cream between her thighs. "I hope you had dinner. It's time for dessert."

"I thought you were always supposed to eat dessert first," Rachel said, feeling drunk with lust. "Because life is uncertain."

"Wise planning."

Chase leaned over her and licked the upper curve of her breast. His tongue was warm, the cream was cool, and her skin was on fire. Rachel let out a moan that was almost a sob, arching into his mouth, wanting more. When his mouth closed over her breast, she felt a surge of pleasure shoot from her nipple straight to her clit. She made a strangled sound of appreciation, her pelvis tilting up of its own volition as if seeking him.

He didn't hurry. He licked and kissed and nibbled at

her, sometimes lapping at her and making lazy patterns with his tongue, sometimes sucking, sometimes scraping her with the edge of his teeth. By the time he'd licked his way down her belly, Rachel was quivering with need.

"Spread your legs wider for me, Rachel."

Best idea she'd heard yet, in a night that had so far been full of really good ones. Rachel bent her knees and moved them as far apart as she could stretch, offering herself to Chase.

"I'm going to lick up all your cream." His mouth moved down lower, hovering just over her vulva, and Rachel groaned.

"God, yes."

His tongue traced the outline of her sex, teasing her. Then he closed his mouth over the swollen bud of her clit and sucked while he flicked his tongue over the bundle of nerve endings. Rachel screeched and bucked her hips, so close to coming from that contact alone, but it wasn't quite enough. She needed more, needed it now.

He gave it to her, eating at her as tremors shot through her and her inner muscles spasmed.

"Chase . . ." His name was almost a wail. She thrashed her head from side to side. "Please . . . Please . . ."

His tongue thrust into her sex, withdrew, thrust in again, and Rachel broke, her spine bowing as she came hard. She was still quivering with aftershocks when he lifted his head and left the bed to grab a condom. She watched through half-lidded eyes as he sheathed himself in latex and came to kneel between her thighs. He cupped her sex with one hand, grinding his palm into her swollen vulva. "This is mine to do anything I want with. Isn't it?"

Rachel made a soft sound of pleasure and agreement.

His hand felt so unbelievably good there, touching her, giving her pressure and contact where she needed it so badly. The orgasm he'd given her had primed her for another, intensifying her state of arousal instead of relaxing her. He rubbed his thumb over her clit, and she squirmed in reaction. She really was greedy. He'd just made her come once and she only wanted more.

When he delivered an open-palmed spank to her vulva, she almost did come again. Her eyes flew wide open in shock at both the unexpected light blow and the intensity of her response to it.

His eyes met hers. His expression had gone hard and demanding. "You didn't answer me."

Rachel licked dry lips and managed to answer. "Yes. That's yours to do anything you want with." *And I hope you want to do* that *again,* she added silently.

He didn't. Instead, he took his hand away and wrapped it around the base of his cock, aiming the head at the soft folds of her innermost flesh, pressing lightly against her opening. "I want to fuck you, pretty Rachel."

He pushed forward just enough to barely enter her, not even half an inch, showing her his intent. He was hard and thick, and even though she was slick and ready for him, she knew it was going to be a tight fit.

Chase held her eyes as he pressed forward, penetrating her only with his head. She felt her flesh stretching to take him and ached with an emptiness that needed to be filled.

"Chase. More," she gasped out, not caring if he wanted her to beg for it. She'd do that willingly. Nothing mattered but the heat and connection between them, the need inside her, the screaming buildup of tension in her body that demanded release.

He lowered his body onto hers by degrees, placing himself over her but using his hands to balance his weight so it settled onto her slowly, letting her adjust to the burden. Then he flexed his hips and drove himself all the way inside her in one long, hard stroke. Rachel planted her feet flat on the mattress, using the leverage to lift her hips to meet him.

"So tight." He paused, resting his forehead against hers, his breathing harsh. "You are so hot and tight. You're squeezing my dick hard enough to make me come right now."

At his graphic words, Rachel felt her sex clench around his thick length and heard his breath hiss in reaction. "Damn, Rachel. I want this to last more than a minute."

"Please," she whispered, her tongue feeling too thick in her mouth, her inner muscles already fluttering with the beginnings of another orgasm. She rocked her hips into him, conveying her urgency. "Please, Chase, don't make me wait."

"I won't." He levered himself up to gain the angle he wanted and drove into her, hard, fast thrusts that made her keen with wordless pleas for completion.

His body against hers, over hers, skin to skin, his cock thrusting into her, the multitude of sensations shattered her. Rachel felt her sex clenching, spasming, felt orgasm rip through her, and she cried out, arching into Chase. She felt him jerk as he started to come with her, finishing them both in a series of hard strokes that drove her past the edge.

He stayed on her, inside her, while they both fought to breathe. Rachel sucked in air in gasping gulps, her heart thudding in her rib cage. She felt Chase move, his lips brushing her forehead. "Need me to get off?"

She gave a short laugh. "I think you already did."

He shook his head and feathered kisses over her eyelids. "Lady, I'd be willing to bet no other man on the planet has gotten off as thoroughly as I just did."

"That makes two of us. Well, I mean, I'm not a man."

"I think I would have noticed," Chase agreed.

"But I have just gotten off as thoroughly as you. Maybe more," she mused. "I came twice."

"I came twice as hard."

"Mmm." She turned her face to seek his kiss, and his mouth settled over hers in a leisurely meeting of lips. She could still feel the length of his penis buried deep inside her, her body cradling his, the wiry matt of hair on his chest teasing her bare nipples.

She felt full and satiated and relaxed, and grateful because this man had set out to fulfill her fantasy. And he'd made her feel like a fantasy come true in return. She'd never felt so sexy, so desired, so aware of her feminine power. This man wanted her, enough to take her, handcuff her to his bed, and fuck her silly.

"Chase." She sighed his name against his lips.

"Very good. You should always know the name of the man who has his cock buried in you to the balls."

She giggled, then sighed. "That should be crude, but it's a turn-on."

"There's a big difference between what a lover says to you in bed and what another person might say in different circumstances." Chase levered himself up to look down at her. "It's not just the words, it's the context. You know

I want you. I find you beautiful and smart and sexy as hell. And I like burying my cock in you to the balls. I like pumping my balls empty inside you, too."

His words made her shiver, not just because the explicit message excited her, but because the way he said it was a promise of more to come. He'd already had her, but he was letting her know he wasn't finished with her. He hadn't lost interest. He wanted her again. The knowledge warmed her, reassured her, made her feel like a desired prize worth holding captive.

Five

"Your arms have to be getting tired." Chase withdrew, and Rachel made a slight sound of protest at the loss. He grinned down at her. "Don't worry, we still have a whole rainbow of condoms. I'm far from through with you, and judging by your reaction, I think we can make our way through more of the spectrum than one color."

"I think so, too," Rachel agreed, trying to keep her face straight. Her lips twitched with humor, in spite of her efforts. Now that he'd made her aware of it, her arms were tired of the unaccustomed position. He unlocked the cuffs, and Rachel stretched in freedom, then moved her arms up and down and across her body to work out the kinks.

"Let me."

His fingers kneaded her upper arms and shoulders. Rachel closed her eyes and melted into the bed, wondering if her body had ever felt so good in her entire life.

"Don't go to sleep on me. I said I'm not finished with you."

She let her lashes flutter up, meeting his gaze with her own. "I don't think I'm finished with you, either."

"You don't think? You're not sure?" Chase raised one brow at her. "Do you need another spanking to be convinced?"

She burst into laughter. "I had no idea I was such a deviant. You smacked my butt and my privates, handcuffed me, licked whipped cream off my naked body, and I loved all of it."

"I fucked you, too." He sounded satisfied and smug, his look possessive as he gazed down at her.

"God, yes, you did." She blinked at him. "Did I thank you for that?"

"Your sweet little pussy milking my cock dry while you come is all the thanks I need."

She shook her head to clear it. "You have to stop saying things like that. I might lose my mind and attack you."

"Ah, ah, ah." Chase shook his head at her. "I'm in charge. You don't get to attack me unless I give you permission."

"Well, damn." Rachel gave him a speculative look. "What will it take to get permission?"

"You want to attack me?"

"I want to lick whipped cream off you," she answered promptly. "I'd settle for that."

"We'll continue this discussion in a minute." Chase rumpled her hair in a playful caress and strolled naked to a door that she realized must be the adjoining bathroom. Right, he'd have to dispose of the condom. Although she thought the bright purple was kind of a good look on him.

Rachel flopped back on the bed and hugged herself, thinking of how he looked, hard and intent, rolling a vibrantly colored condom down the thick length of his cock.

"You must be thinking happy thoughts."

His voice brought her back to the present in a rush. Rachel blinked at him and sat up, putting her hand into his when he extended it to her. He drew her upright and tugged her closer until their bodies brushed. "Yes," Rachel said, trying to focus on the conversation and not speculate on how long it might take him to recover enough to start over.

"How do you feel?"

"Exciting." She smiled at him. "Like maybe there's an exciting side to me. Maybe I'm not just a person who sells insurance and makes the numbers and gets the paperwork in on time. Nobody would believe it."

"Nobody?" Chase tilted his head to study her face. "Aren't there any friends in your life who know the real you?"

"Well, yes. The one who told me about the Capture Agency in the first place. And you know, I really think it surprised her that I wanted to do this." Probably because the real her wasn't this exciting, abandoned, wanton woman, naked and greedy for pleasure. Rachel pushed the thought away and nestled into Chase, turning her face into the column of his throat so she could breathe in his scent and lose herself in the fantasy.

"Lots of people like sex. Lots of people enjoy adding a few variations to the traditional tried and true." Chase wrapped his arms around her, one hand moving up to toy with her hair while the other moved lower to stroke the curve of her ass. "Why should it surprise anybody that you wanted to enjoy your sexuality?"

"Well. You know. Lifetime member of the button-up club, conservative professional image." Rachel shrugged.

"I'm conservative."

Rachel laughed outright. "You spanked me. You cuffed me to your bed and licked whipped cream off my, er—"

"Pussy," Chase supplied helpfully.

"Pussy." She said it almost defiantly and felt an inner rush of glee at using the explicit word.

"Yes, I did. You taste delicious, by the way. But that doesn't mean I'm not conservative." He pressed her body closer to his, and Rachel felt his cock twitch against her belly. Hmm, it seemed his recovery time was pretty fast. "Men like to pursue and capture. A lot of men like to be in charge, to be dominating. In today's world, it's not exactly politically correct to have those tendencies outside of the bedroom, but in bed, I think it's an expression of a natural instinct to conquer."

"You can conquer me." Rachel sighed against his bare skin and kissed the pulse point at the base of his throat. "I never imagined it could be such a turn-on."

"Think you can take more?" Chase cupped her butt with both hands to hold her steady and thrust his cock against the smooth skin of her belly in rhythmic strokes, demonstrating exactly what he wanted her to take.

"I'm your helpless captive." Rachel lifted her head to flutter her eyelashes at him. "You have me naked. Whatever are you planning to do with that enormous erection?"

"Use it on you." He gave her a heated look. "Now that we've taken the edge off, I think we can make the next time last a little longer."

"You think?" Rachel burrowed into him and ran her tongue down the line of his shoulder, liking the salty taste of him.

"Like the taste of me?" Chase asked her.

"Mmmm."

He brought his hands up to her shoulders and pushed down. "Let's see if you do. Get on your knees and suck my cock. Show me how much you like the taste of me in your mouth. If you convince me you love it, I'll fuck you again."

All the air left her body. It was a good thing he wanted her to kneel because her legs collapsed and she dropped, struck down by lust and sheer incredulity that a man so raw and sexual, so in command of himself, had chosen to capture boring Rachel Law.

Except he doesn't think you're boring, she reminded herself. He thought she was sexy, so she felt sexy. He thought she was adventurous, and desirable, and he wanted her mouth on him before he took her again.

Just the thought of having him in her mouth excited her. The further thought of experiencing every inch of that impressive hard-on between her legs, penetrating her, made her suck in air and wheeze.

"Rachel? All right down there?" His hands tangled in her hair and rubbed at the base of her skull.

"Fine," she gasped. "It just hits me once in a while and I have to take it in. You want me."

"Hell, yes, I want you." He pulled her head closer to his cock. "Now put your mouth on me. Wrap your lips around my cock and suck me like I'm your favorite candy. I want you to eat me up until my balls are bursting with the need to come. And then I'm going to fuck you. I'm going to pump your pussy so full of come, you can't hold it all and it spills out."

"Chase." She shuddered as he fed her his cock.

She traced her way around his rounded head with the tip of her tongue first, then closed her lips around his warm, smooth flesh and sucked him as far into her mouth as she could take him. He tasted so elementally male. A hint of musk, a tang of salt on her tongue. She rolled her tongue around his member, licking at him, sucking, nibbling, drawing him in and out of her mouth, kissing the sensitive tip of his head.

Rachel ran her tongue over the small slit that seeped salty pre-come and lapped it up, feeling drunk on him, starved for him. Starved for *this*. Whatever this feeling was, she was hungry for it, for him, and she showed him just how much with her mouth and lips and tongue.

"Stop." Chase urged her head up, using his hold in her hair to pull her away. She let his cock slide out of her mouth and stood, waiting for him to direct her.

"Spread your legs." Rachel complied, shifting her feet apart shoulder width. Chase palmed her sex, testing her, groaning when he found her slick and ready. He plunged a finger into her, and she let her head fall back, panting, as he thrust it in and out. "You are so wet. So hot. You sucked me so good, Rachel. Maybe next time I'll spill myself down your throat and let you swallow every last drop."

"Mmm." Rachel ran her tongue along her lower lip. "Now?"

"No." He added a second finger to the one buried inside her, stretching her open. "Not now. Now I want this." His penetrating fingers twisted and found the spot deep inside her that made her gasp and writhe.

"Chase." She grabbed for him, needing support as the world spun out of control.

He withdrew his fingers and turned her, giving her a sharp slap on the ass. "On the bed, hands and knees. Now, Rachel."

She practically fell into position, feeling awkward and urgent and so very aware of him right behind her. She felt his hands grip her hips, his cock nestling against her bare ass, riding between the twin globes. "Do you want me to get a condom, Rachel?"

"No." The word burst out of her, and she pushed her hips back toward him, arching her back to offer her sex. "You said you wanted to pump me full of come. Do it, Chase. We both had to do the testing, I'm on the pill. I want to feel you inside me, just you, and when you come I want to take it all."

His hands tightened on her hips, and she felt his cock pull back, nudge against her opening, then press forward until the head rode inside her. "Be sure."

"I'm sure." Rachel squeezed her inner muscles, gripping his head as if to keep him from withdrawing.

"Then take this." Chase drove into her, hard and fast and deep, until she felt him at the opening of her womb. Her flesh stretched around him, yielding for him, taking the full length of him inside her, and Rachel closed her eyes at the sensation of being so thoroughly filled.

The universe shrank down to a bubble inhabited only

by the two of them, the rhythmic slap of flesh meeting, the intense physical awareness of Chase that made pleasure almost too much to bear. His hands on her, his body behind hers, rocking into her again and again.

Rachel made a soft sound and laid her cheek against the bedspread as she half collapsed, her chest touching the bed as she rested there, back arched and butt upraised, being taken so completely that it made every other experience she'd had seem unreal. Unimportant.

"Time to change position." Chase withdrew, and before she could protest the loss, he rolled her onto her back and lowered himself onto her. "I want to look into your eyes while I have you."

She swallowed. Her mouth had gone dry, and her eyes felt heavy and swollen. "I'll try to keep them open."

He pulled her arms above her head and pinned her wrists with his hands as he positioned himself and thrust into her again. The slick folds of her vulva gave way to his invasion, welcoming him.

"Rachel." He scraped his teeth over the curve of her lower lip. "If you could only see how you look right now. Your face flushed, your eyes half-lidded. Your nipples so hard and tight. Your legs open for me, taking me. You look like a woman surrendering to pleasure, on the edge of orgasm. Absolutely beautiful."

"You look different, too." Rachel lifted her head to kiss him. Their lips met and clung, then slid apart. "You look like you left civilization with your suit."

"I don't feel very civilized right now." He held her down as he continued to thrust into her. "Put your legs around me."

She shifted under him and did as he asked. The slight

change in angle opened her more fully to him and made his penetration even deeper. "Chase."

"Yes. Like that." His voice was rough. The way he held her wasn't gentle, and she didn't want it to be. She wanted to be taken hard, marked, claimed.

"Harder," she whispered as her body wrapped invitingly around his, offering anything he wanted.

"Tell me who you want to fuck you harder."

"Chase." She said his name in a hoarse voice. "I want Chase to fuck me harder."

"Do you want to come now, pretty Rachel?" His voice rasped as he drove into her with increased force.

"Yes. I want to come. Make me come, Chase." Her body was tightening under and around him. She could feel the wave building and building, but release stayed just out of reach.

"I'll make you come so hard, you'll see stars."

Rachel closed her eyes, unable to keep them open any longer. She was falling, drowning in sensation, in need, and Chase was her anchor. He held her, grounded her, and pushed her past the limit of restraint as he took her in hard, demanding strokes. Some internal barrier was battered down and she went liquid under him, feeling the completeness of her surrender. Her body was his to take. She was his to take.

"Chase." She wasn't sure if she actually said his name or only thought it before the pleasure took her like a storm. The intensity stole her breath and seized her muscles, leaving her helpless and unable to move while Chase continued to surge inside her. She felt his shaft grow even more engorged as he started to come, then a hot, liquid rush that sent her off on another crashing wave of sensation and an orgasm so violent, it was almost painful.

It was so primal, so basic. His body on hers. His seed filling her. His strength holding her, the heat and need between them holding him just as surely. She jerked and twisted underneath him, and he rode her down, bringing them both through the eye of the hurricane and finally coming back to rest together.

Chase stayed on top of Rachel for what seemed like eternity, his body heavy with release. He was still buried in her to his balls, a position he was loath to relinquish. It filled him with satisfaction to have her trapped under his weight after he'd taken her. He'd pumped himself empty into her, both of them wanting the deepest, fullest contact with no barriers between them. Coming inside Rachel was a pleasure all its own.

The way she looked while he took her was another. He didn't think any other man had seen her looking that way. She'd been lost to sensation, lost to the moment, surrendering to him and to her own passion. She'd looked like a goddess. He'd made her look like that. He'd made her come until she couldn't take any more.

And he'd nearly sent her away from the Capture Agency. The thought twisted his gut.

"Chase." His temporary captive stirred under him, and Chase rolled onto his back, taking her with him so their positions reversed, Rachel lying sprawled on top of him. He wrapped his arms around her and stroked her back, liking the feel of her against him and the smooth silk of her skin under his hands. "Is that better?" he asked her.

"Um." She rubbed her cheek against his chest in a lazy caress. "Yes. You were getting heavy."

"I'll move sooner next time." He slid one hand into her hair and toyed with the length.

"No, don't." Her voice was low and drowsy but audible. "I liked it. You feel good lying on me like that. In me. After."

"After I fuck you senseless, I'm in no hurry to go anywhere." His body rocked against hers, and he heard her sigh in response. "We used each other up. That calls for a little recovery time."

"Mmm," she said.

From the boneless sprawl of her body and the sound of her voice, Rachel was on the verge of slipping into sleep. That amused him and charmed him, too. Ms. Urban Professional had transformed into a vixen and now was fully sated and as cuddly as a cat.

He continued to stroke her back in slow, soothing motions. Her breathing deepened and settled into a steady rhythm as she slept in his arms, limp and spent.

It occurred to him that he couldn't remember the last time he'd felt so relaxed. Being at the cabin was always peaceful, but for the first time he wasn't alone in his private retreat. It pleased him to have Rachel here, like a treasure he'd carried off to his lair to hoard with dragonish lust. The image made him smile. Something about her certainly brought out the animal in him.

She shivered in his arms, and Chase realized her skin was cooling after the heat of exertion. He didn't want her to get chilled. He eased back the covers and settled her under them, tucked them snugly around her, and went to see to the fire.

Rachel woke up in a strange bed, reached out for Chase, and found the sheets cool. She blinked her eyes open to confirm what her other senses told her, that she was alone. An unexpected pang of uncertainty hit her and she sat up, pulling the covers with her. From her upright position, she could see out of the open loft to the wall of windows on that side of the A-frame cabin that looked out over the Hood Canal, now illuminated by the nearly full moon. The view made her catch her breath. Water and the wooded landscape on the far side of it made a stunning panorama. In the full light of day, it would be even more striking.

The sound of a door opening and closing downstairs was followed by heavy footsteps and a thudding noise as Chase dumped an armload of logs into the woodbox by the fireplace. Well, that explained where he'd gone. He must've wanted to make sure there was enough wood to keep the fire going through the night.

She heard the rhythmic steps that told her Chase was climbing the stairs to her and felt her wavering uncertainty clutch into self-conscious shyness. She started to remember everything they'd said and done, and by the time Chase came into view, her face was burning as hot as the fireplace.

He stopped short at the sight of her, sitting up with the covers clutched to her chest and her cheeks flaming. "Hey."

He was dressed in jeans and a sweater. Whatever shoes he'd worn out to get firewood had been left downstairs since he wore only socks. He looked masculine and imposing and far too attractive. While she probably looked as though her hair had been slept in, since it had, and she wore nothing but blankets.

Rachel opened her mouth wordlessly and then closed it again, unable to form any sort of response. Not knowing what else to do, she fell back and pulled the covers over her head.

"Rachel." Chase came closer and tugged at the covers. She held on and burrowed into the pillow, wondering where her inner wild woman had gone. The Rachel who had acted out her fantasies with pure abandon had disappeared and left the Rachel who always did the responsible thing to hold the bag, apparently.

"Rachel. Come out of there."

"No."

"You're embarrassed."

"You think?" Her voice came out in a half shriek. "Oh, my God. You did—and I liked—and I said—." The words tumbled over one another incoherently, and she gave up.

"Rachel." He pulled at the covers again and she let go, recognizing the futility of hiding under them forever. He drew them down to her waist and looked at her bared breasts. "Nice."

Rachel shook her hair forward to cover them. Chase slid one hand under the screening fall of hair and found her nipple, tweaking it. "Are we playing hide-and-seek? Bet I can find something else interesting hiding in here."

Before she could block him, he threw the covers all the way back with his free hand. He cupped and squeezed her breast while his other hand wedged in between her thighs and burrowed forward until his thumb nudged her clit. "Just like I thought. Very interesting." His thumb rubbed up and down over the sensitive bud, and Rachel jumped.

"Open your legs for me, Rachel."

"Chase, I can't. I feel so stupid."

"You feel sexy to me, not stupid." Chase found her opening with one fingertip and probed inside her.

She groaned. "You're trying to make me feel better about this."

"That, and I like looking at you naked almost as much as I like touching you. Open your legs for me, Rachel. Let me see your pretty pussy. Or do I have to spank you again?"

She made a strangled sound and let her knees move apart, not all the way, but complying enough to show him what he wanted to see.

"Watch, Rachel. See how beautiful you are, how sexy."

His thumb circled her clit as he slowly buried his finger inside her, drew it back out, and plunged it in again. Rachel watched him do it, feeling exposed and unsure and turned on despite it. He pinched her nipples in turns, not hard enough to hurt, but enough to get her attention, and she felt the response in her womb as everything tightened. Her sex clenched around his finger as it penetrated her.

"I could do this for hours." Chase pushed a second and then a third finger inside her, wiggling them until she squirmed into his hand in reaction.

"Your hand would probably cramp," she muttered. She was enjoying it in spite of herself, in spite of her mental discomfort, and half hoped he'd keep going. It was starting to feel really interesting. She realized with a jolt that he could coax her into orgasm without much more trouble, when she'd been hiding under the blankets from him minutes before.

"You won't last long enough for that." Chase gave her a knowing look, and Rachel felt her cheeks burn with renewed embarrassment. "Want to come again?"

She must've taken too long to answer him while she thought it over, making him think she needed to be convinced, because he lowered his head to her breast and sucked hard at her nipple while his fingers continued to play her sex. It felt too good. Rachel dropped her head back and let her legs fall open all the way. "Yes."

"That's the right answer," he said, letting her nipple slide out of his mouth. "I like making my pretty naked captive come."

Making her come again was something he could do all too easily, she realized. He'd seduced her from hiding under the covers to lying naked and splayed open for him while he played her body like a master. And he'd done it so quickly, arousing her all over again so completely. That unnerved her, but it felt too good to want to stop. *You deserve this, just this once,* she told herself, pushing aside the fear that said she was losing control and losing herself to the fantasy.

"Ask me to make you come, Rachel."

She drew in a shuddering breath. "Make me come, Chase. Please."

Six

Chase felt his blood rush from the picture she made. Rachel with her hair sleep-tousled, her nipples swollen from his attention, her sex soft and wet and giving as he worked her with his hand. This aroused, sensual woman was such a contrast to the controlled, cool image she presented to the world.

She was still clinging to a vestige of self-control as anxiously as she'd clung to the blankets, but he was going to rip it away from her and send her skidding into erotic abandon. He wouldn't stop until he'd erased every vestige of the anxiety that had sent her burrowing under the blankets with pleasure. She wasn't hiding just from him, she was hiding from herself, from who she was and what she wanted. While she belonged to him, he wasn't going to allow that.

"Touch your breasts, Rachel."

"What?" She blinked at him, as if unsure she'd heard him right.

"Put your hands on your breasts. Roll your nipples between your fingers. Show me how sexy your pretty tits are, how hot it makes you when they're stimulated." He pressed lightly against her clit as he continued to pump her with his fingers.

She put her hands to her breasts, her movements hesitant. Her fingertips brushed over her nipples, and she gave him an uncertain look.

"Yes. Just like that." He leaned forward and nipped at the curve of one breast. "Do you masturbate, Rachel?"

"Well . . . you know. I have a vibrator." She cupped her hands over her breasts and looked down, her hair falling forward.

"Are you more comfortable with your body when you're alone? Do you touch yourself when you get yourself off, or do you just let the vibrator touch you?"

"Um. Pretty much, well, it's not like I spend a lot of time practicing my technique." She shot him a disgruntled look, and Chase grinned back, pleased to have gotten a rise out of her.

"Practice now. I'm ordering you to. You're my captive, you have no choice. Play with your pretty breasts, Rachel. Feel how soft they are, how smooth, how hard your little nipples are."

Chase felt her inner muscles grip his invading fingers, felt her lubrication increasing, and knew that whatever mental barrier she'd run into, physically she was having no problems.

It had been a mistake to let her wake up alone. She had no experience with playing these kinds of games, and her own lack of inhibitions had surprised her. He should have predicted that she'd react by trying to pull back from him. He didn't intend to let her.

Rachel touched herself at his command, exploring her breasts, the curves, cupping and lifting them, squeezing. She rolled her distended nipples between the thumb and forefinger of each hand, and he saw her eyes widen with pleasure and surprise. Her self-consciousness gave way to natural grace, her hands falling into a rhythm that mirrored his as he took her with his fingers. Her breath came faster and her back arched as she rocked into his hand. "Chase . . ."

"You want to come all over my fingers, don't you, pretty Rachel?"

"Yes." She pinched her nipples hard and moved her hips with increased urgency. "God. Chase."

"Just Chase is good enough."

She let out a surprised laugh that turned into a moan as he bent his head and tongued her clit while keeping up the tempo of his thrusting fingers. She nearly came off the bed, and he felt a primitive surge of satisfaction at the strength of her response.

Chase flicked his tongue over the tight bud of her clit again and again, determined to drive her further than she thought she could go. He felt her writhing and shuddering, heard her gasps and moans, and knew she was right on the brink. He withdrew one finger from her. It was coated with natural lubrication that he rubbed over the puckered rose of her anus once before sliding the tip of it into the tight opening.

"Chase," Rachel wailed. He felt her sex spasm, clamping down tight on his fingers. "More."

He sucked her clit hard, plunged his finger fully into her ass, and twisted the fingers buried in her until she broke and bucked wildly, coming apart for him, coming in a rush.

She fell back panting, legs splayed. Chase felt a wave of fierce, possessive satisfaction at the sight of her sprawling boneless in the aftermath of pleasure he'd given her. She deserved it. She'd given him everything he'd asked for without restraint. He'd demanded that she give herself to him, and she had. The completeness of her surrender made his neatly ordered world tilt on its axis.

He kissed the delicate skin of her belly and felt it quiver under his mouth. "Be right back," he murmured against her stomach. "Don't move."

"Couldn't if I wanted to," she said, waving a limp hand at him.

Chase used the adjoining bathroom to clean up, then stoppered the tub and let it fill while he rejoined Rachel in the bedroom. She hadn't moved, as ordered. He leaned down to kiss her forehead. "Feeling better now?"

"Well. More relaxed physically, anyway." She looked up at him. "Mentally? Emotionally? Hard to say."

"What upset you?" He sat beside her, his hip bumping up against hers, and took her hand in his, rubbing his thumb in lazy patterns on her palm.

"I don't know. It's not that we don't know each other. That actually makes it easier. I think it's because, well, I'm not like this."

Chase fought to keep a straight face. "Who bought the whipped cream? Who picked out the neon latex rainbow?"

Rachel bit her lip. "I *wanted* to be like this. I wanted to be the kind of woman who had fun sex, who did something unexpected."

"I have news for you." Chase lifted her hand to his lips

and planted a kiss in the center of her palm. "You are like this."

She shook her head. "I'm not. I'm boring, Chase. This naked handcuffs thing is not me."

"Yes, it is. Who you are in bed is who you are, Rachel. If this wasn't you, you wouldn't have had a good time." He placed her hand against his chest, cupping his over it to keep it there, and studied her for a minute while he considered his next words. How could she be so blind to something that was so clear to him? "Maybe your self-image needs a little readjusting."

She frowned, doubt and disbelief plain on her face. "That would take a lot of readjusting."

"I'm up for it." He kissed her because he wanted to and because he could, then stood and tugged her up by her hand. "Come on."

He led her into the bathroom and watched as she climbed into the tub. Part of him wanted to get naked and join her in there. That part was half-hard and straining against his zipper. Better to think with his head than his dick if he wanted to keep the ground he'd just regained, though. Instinct told him this was not the time to push.

"Relax and soak. When you're ready, there's a robe hanging behind the door. Put it on and come join me downstairs."

"I could just get dressed." She gave him an uncertain look. "You are."

"I got dressed because I had to go outside for wood." Chase leaned forward and feathered a row of kisses along her forehead and then placed one on the tip of her nose. "I don't want you to get dressed, Rachel. I don't want you to leave yet. Do you trust me?"

"Yes," she answered without hesitation. A surge of relief caught him by surprise, and he realized her answer was much more important to him than he'd expected. He wanted her trust, wanted her, and not just for a weekend. Which meant he'd have to show her what he wanted and hope it was enough to convince her they had something real when he told her the truth.

"Come downstairs when you're done in here, and leave your clothes where they are."

A stunned look came over her face. "I just realized. I don't know where they are."

"That's because you're a wild woman." Chase grinned at the look on her face and tweaked her nipple before he left her to bathe and regroup. Although if she took too long, he decided as he thudded down the stairs, he'd come and drag her out of the tub. He didn't intend to let her pull away from him again.

He wasn't going to make the same mistake twice. Giving Rachel a little privacy was one thing. Leaving her alone in a vulnerable state was another. He didn't want to leave any more room for doubts to grow.

Rachel closed her eyes and ducked under, then rose up so that her head was above the water level. The water was just right, not too hot, not too cold. Although she could tell it would cool quickly. She wondered if Chase had set the temperature that way on purpose, so it wouldn't encourage her to linger overlong in the tub.

Chase. She washed herself with lazy movements as she thought about the fascinating man who was waiting for her.

He really thought she was the handcuffs type? She could see how he'd gotten the idea, given the way they'd met and what they'd done on their first date. But he also had to know this was fantasy and her real life was a world apart.

That thought sent a sharp pain through her midsection, and Rachel realized she was dangerously caught up in the fantasy herself. She wanted to think she was sexy and fun. And maybe she wanted Chase to think so, too.

Maybe she just plain wanted Chase.

She sighed and ducked her head under the water again. No maybe about it. He sent her into sensory overload. Maybe that was just chemistry. If so, there was obviously a lot to be said for chemistry. He kept surprising her, and that engaged her interest fully. She'd never met a man like him.

Although come to think of it, she knew next to nothing about him. Aside from what car he drove, which could be a rental, and that he had this cabin, what *did* she know about Chase?

She knew he tasted good, but that kind of information didn't fit neatly into any classification. Unless she put it under the mental heading "Why Sex with Chase Is Fantastic." There was a very long list of items she could file there.

She knew he was deliberate, that he had a habit of thinking things through before he spoke or acted. That was better, a character-revealing trait. What else?

She knew he kissed as if he meant it, he had a sexually dominating streak a mile wide, and he was a very skilled lover. That made her stomach churn because of the implication that he'd had a lot of practice. On other women. Women who were more fun than she was.

Stop comparing yourself with imaginary women, Rachel

lectured herself. The last thing she needed was a trip to mental purgatory because she was making negative comparisons and imagining the worst. For all she knew, the women Chase had practiced on were lousy in business, had no ambition, couldn't run a board meeting. Dressed badly.

That made her feel a little better, but she really wished she'd thought to bring along some Häagen-Dazs for emotional support.

The whole line of thinking was silly, anyway. They didn't have a relationship, so she wasn't in competition for his attention with any other women, past, present, future, or wholly imaginary. What they had was an arrangement. She'd wanted fun sex, and Chase had certainly delivered there. Way beyond her expectations.

Did it matter that he didn't know the real Rachel? Did she care if he'd still want to handcuff her at the end of the day if he did?

Yes. It mattered. And she cared. It was dumb, it was probably going to get her hurt, but in her defense she couldn't have known she'd feel this way when she'd planned it.

In her admittedly limited experience, sex had never been so raw, so all-encompassing. So intense. So shattering. There hadn't been any distance, any boundaries. Just the two of them and an explosive physical response she couldn't have predicted.

And if she was honest, it wasn't just physical. Maybe it was because she'd never done anything remotely resembling domination and submission in the past, maybe that kind of sex play created an intense emotional element by its nature. But if so, what about the people who did this kind of thing regularly? Did they fall a little bit in love with all their part-ners and feel abandoned when playtime was over?

That thought stopped her dead and prompted a harsh internal lecture. *Get a hold of yourself this minute, Rachel Law. You are not in love. You're infatuated, and the sex is amazing, but when it's over you will not be abandoned because this is not real.*

She could admit to herself that she wanted it to be real, however. And she wasn't sure how much of that was because she wanted to be the woman he clearly thought she was and how much was because she wanted him. It seemed like a fifty-fifty split, and it occurred to her that maybe the combination was the elusive missing something she'd come here looking for. A missing side of herself and a man who brought it out.

Well, whatever she wanted, she wasn't going to find it by staying in the tub until she turned into a prune. Rachel pulled the stopper free to drain the bathwater, climbed out, and toweled herself off. She found the robe hanging where Chase had said it would be, belted it around her midsection, and headed downstairs.

She found him in the kitchen, holding a spatula. He gave her a warm smile and used the spatula to wave her to a seat at the bar that divided the kitchen from the rest of the living area. "Sit. It's almost ready."

He'd cooked for her while she took a bath? No wonder she felt as though she were falling for him. How was she supposed to keep her head when he did things like that? Rachel slid into a seat, and a minute later Chase put an omelet with toast in front of her. He set an identical plate next to her and then poured two glasses of orange juice be-fore joining her.

"Eat," he said. "You burned a lot of calories up there. Time to refuel."

"Thank you." Rachel picked up her fork and cut into the omelet. "You didn't have to do this."

"Yes, I did. It's all part of my master plan." He leaned over and kissed the sensitive hollow just below her ear.

Plan to do what? Drive her insane? Make her hopelessly lost in the fantasy? Since she couldn't fathom Chase, Rachel focused on something concrete she could sink her teeth into and ate her omelet.

While they shared the impromptu meal, Chase kept up a steady campaign of little touches. Smoothing her hair back over her shoulder. Brushing his arm against hers. Small points of contact that made her feel very aware of his presence and very much the focus of his attention.

When they finished, Chase stacked the dishes in the sink and then came around to stand behind her. He drew the robe to the side just a little, baring the curve of her shoulder, which he covered with a series of kisses that sent shivers down her spine and made butterflies dance in her belly.

"Come lie by the fire with me, Rachel."

She stood with him and let him take her hand to lead her over to the fireplace. He grabbed a couple of pillows off the couch and dropped them on the carpeted floor, then sat on the floor and drew her down with him. Chase nudged her to lie back with her head on one of the pillows and stretched out beside her, propped up on one arm, another pillow tucked under him. He carried her hand to his mouth and kissed it in a series of soft, lingering brushes of his lips that sent heat curling through her and made her feel cherished.

Rachel looked up into his eyes and found herself caught

by his intent gaze. His lips quirked in a faint smile as he lowered her hand to rest on his chest. "You look surprised."

"You kissed my hand," she blurted out in response.

"Your hand is very kissable." Chase loosened the top of her robe a little more and began a lazy exploration of the curves and hollows of her shoulders and collarbone. "Every inch of you is delectable."

"You use words like that, and then you say things like—" Rachel broke off, finding herself unable to repeat some of the things he'd said upstairs now that the heat of the moment was past.

"I have a broad vocabulary." Chase dipped his head to hers and kissed the curve of her cheek, then the hollows of her throat. "Pretty Rachel. So beautiful here in the firelight. Will you let me see more of you?"

Rachel untied the robe with fingers that felt thick and fumbling and then pulled it open.

"Look at you." Chase admired her with his eyes, and Rachel felt herself blushing again as he took his time looking over her naked form. He let one hand trail from her throat down the center of her torso, pressing lightly into her navel, coming to rest when his fingers brushed the soft thatch of hair that covered her pubic bone. He toyed with her pubic curls for a moment, stroking and petting, making no attempt to touch her more directly. "You're a natural blonde, I see."

Rachel felt herself blush darker red. "Yes."

"Close your eyes, Rachel." His voice was a soft, seductive whisper. She let her lids shutter her eyes and found herself even more aware of his touch, as if that sense were heightened by the loss of vision.

His mouth and hands moved over her in a mind-numbing series of kisses and caresses. He worked around the obvious spots, neglecting her breasts and mons in favor of exploring her rib cage, her belly, her arms, her thighs. Rachel felt herself sinking into a dreamy haze of sensation and emotion. He was so tender, so gentle, paying homage to her body as if he found her worth worshipping with lips and fingers.

"My pretty captive." He kissed the lower curve of her breast, and Rachel sighed in pleasure. "Stay here. I'll be right back."

She waited, drifting in lassitude, hearing his footfalls moving up and back down the stairs. Maybe he'd gone to get another colorful condom. She felt herself heating at the thought of him preparing to slide into her again.

When Chase returned, he sat at her feet and lifted them into his lap. She felt something cool touch her skin, and then he worked what must be lotion into her feet with his thumbs and fingers, kneading and pressing and stroking her from ankle to toes in a massage that drew little moans of enjoyment from her.

"That feels unbelievably good," she said, sighing.

"It's supposed to." Chase worked his leisurely way up her calves as he spoke. "Did you know that feet contain the pressure points that can stimulate every part of your body?"

"The science of seduction." Rachel felt herself smiling as he stroked down to her heels again. "I love sex with a smart man."

"This isn't about sex." Chase finished with her feet and placed them back on the carpet, then ran his hands up her legs to slide between her thighs and pull them open. His mouth explored the sensitive insides of her thighs until Rachel was quivering and ready to beg him to kiss her between her legs.

"What is it, then?" she managed to ask.

"You can't tell?" Chase stretched out beside her again, leaving her equal parts relaxed and frustrated, and stripped off his sweater. He pulled her into his arms, and she felt the rough fabric of his jeans rasping against her bare hips and legs, the snap of his fly cool against her belly, and the heated expanse of his chest against her breasts. "I'm making love to you, Rachel."

Seven

"Oh," Rachel said.

"You sound surprised." Chase sounded amused. He stroked one hand down the line of her spine and cupped her bottom, pressing her more tightly against him.

"Confused." She kissed his chest because the spicy, masculine scent of him was filling her nostrils and intoxicating her, and because she needed to.

"Did you think what just happened between us was meaningless sex, Rachel?" His hand tightened on her butt, digging into the soft flesh with his fingers just a little.

"I don't know. And that wasn't *just* anything up there," she mumbled against his skin. "It was more and better than I've ever had before. If that's meaningless sex, my relationships have been truly pathetic and I can't imagine what meaningful is like."

"Since you don't seem to know what a goddess you are in bed, I have to conclude your relationships have been pathetic. Or at the very least you've been badly mismatched.

And sex should always mean something." Chase moved one hand down between them to unsnap his jeans and draw down the zipper. "Touch me."

Gladly. Rachel slid her hand into his open pants and grinned at what she found. "I never would have expected you to go commando."

"I didn't want another layer of fabric between my cock and you." He kissed the top of her head as Rachel wrapped her hand around the base of his penis, enjoying the warmth and smoothness of that part of him.

She moved her hand up and down in a leisurely stroking rhythm, loving the way he thickened in her grip and the way his breath hissed when she stroked a sensitive point on his shaft.

"I like your hand on my cock," Chase said. "I want to touch you, too."

"Please." Rachel lifted one leg and hooked it over his hip, opening herself to him.

He cupped her sex in one hand, the other still holding her ass from behind, and Rachel sighed at the sensation of being touched in both places at once. His palm pressed into the swollen flesh of her vulva, rubbing in a slow circle.

"So wet. So sexy." He stroked one finger along her nether lips, opening her before sliding it inside. It was a gentle entry, coaxing and seducing. Such a contrast to the way he'd stormed her gates with his hands after she'd hidden under the blankets from him. He worked his way in and out in several slow, careful thrusts and then let his finger travel up to circle her clit before rubbing directly across it. The contact made her gasp and squirm.

He was hard and engorged in her hand, and she could feel the tension in his body as he restrained himself to focus on making her ready by careful stages.

"I want inside you again, Rachel." Chase moved away from her long enough to strip off his jeans, then lay back and patted his chest. "Come up here. You're on top this time."

"Saving me from rug burns?"

"It's the chivalrous thing to do." He smiled at her, and Rachel felt her heart ache with emotion. She slid onto him, pulling her arms free of the robe to leave it behind so that only her hair covered her.

She opened her thighs to brace against each side of him, resting on her knees and his torso. A hitch of her hips brought her slick vulva into contact with the hard, hot length of his erection. Experimenting with the position, she moved to rock her sex along his shaft. The intimate contact made her breath stutter, made her vaginal walls clench in anticipation.

"Rachel." Chase cupped her ass with his hands and pulled her hard against him. "Take me inside you. Now."

She raised her hips, felt the width of his head nudging against her opening, and lowered herself to sheathe him in a rush of hot, slick flesh. A soft gasp broke from her lips at the exquisite sensation of being so filled, caressed deep inside by his length. "Chase . . ." Her voice was low and hoarse.

"Ah, that feels so good." She felt his fingers dig into the twin globes of her butt, felt him push even farther inside to probe at the opening of her womb. "I want to make it last for hours. And at the same time, I can't wait to come in you again."

His words brought back the visceral experience of

coming with him buried inside her with no barrier between them. The hot liquid jet of his semen in her sensitized flesh had triggered another orgasm, and the muscle memory of it had her clenching around him, trembling on the brink.

"Oh no, you don't." Chase held her hard, not letting her move when she tried to rock on him. "Wait. If you come now, I will, too."

"I don't want to wait," she groaned, turning her head into the curve of his shoulder.

"It'll be better if you do." Chase kneaded her butt, then worked his hands up each side of her spine, relaxing her, soothing her back from the edge.

"I don't believe it gets better." But she smiled into his skin, letting him direct the pace, willing to wait because he wanted it.

"Trust me."

"I do, Chase."

At her words, he wrapped his arms around her in a tight hold and ground his pelvis into hers. "Rachel . . ."

She moved in response, finding a gliding rhythm that brought them together, moved apart until only his head remained inside her, then back together as he filled her again. It felt warm and comforting, satisfying, and more than a little intoxicating having Chase under her, so many parts of their bodies touching. Feeling Chase hard and thick inside her, engorged with need. She reached back to touch his balls and found them drawn tight. "You want to come," she said in a husky voice.

"More than you can imagine. But don't stop. I love the way you ride me. Love feeling you close around me, so hot and tight and wet. I love being inside you."

"I want to come, too." She shivered as she said it, feeling her inner muscles beginning to quiver as a precursor to orgasm. He rocked into her again and hit the pleasure point deep inside her that made her gasp. "Chase."

"There?" He held her tight as they rocked together, their rhythm accelerating, the ridge of his cock thrusting against the spot that made her groan and tighten around him and slide over the edge, helpless in the grip of seemingly endless spasms of pleasure. "I'm coming, Rachel. Take me."

"Yes," she panted, and then let out a low cry as he pumped the hot spray of his seed into her again, pushing her into another pulsing wave of ecstasy.

When they finally stopped, she rested on him and burrowed into the comforting solidity of his arms wrapped around her, breathing him in, feeling him planted as far inside her as he could go, and wondered if she'd ever feel complete without this again.

Eight

Rachel woke up alone again, but this time instead of reacting with self-conscious panic over her uncharacteristically abandoned behavior, she stretched and rolled across the bed in a giddy expression of happiness. She felt muscles twinge and pull as she moved, and the evidence of her debauchery made her smile.

Rachel belted the robe around her waist and headed down to get a cup of coffee and a good-morning kiss, serenely confident that the morning after would be as enjoyable as the night before.

Her first hint that her confidence might be misplaced came when she saw Chase's closed expression. Her smile faltered, then faded as she came up to the kitchen area. "I thought I smelled coffee?"

"You did." He turned and opened a cupboard to take out a mug for her, filled it, and held it out to her. Rachel came closer to take it. Her fingers brushed against his in the process, and she drew back in confusion, not sure if the

casually intimate touch was welcome or appropriate in the
cold light of day.

"Rachel." Chase frowned at her and turned the cup so
she could take the handle without any awkwardness. "Here."

"Thank you." She took the mug and clutched it to her
chest, unconsciously moving into a self-protective stance.

He looked at her and shook his head. "I'm sorry. I'm
making you feel uncomfortable. That wasn't my intention."

"No?" She sipped at the coffee. Whatever the morning
held, all signs indicated that she was probably going to need
some caffeine to get through it. "You looked like maybe I
was intruding. Or maybe you just woke up and realized
you'd brought a strange woman with bad taste in condoms
home with you."

"I thought the electric blue was interesting," Chase
said, his face unreadable. "And you seemed to like the
purple."

Rachel swallowed, trying to get rid of the lump that
seemed to have formed in her throat. "It looked good on
you," she said carefully.

She set down her cup and wrapped her arms around her
midsection. "Chase, I feel like I'm getting some mixed signals
here. We made a date to play captive and captor. We had
great sex. And then you started talking about making love
and gave me definite indications that you were looking forward to seeing me in the morning, and now, well . . . Now I
get the feeling that I should have put on my clothes instead
of this robe before I came downstairs."

He shook his head. "There's nothing wrong with what
you're wearing, Rachel. I want to see you this morning very
much. I'm just not looking forward to certain aspects of it."

"Oh." Rachel licked her dry lips and nodded. "Like the part where you tell me you're sorry if you gave me the wrong idea because I've jumped to conclusions, read too much into what was just sex. Just fun. It's okay, Chase, I'm a big girl. I knew what I was getting into from the beginning."

"No, you didn't." Chase came toward her and settled his hands on her arms. "You thought you had an agency date. You thought you had a match who wanted the same thing you did."

She stared at him, uncomprehending. "I don't understand."

"I know." Chase sighed and said, "You're owed a refund. You were a hard match, and there wasn't any profile in the company's client database that was compatible."

Rachel shook her head. "No. Mark told me there was a match."

"Not in the client database."

She shook her head again, swimming in confusion. "What are you trying to say, Chase?"

"That I'm not a client of the Capture Agency. But I am your match, Rachel. Mark didn't lie about that. He just didn't tell you that he ran your profile against something other than the client database."

"What?" Rachel's stomach felt clenched and hard. "Then how did you come into the picture?"

"My profile was stored in the original test database." Chase rubbed her arms as if he could feel how cold she'd gone under the thick fabric of the robe. "It's been there since the early design stages, when I wrote the compatibility matching program. I had to have something to work with, so I entered my data. When Mark couldn't find a client

match for you, he ran my profile against yours. I was coming to tell you that there'd been a mistake when I joined
you in the conference room."

Rachel opened her mouth and closed it again, speech-
less. She shook her head and tried again. "Why?"

"Why did I let you believe I was a client? Because I
wanted you. Because I didn't want you to go looking for
sexual excitement with another man when I could give you
what you wanted." His hands tightened on her arms and his
eyes bored into hers, his pupils dark and dilated with emotion. "Because you fell into my arms and I didn't want to let
you walk away."

"Oh." She nodded dumbly. "Good reasons. I think."

"I didn't expect this, Rachel." His hands gentled on her
arms and stroked up to her shoulders to nudge her forward.
Rachel took a half step that brought her up against him, and
his arms circled her, keeping her there. "I thought I could
play my part, give us both something we needed, send you
on your way with your curiosity satisfied and some happy
memories. I didn't expect to want more, and you probably
didn't, either."

He brought a hand around to cup her chin and lift it up.
"You do want more, don't you?" His eyes searched hers, and
Rachel saw the hint of vulnerability there and realized that
her answer was important to him.

"Yes." She gave him her answer without hesitation. "I
want more. I didn't expect that, either. I didn't expect to
feel so tangled up with you, so immersed in the fantasy. But,
Chase, how much of that is just sex and how much is real?"

He gave her a half-smile and tossed her own words back
at her rephrased. "There's no *just* about the sex we've had.

And everything that's happened between us was real. It doesn't get any more real." He lowered his head to kiss her with deliberate thoroughness. Her lips softened and parted for his, unable to resist, unwilling to shut him out. Chase deepened the kiss until Rachel felt her heart racing and blood rushing in her ears.

When he finally ended it, he rested his forehead against hers and rocked her in his arms. "I'm aware that we need time to get to know each other better, but I do know the real you, Rachel. And I know that I want you this morning more than I did yesterday."

"I want you, too," Rachel admitted. Not much point in denying it, since she'd just finished playing tongue tag with him. "But you lied to me. Or at least, didn't tell me the whole truth. So where do we go from here?"

"Where do you want to go?" Chase walked her backward until she came into contact with the kitchen counter.

"I don't know." She took a deep breath and let it out, trying to think. "You could tell me just exactly who you are, for starters. Why would Mark set us up like that?"

"Mark worries about me. He's been looking for a match for me for years, apparently, and you finally fell into his clutches. I'd apologize for that, except that it brought us together and I'm not at all sorry you're here with me now."

"Then you're a hard match, too."

"Just like you. To answer the rest of your question, I own the agency," Chase said. "I wrote the compatibility matching program and used it along with the money I made at a more conventional software company to start the business."

"So you're a programmer." Rachel took a minute to absorb that. "I did want a smart man."

"That was in your profile," Chase agreed.

"You don't dress like a programmer." She gave him a guarded look.

"Mark is my personal shopper. He has excellent fashion sense. Or so he tells me."

Rachel nodded slowly. "Should I be jealous of Mark? Is there some history between you two?"

Chase raised a brow at her. "If you don't believe I'm firmly in the hetero camp, I'd be happy to lay you and any suspicions you have about my sexual orientation to rest."

That made her go light-headed, but Rachel drew in a deep breath and forced herself to focus. "Good to know. But not an answer. Why would Mark be looking for Ms. Right for you?"

"He's a good friend, and he worries." Chase rocked his pelvis into hers and tightened his arms around her simultaneously. "And there has not been a woman, right, wrong, or indifferent, in my life for longer than I care to admit."

"Which brings up another point." Rachel laid her palms against his chest and pushed back, not hard but enough to get his attention. Chase loosened his hold and let her put a little space between their bodies, which allowed her to look into his eyes more easily. "We had sex without condoms. Twice. I assumed you'd been through the same testing I had."

"I have been. You can see the records if you want. When I used myself as the test profile, I went through the whole process."

It took a beat for the implications of that to register, and when it did, Rachel felt her jaw sag. "You haven't had sex with anybody since you set up the company? Why?"

"No, and thank you for reminding me how long it's been." He scowled at her, and Rachel fought the urge to laugh.

"It's only been a few hours," she pointed out.

"I have a lot of time to make up for." Chase kissed the corner of her mouth.

"Which doesn't answer my question," she said, unable to resist turning her head just enough to let her lips brush his.

"The why is pretty simple. There wasn't anyone I wanted, and I didn't try very hard to change that," he answered. "I'm willing to bet that you went the same route I did. Lived in your intellect, because that was your strength. Focused on goals. Had a long-term plan. Achieved everything on it. And then suddenly something changed and you looked around you and wondered why it wasn't enough."

"That pretty much sums it up." Rachel closed the space between them and pressed into his body with hers, sliding her arms around his waist. "Why wasn't getting everything I thought I wanted satisfying?"

"Because there's more to life. More than you might even know you're missing until the moment it falls into your arms." He tucked her head under his chin and cuddled her. "Emotional needs." His hand roved down her hip. "Physical needs. Connection."

"Um," Rachel agreed, feeling very aware of her physical needs. "About that *more* . . ."

"This counter is a nice height," Chase observed, and she found herself torn between laughter and the urge to find out if the counter was, in fact, an accommodating height for satisfying certain physical needs.

"Chase." She shook her head and burrowed into him, not sure what came next but positive she didn't want to let go.

"I'm asking you to give us a chance, that's all." He placed his hands on her hips and lifted her onto the counter, slid his hands between her thighs to urge them apart, and stepped between them. His arms closed around her, and his lips searched hers out. His body rocked into hers, and Rachel didn't want to think anymore.

She broke the kiss long enough to find the knot she'd tied the sash into and loosen it. That done, she pulled open the robe and sat there, baring herself to him.

Chase cupped the sensitive undersides of her breasts with his hands, rubbing his thumbs across her nipples. "I take it this means yes?"

"Yes." Rachel felt her belly tighten and her breasts swell in his hands, nipples growing pebble hard from his attention. "We'll give it time. Date, I guess."

"Exclusively." Chase freed one breast to plant his hand over her mons in a possessive hold. "If you want to take it slow, put the sex on hold after this weekend, that's your right, but no other men, Rachel."

"There weren't exactly hordes of sex fiends beating down my door before," Rachel managed to say. It was getting harder to focus on the conversation when his hand was cupping and squeezing between her legs and all she wanted to say was *more*.

"That's because they never saw the real you." He found the sensitive bud of her clitoris hidden under its protective hood of flesh and stroked it in a gentle, coaxing caress. "The woman who wanted to be handcuffed and taken, the one who makes love like a goddess, the passionate, uninhibited you."

"I never thought I was that person." Rachel tilted her pelvis forward, arching into his hand. "I might not be. This could be an aberration. You might be really bored with me once you get to know me and the initial novelty wears off."

"I'll take the chance." Chase drove a finger into her, and Rachel gasped. "Right now I'm going to take *you*. I'm going to fuck you right here on the kitchen counter, and I'm going to do it hard and fast."

She gulped in air. "There's a problem with that."

"What?" He froze into rigid control.

"Your pants. They need to come off."

Chase relaxed again, the tension easing from his body. "That's not a problem."

"Well, actually, it is." Rachel reached down to fumble at his button and zipper. "Because it takes two hands and one of yours is really busy. But I am pretty good at problem solving." She tugged down the zipper, and Chase laughed.

Then her hand closed around his shaft and the laugh turned into a groan. "Rachel . . ."

"Maybe they don't have to come off," she panted. She needed all of him filling her, and she needed it now. "Open is good enough. Fuck me, Chase. Right now."

"And you think I'm going to get bored with you." He gave her a look of disbelief, then pulled her closer to the edge of the counter and guided himself to her opening, replacing his fingers with the thick head of his cock. He gripped her hips and thrust forward. Rachel wound her legs around his waist and held on.

Six months later, Rachel stared blindly out the windows of her corner office. It was bright and sunny out, and she was itching with spring fever. Over breakfast that morning, Chase had suggested spending the weekend at the cabin, and she'd been distracted by the idea all day.

Images of her naked lover and fantasies of all the deliciously wicked things he might want to do to her and with her kept intruding as she struggled to keep her mind on business. Not easy to do, when Chase had found so many creative ways to demonstrate that her taste for handcuffs and unconventional sex wasn't a temporary aberration.

He'd been right all along: He'd seen the real her that first weekend. It had taken her time to adjust her image of herself to include a kinky streak, but Rachel no longer had any worries that they'd prove mismatched over time or that she'd disappoint Chase in bed. She wasn't nearly as conservative as she'd thought she was. She'd just needed the right partner.

By the time the clock read 4:00, she wanted nothing more than to shut down her computer, abandon the reports waiting for her, and leave early. She'd found what she'd been looking for six months ago, and she wasn't missing anything now except Chase. There was something she wanted to tell him.

A pair of arms came from behind her and closed around her in a hard, uncompromising grip. A low, masculine voice rasped against her ear, "Get up, nice and slow, and come with me."

Her pulse leaped in her throat, and her breath went away. The man holding her pulled her into a standing position. Once he had her upright, he tightened his grip to pull her hard against his body. The unmistakable bulge of his erection pressed into her ass. He thrust his hips into her, blatantly showing her what he wanted. Rachel felt traitorous heat stealing through her body. He brought one arm down her body to cup his hand over her sex through the thin fabric of her dress.

"Leave with me now, or I'll bend you over that desk, bunch your skirt up around your waist, and tear off your panties. Then I'll touch you until you're so hot, you're squirming. I'll use your skirt to tie your hands behind your back so you can't fight it, can't get away. And then I'll fuck you. Right here. If anybody comes into your office, they'll find you bent over your desk with your bare ass in the air and your legs spread open, taking every inch of my cock."

She whimpered and felt her knees folding, her sex swelling, growing slick and hot at his erotic threat. "Chase . . ."

"I'm taking you captive." The hand cupping her between her legs squeezed her mons, and Rachel rocked her hips into his hold. "You've been working long hours all month. So have I. Work will still be here waiting Monday morning. Right now, it's playtime."

She wet her lips with her tongue. "I want to play."

"Then come with me." He moved his hands up to cup her breasts, and she made a low sound of pleasure. They felt heavy and aching, needing his touch. "Like that?" He rubbed his palms in teasing circles over her nipples, making them swell and harden.

"Yes." Rachel let her head fall back on his shoulder. "I like that."

"You don't seem to be moving, though."

"That's your fault," Rachel complained. "You come in here when I'm staring out the window, all distracted, thinking about being at the cabin with you. Then you grab me and rub your hard-on into my butt and threaten me with unspeakable things that make me hot, and now I can't walk."

"I could carry you, but it might look funny." Chase slid his hands away from her breasts, down to her arms, and stroked her from wrist to shoulder in a soothing caress.

"Just give me a minute and I'll get control of my knees back." Rachel grinned and leaned against him, letting him support her. She knew he wouldn't let her fall. He'd caught her the first time they'd met, and he'd never let go. She'd been certain for months that she never wanted him to.

"Take your time, as long as you're aware I'm going to take *you*." He lowered his head to kiss the vulnerable nape of her neck, exposed to him since she wore her hair swept up in a clip. "Every way I want to. Standing. Sitting. Bending. Kneeling. Lying. Hard and fast, then slow and deep. Again and again."

She shivered at the erotic promise in his words. His lips on her bare, sensitive skin made gooseflesh dance down her shoulders, and the combination made her melt into him. "That isn't helping. I'm going to collapse in a heap of mindless lust if you keep this up."

"Just lust?" He caught her earlobe between his teeth and scraped them lightly against her skin, making her shudder in reaction.

"No." Rachel closed her eyes and hoped he'd catch her as she fell this time. "I love you."

"Ah." Chase wrapped his arms around her again and held her tight. He rubbed his chin against the top of her head and let out a long breath. "Do you have any idea how long I've waited to hear you say that?"

"I wanted to be sure." She gave a slight shrug. "It's not like we met under conventional circumstances, and we really haven't known each other all that long."

"Long enough. I've been sure since the first week." Chase took her by the shoulders and turned her to face him. "I started falling in love with you the first time we met."

"In that conference room? When I was wearing business clothes and granny panties?" Rachel sent him a look of amazed skepticism. "I was so not dressed for seduction. I had to buy something sexy to wear for our date because I didn't own anything I wanted you to see underneath."

Chase laughed out loud. "I didn't know about the granny panties, but I promise you I wanted to take them off you no matter what kind you wore."

Rachel shook her head. "Granny panties are the direct opposite of sexy, Chase."

He gave her an interested look. "Maybe you should wear them for me and let me judge. Just the panties. Nothing else."

She blinked. "That might be enough to make you overlook the style."

"We'll have to find out. In the meantime, I have something else I want you to wear."

"Really?" She blinked at him and reached up to fit her

thumb into the dent on his chin while she came up with a guess. "Handcuffs?"

He shook his head. "Something you can wear in public." He reached into his pocket and took out a small box, and Rachel felt her heart flip over.

Then he knelt in front of her, and she bit her lip as tears pricked her eyes. "Chase."

"Very good." He raised a brow at her. "You should always know the name of the man who's proposing to you."

She held her breath as he took out the ring and slid it over her fingertip. "I love you, Rachel. I want to keep you forever. Be my wife."

She blinked a shimmer of moisture from her eyes and whispered, "Yes." He slid the ring all the way on, and Rachel pulled her hand up to look at it. The marquise-cut diamond sparkled in the sunlight. "It's beautiful, Chase."

"So are you." He stood and took her hands in his. "It looks very right on your finger."

"It feels right." She smiled at him, feeling light and happy and certain that he would never stop surprising her.

"This is the part where I steal you away and have my way with you," Chase informed her.

His mouth claimed hers in a hard, hot, thorough kiss, and Rachel surrendered to it, ready to be taken.

The Perfect Stranger

Nine

Sabrina Daniels breathed in the cool morning air and felt the spray misting her face as she stood at the bow of the ferry. Bainbridge Island was already in view. As she watched, hands buried in the deep pockets of her thick wool coat to ward off the winter chill, it loomed larger. More detail emerged as the ferry neared its dock. She could see the sailboats and yachts in their slips. Which one was her destination?

One of those bobbing masts represented her goal. The *Rebecca,* which struck her as both a romantic name and a good omen. She had a date with a pirate. Or at least with a man who wanted to play the part while she played his captive. Excitement bubbled up inside her, and she found herself grinning, almost hugging herself with happy anticipation.

Maybe it was silly to have gone to such lengths to fulfill a fantasy. She didn't care. She was entitled to be silly if she wanted. And she had gone to some lengths. Engaging the services of an exclusive dating agency that catered to clients with capture and bondage fantasies. Going through all the agency paperwork, tests, and requirements. Meeting her prospective match to see if they hit it off.

Sabrina curled her toes in her deck shoes at the thought of that first meeting with Kane.

Her first impression had been that he didn't look at all like her usual type. He wasn't an executive, with one of the three variations on the conservative male haircut. He wore his wavy black hair long, secured with a leather thong at his nape. The hairstyle showed off a solid gold hoop dangling from one earlobe.

His blue eyes framed by thick black lashes were almost pretty in contrast with his very masculine face. His skin showed the signs of long exposure to sun and wind. He'd worn jeans and a bone-colored fisherman's sweater instead of a suit, deck shoes instead of polished dress shoes.

And he was big. At least six feet four, with a well-muscled proportionate build. He'd filled the little conference room where they met, making the space around her seem too small. The height difference between them was noticeable, even sitting. His shoulders were easily twice as broad as hers. He lounged beside her, dropped her a wink, and said, "Arrrrr," in his best pirate voice.

Sabrina had burst into laughter and relaxed. She'd known then she didn't need to meet any of the other candidates on her match list. Kane might have been larger than she'd expected, but he didn't use his size to intimidate, and he had a playful sense of humor.

They'd arranged the date. She'd agreed to come to him this morning, board his yacht, and then, well, probably spend a lot of time in his cabin. Who knew what a pirate would demand of her?

She felt warm in spite of the winter chill as she imagined the possibilities. Maybe he'd start with finding out if she'd met his condition. In fact, she'd gone one step further. She felt her inner muscles tighten in anticipation and knew that she'd done the right thing for herself, no matter how silly it might be.

She felt alive. Excited. The frustration she'd been fighting for months had evaporated as soon as she held the Capture Agency's brochure in her hand. She'd known it was what she needed to do. After the Richard fiasco, she'd given up on finding what she wanted in a relationship. She wasn't about to set herself up for that kind of rejection again. The agency offered her another option—everything she wanted with no emotional risk.

It was a little unorthodox, true. But she'd always known she was a little bit different. One of these things is not like the others, she thought, looking at the group of ferry passengers. Students and businesspeople, some with books, some working on laptops, some using their BlackBerrys as they maximized their time during the half-hour ferry crossing.

Maybe she wasn't cut out for the traditional happily ever after of life in the suburbs playing soccer mom, but she could be a pirate's captive for a day. Kane's captive.

A shudder went through the ferry as it docked. Sabrina headed toward the stairs, joined the line of foot passengers, and disembarked.

"Permission to come aboard."

Kane Woods heard the pert voice and smiled to himself. So, she hadn't changed her mind. Sabrina was here.

It wasn't hard to picture her waiting on the dock. She'd

made a vivid impression on his memory with her stylish fringe of dark hair that just brushed the curve of her shoulders, gamine features, and doe eyes that had lit several times with mischief while they'd talked.

Her kissable bow of a mouth had captivated him. And while she was slender and petite, even her conservative business attire couldn't hide the fact that she curved sweetly in all the right places. A little pocket Venus. And today this treasure was his for the taking.

After a lifetime of denial, he was about to experience his ultimate sexual fantasy, and he owed it all to his agent and an unusual dating agency.

"You're holding back, Kane," Maddie had informed him after he'd turned in his last book. "Your books are solid, but writing at this level, you'll stay in midlist. You'll never break out as long as you're keeping a leash on your passion. If you want to take your career to the next level, you have to let loose. Do the thing you've never let yourself do but always wanted to. Stop holding back in life, and you'll stop holding back in your work."

Maddie was right. He knew she was right. But by the time he'd reached puberty with the typical teenage hormonal overload, he was already too tall, too big, too intimidating. He'd had to be so careful just to get a girl to talk to him, forget anything else. In college, he'd gained enough experience to know what he wanted sexually. He'd also known that it was off-limits. If he'd told any of his dates his true desires, they would have run screaming. So he'd harnessed his sex drive and practiced restraint his entire adult life. Now that habit of rigid self-control was interfering with his goals.

He was more than ready to unleash his desires on a

willing woman. But where could he find one who wanted to be made passion's captive, who wouldn't be unnerved by his size and superior strength, who wanted the fantasy as much as he did? He'd also needed a woman who wouldn't expect commitment or emotional entanglement. He could hardly use a woman he was dating for research. But an anonymous fling who'd never know, let alone be hurt by his motives? That would fit the bill.

Some determined Web searching and investigation had uncovered the Capture Agency. The solution he needed and the experience he craved. Anticipation shot through him at the thought of acting out his every forbidden desire on the woman who was waiting for him now.

Kane swung his feet off the bench they'd been resting on and went to greet Sabrina. She had her hands buried in the pockets of a wool coat that made her look even smaller than he remembered, and he felt a momentary twinge of misgiving. She looked young and defenseless, in need of protection. Why wasn't somebody protecting her from the big bad wolf?

He held out his hand, and she slid hers into his without hesitating. He gripped her fingers and steadied her as she joined him on the deck.

"Hello, Kane. May I say you're looking very able." She grinned at him, full of mischief and excitement, and he felt old and debauched just looking at her.

"I should send you home," he said, staring down at her. She wasn't wearing any makeup today, and in the sunlight she looked impossibly young and vulnerable. She didn't even come up to his shoulder. Use this woman for sexual excess and experimentation? What the hell had he been thinking?

"But I met your requirement." She batted her eyelashes at him. "Want to check?"

He should. He should show her what she was in for, what he wanted from her, and then watch her run away. Let her find out what it was going to be like to have his hands on her now, while she was free to change her mind and leave.

Kane let go of her hand to unbutton her coat, starting from the top. Nothing but bare skin waited for him underneath it, and he almost gaped in disbelief as he continued to open buttons down to her waist. At least he knew she'd worn pants, he could see blue denim covering her from the knees down.

"I said no underwear," he said, his voice coming out like a low growl. "I didn't say freeze your ass off in the middle of winter."

"My ass is fine." She smiled up at him, and he wondered how she could look so damn happy to be in the clutches of a stranger who intended to make her his captive to passion. Did she have any idea what he wanted to do to her? She was tiny and fragile, and he felt like a huge brute with his hand on the button of her pants.

More so because he wanted to undo those jeans and make certain she really wasn't wearing any underwear. The thought of looking at her and touching her like that made him grind his teeth. "You're too young to be doing something like this," Kane informed her.

Her bow mouth drew down in a stubborn line. "Am not." Then she switched tactics and opened the coat, flashing him with twin peaks of naked perfection, her pink nipples drawn into hard little buttons from the cold air. "Do these look underage to you?"

"No," Kane was forced to admit. "You're still just a kitten. What are you, twenty?"

"Twenty-nine, as you know perfectly well. And what are you, the Ancient Mariner?" She rolled her eyes at him and planted her hand on his crotch before he could guess her intention. Her hand felt far too good on him, and his reaction showed it. She gave him a triumphant look and slid her palm up and down his hard shaft. "Either you're not too old for this or you've got Viagra."

"Mouthy woman." He shook his head at her.

"The better to kiss you with." She wiggled her eyebrows at him and leaned forward to add, "The better to suck this very hard cock with, too."

"Jesus."

"Tell me you don't want to find out what my mouth wrapped around you would feel like," Sabrina said.

"You are determined to go through with this, aren't you?" Kane asked her.

"Yes, and I'm not going to let you get cold feet." She moved closer to him. Her coat hid her from view from anybody but him, and the open sides of it hid his hand on her button, her hand on his crotch. "Don't you want to see if I'm wearing anything under these pants, Kane?"

"I don't have cold feet." He scowled down at her. "I'm trying to be a gentleman now, because once I have you naked I can't promise I'll be capable of it. And then what will you do, kitten?"

"Enjoy myself." She gave him a wide, feline smile and

wiggled her hips seductively. "You're not too old for me, Kane. You're forty-two, which is a long ways from over the hill. And I appreciate the gentlemanly streak, but I don't need it. Now, are you going to answer my question?"

"Yes." Kane undid the button, feeling doomed. She wasn't wearing any panties. He would be willing to bet his boat on it. "I want to find out what's inside your jeans."

"Please do." She shifted her stance so that her feet were slightly apart, making herself accessible to him as he opened her pants and slid his hand inside. Nothing but smooth, bare skin greeted him. His fingertips brushed a tiny landing strip of carefully trimmed pubic hair and slid lower to find her sex completely hairless, bare, slick, and ready for his touch.

"Hell." He stared at her, and she looked back in brazen interest, her lids lowering slightly in pure seduction. She traced the tip of her tongue along the curve of her lower lip, and Kane wanted to take her right there. Instead, he cupped his hand over her bare sex inside her pants and considered his options.

"No underwear, Kane." Her voice was low and throaty. "Just like you demanded. I'm here for you, and you can feel how willing I am. I even got a Brazilian wax for the occasion. Why are you being stubborn and trying to ruin everything?"

"You didn't look so young in that office." He stroked a fingertip along her soft, slick folds. "You look young now. Small and helpless." And her sex was totally bare. His cock throbbed just thinking about that. Waxed smooth. Was she trying to make him insane?

"Isn't that what you wanted?" She tilted her pelvis, making his fingertip press lightly into her. "A helpless captive for the pirate in you to carry off and ravish?"

"I don't want to hurt you."

She tipped her head to one side, considering him. "If I were ten years older, six inches taller, and weighed another thirty pounds, I bet we'd still be having this conversation. I bet you've held back all your life, convinced no woman could take everything you wanted to unleash, because you're big and strong and you want to do such very politically incorrect things in bed."

Sabrina placed her hand over his, between her legs, pressing him into her. "I want you to do those things to me, Kane. I'm stronger than I look. I promise you I won't break. And I can take a little pain. If you don't believe me, try waxing *your* privates."

She was right about the first part. Was she right about the rest? Kane slid his hand out of her pants, taking his time about it and giving her sex a lingering stroke in the process, then gripped the lapels of her coat in each hand, pulling it shut and protecting her from the cold air. "Why don't you come down into the galley, have a cup of hot cocoa, and we'll talk about it."

She snorted. "I'm old enough to drink, grandpa."

"If I'm going to take advantage of you, you're going to be sober while I do it." Kane kissed the tip of her nose because she charmed him and led her below by his grip on her coat.

He settled her on the seat he'd abandoned when she came aboard and turned to the kettle on the little stove. Steam came from the tip of the spout. The water was hot enough. As Kane pulled out two mugs and two packets of hot cocoa, he tried not to think about anything but the task at hand. When he turned back to her, he found Sabrina sitting with her coat still on but hanging open, one breast fully exposed to him. He could see a seemingly endless expanse of bare skin from her throat to her belly. He curled his hands around the mugs to keep himself from putting them on her and then set her cup in front of her. "Here."

"Thank you." She took a sip and then stretched like the kitten he'd called her. "Pretty warm in here." She shrugged off her coat and sat there, naked to the waist, her jeans still unfastened, sipping her cocoa in blithe unconcern.

"Sabrina."

"Hmm?" She blinked up at him, all innocence.

"You won't distract me by flashing skin at me."

"Damn." She pouted. "I was hoping you'd forget about talking, fall on me, and rip my pants off all the way."

"Bad girl." He shook his head and sat across from her, stretching out his long legs. They bumped into hers, and she took the opportunity to insinuate one leg between his.

"Very." She gave him a wide-eyed look. "What happens to bad little girls on this boat?"

"Hard to say. You're the first."

"You haven't had any women here?" Her brows shot up. "Why not?"

"I didn't say no women."

"Ah." She nodded. "So it's bad girls you draw the line at."

He took a sip from his own mug before he answered her. "Never said I drew the line. Just that you're the first."

She gave him a bright, happy smile. "That makes me feel special."

Kane found himself shaking his head at her, smiling in spite of himself. "You are relentless."

"Determined." Sabrina set down her mug and leaned

forward, her hands on the table between them. "I want this, Kane. It's not a whim. I went to a lot of effort to find a compatible sex partner. We're not required to have sex, of course, that's entirely at the discretion of the clients who agree to date. But I came here fully intending to have sex with you, any way you wanted it. Barring a threesome."

"So you do draw the line somewhere." His lips twitched, although he had to admit the image of Sabrina sandwiched between two men made a very interesting mental picture. But there was only one of him, and the last thing he intended to do with the half-naked woman in his kitchen was share.

"Sure, it's a hot idea. It's a very popular fantasy, and great to imagine while I'm getting close and personal with my battery-operated boyfriend," Sabrina said. The admission made his cock throb. His imagination willingly sketched out an image of her naked, eyes closed, pleasuring herself. "But in reality? Not. People don't share their toys well, let alone lovers. Emotions get tangled, people get jealous. And that's just the emotional downside. Physically, you run even more risks. I'm not into risks."

"Liar." Kane reached across the table and drew a line down her breast, stopping just short of touching her nipple. "Your profile said you skydived."

"There's risk, and then there's risk." She grinned at him. "Jumping out of an airplane with a parachute and thoroughly checked gear after safety training and all the other steps you have to go through isn't as risky as it sounds. Sure, something could go wrong. But the odds are against it. It's a calculated risk. Not unlike our date."

"I'm a calculated risk?" Kane circled her nipple twice,

then stroked over it. He watched her eyes unfocus briefly and hid a smile at her reaction.

"Yes, Kane, you are. I know you're not a psycho, you don't have a police record, you don't have any horrible diseases, and you don't show any tendencies towards abuse or cruelty. Although you are being very cruel to me right now. You haven't touched this one at all." Sabrina indicated the neglected breast.

"I'll get around to it." He smiled at her and continued to toy with her nipple, tugging at it. "If you wanted to play sex slave, why the Capture Agency? Why not just find yourself a man at a BDSM club to experiment with?"

Sabrina closed her eyes and wiggled in reaction to his fondling. Her open response to him made him even harder.

"I wanted to experience being held captive and seduced into surrender in bed. That doesn't mean I'm ready to sign a submissive contract and spend my weekends chained in some executive's Bellevue dungeon getting hot wax dripped on my nipples to relieve his midlife crisis. I'm also not about to put myself in a vulnerable position with somebody who might be dangerous. I investigated the BDSM lifestyle, and to be honest, most of the people living it are too serious about it for me. I'm not that serious about anything. Except maybe Nordstrom."

Kane let go of her breast and toyed with the one she'd accused him of neglecting while he continued the conversation. "You like shopping?"

"Oh, that's nice . . ." She sighed, arching her back to thrust her breasts forward. "And yes. I'm a girl, I like to look pretty, I like fashion, and I like to shop. I'm not obsessive about it, but then, I'm really not the obsessive type."

"So what do you like?" Kane pinched her nipple and watched a flush of heat spread over her face. Her lips parted and her eyelids lowered.

"I like variety. Sleepy-time sex, when you spoon up and do it in slow, rocking movements. Comfort sex, cuddly sex, marathon sex, a hard and fast quickie. I don't want a relationship where it's all one flavor. I can think of a lot of times when emotionally or physically I just would rather do the straight vanilla thing than feel like I had to swing from the chandeliers or go through some ritual to have sex. Sometimes you just want your lover to hold you, touch you, without playing any games."

"So you don't want to play games?" Kane used his leg to push hers apart, then slid his knee between her thighs.

"I didn't say that." Sabrina licked her lips and scooted forward to press her sex against his knee. "I want to play games. I just don't want to be locked into a relationship that's nothing but. And the relationships I've had didn't lend themselves to game-playing. So I looked for what I wanted outside of a relationship."

"If you want to play games with me, Sabrina, you'll play by my rules."

She nodded. "I'm prepared for that."

"Are you?" Kane let go of her and sat back. "Then stand up and take those pants off."

Ten

Sabrina felt a thrill go through her at Kane's erotic command, and her legs actually trembled as she got to her feet. She didn't intend to show it, though. She wasn't going to give Kane any reason to hold back, and if he thought he was scaring her, he would.

It wasn't fear that made her tremble, though. It was excitement. She worked her jeans over her hips, down her legs, kicked off her shoes, and pulled her feet free. Then she stood up, fully naked, and met Kane's eyes. Which was easy to do, with him sitting down. If he'd been standing, she would have had to tilt her head far back.

The size difference between them didn't bother her. She liked it. Liked feeling fragile and feminine next to him. Liked the size of his hand engulfing the curve of her breast or palming her sex.

"Nice." His blue eyes ate her up. She could feel her nipples tighten and her sex soften at his blatantly sexual regard. "Come here." He patted his lap in invitation.

Sabrina closed the distance between them with a couple

of steps and perched on his thighs. The rough fabric of his jeans rubbed against her bare butt and the backs of her thighs. He felt big and unmistakably male under her. He wrapped one arm around her and pulled her back against his chest. "You didn't finish your cocoa."

"Do you have a hot chocolate fetish I should know about?" Sabrina asked him.

"What, like this?" He dipped a fingertip into his mug, painted her nipple with warm cocoa, then shifted her in his lap. "Straddle me."

"You're the boss." She faced him and hooked her thighs over his. He gripped her waist and lifted her up as he bent his head to draw her cocoa-tipped breast into his mouth. The position made her open and accessible to him, and Sabrina felt heat curl through her belly as his tongue curled around her nipple.

His hands were hard and insistent on her bare waist. She wanted to feel them on her sex. Removing the protective pubic curls had left her most sensitive skin exposed, and it amplified every sensation. In the week since she'd had the waxing done, she'd discovered that even something as simple as walking had become an erotic experience.

What would it feel like to have Kane touching her there in earnest? His fingers had barely brushed her, and she ached to feel them explore her more thoroughly. She wanted to feel his hands and his mouth all over her and that impressive cock of his between her legs. "Kane," she said with a sigh.

He let her nipple slide out of his mouth. "Sabrina."

She caught her breath in anticipation, craving his lips and tongue on her other breast. "Yes?"

"This is your last chance to put your clothes back on and walk away."

She shook her head and leaned forward to kiss him. Her lips met his and clung, then slid free. The taste of him stayed on her mouth, chocolate mingled with the seductive flavor of male. "I don't want to walk away. And you can't honestly tell me you want me to."

"I don't want you to." His hands tightened on her. "I want you to stay. I want to keep on touching you and tasting you, and that's not all I want to do to you, Sabrina."

She felt a quiver go through her and leaned closer, rubbing her bare breasts against the slight scratch of his wool sweater. "Do whatever you want to me, Kane."

"I want a lot." He pushed her back down onto his lap, freeing a hand to touch her mouth. "I want to take you here."

Sabrina could almost taste him, hard and hot in her mouth. She nodded, giving him her wordless permission.

"I want to take you here." He touched the soft skin at the apex of her thighs, and Sabrina ached for him to touch her more directly. She nodded again. He moved his other hand around her back, down to press against the soft, rounded curve of her ass. "And I want to take you here."

She felt her sex clench and her inner muscles tighten in reaction. "You want to do me in the ass?"

"Yes, kitten, I do." He traced a finger down the line that separated the twin cheeks of her butt and stroked lightly over her puckered anus.

Sabrina considered the sensation of his fingertip gliding over that sensitive point. It didn't feel unpleasant. It felt good. Maybe this had possibilities. And frankly, she was curious. "What else would you be doing at that point?"

"What else would I be doing?" Kane pressed against her anus while he spoke, and Sabrina felt herself growing hotter from his words as much as from what his hands were doing. The hand touching her mons slid lower and probed between her legs, cupped her sex, then penetrated her with a finger. "I'd be doing this. Filling you with my fingers. Fucking you with my hand in front while I fuck you behind. Two ways at once."

She shuddered and closed her eyes at the vividly erotic picture he painted. "Wow." She felt her inner walls clamp down on his finger, gripping him tight. "That's hot."

And the closest thing to the two men at once fantasy she'd ever experience in reality. Why hadn't she ever thought of trying that before to spice things up? Oh, yes. She would have had to ask one of the straitlaced executive types she'd dated to do it. Sabrina could just imagine how that would have gone over. Richard would have been horrified. He would have run even faster.

"Not nearly as hot as doing it will be." Kane withdrew his finger, then thrust it back into her again. "Finish your cocoa."

She gave him a disbelieving look. "Like I can swallow anything right now."

"You'd better start practicing." Kane gave her a slow smile full of sensual intent. "I expect you to swallow every last drop of me when I come down your throat."

Sabrina gave an audible gulp.

"It's not too late to run."

"If you keep saying that, I'm going to think you don't want me." Sabrina rocked into his hand, pushing his finger deeper inside her. No way did she intend to let his misplaced gentlemanly instincts get between them and what they both wanted.

"I want you." Kane worked a second finger into her. "You're so small and tight."

"Think how good that'll feel to your cock," she pointed out, panting.

"As long as it feels good to you, too." Kane frowned at her. "If anything doesn't feel good, if I hurt you in any way, you will tell me to stop immediately."

Sabrina shook her head. "Ever heard the saying 'Hurts so good'? If I like it, I'm not going to tell you to stop."

"Okay, then, anything not a good hurt." The concern in his voice and his expression spoke volumes.

"Kane." Sabrina smiled at him as she moved her hips impatiently, wanting more. "I don't believe for a minute that a lover who has a care for his partner's pleasure and well-being is going to do any unintentional injury. I may be small, but you obviously found me appealing or you wouldn't have made a date with me."

"Appealing is too pale a word." Kane stared into her eyes. "You are nothing like any woman I've wanted before, and exactly what I want to take and conquer and overpower with sex."

She blinked as she took in that statement. It packed an erotic punch to hear that this man wanted to seize her and screw her into submission. "Not seeing a problem here. You're nothing like any man I've been with before and exactly the one I want to capture me."

"My size doesn't bother you?"

Sabrina laughed out loud, then sighed as he caressed her, very expertly, deep inside. "Your size is a turn-on. I bet your cock is huge. Your hands are big, your fingers are thick, and I love having them on me and in me."

"You are very small." He frowned at her, but she noticed he didn't stop sliding his fingers in and out of her sheath, working her, stretching her, opening her.

"You keep harping on that. Quit before you give me a complex." She nipped at his lower lip, scraping the sensitive flesh with the sharp edge of her teeth. "I can accommodate you, big boy. Try me and see."

"Patience." He kissed her cheek and pulled his fingers out of her. She made a sound of regret. He pulled her mug within reach of her hand. "Drink."

Sabrina picked up her cup and drank, watching him over the rim as she savored the rich flavor of chocolate.

"So you want to be a pirate's captive," he said.

"Yes."

"Know anything about boats? Ever sailed?"

"Some, and frequently. I can do the job if you need an experienced deckhand." Sabrina suppressed a moment's worry that he'd look for another excuse to send her packing. Did she really look so young to him that he felt guilty debauching her, or was he just the overprotective type in general?

She should have worn makeup. She looked older with makeup. But she'd thought it would be impractical for a weekend on the water, so she'd skipped it and come barefaced except for moisturizer.

"A naked deckhand isn't much use to me. I'm seeing you more in the role of cabin girl." Kane drained his mug and set it aside.

"I like the sound of that." Sabrina let herself relax a

little, satisfied that he intended to keep her as his capture date. She finished the last swallow of cocoa and peered down into her cup. "But why is the chocolate gone?"

"Very funny." He shook his head at her play on the highly recognizable line from a popular pirate movie.

"I like pirates." She smiled at him and set her empty mug next to his. "You look like a pirate. The earring, the long hair, the ponytail. Do you have a tattoo?"

"You'll find out." Kane winked at her. "Do you need to visit the head before I officially lock you up?"

"Yes, thanks, and are you going to lock me up?" Sabrina rose up on her knees, brushing her breasts against him deliberately, then climbed off him to stand beside him.

"You don't know, do you?" Kane unfolded his length and stood up, towering over her. "I can do anything I want with you. What would you do if I locked you in my cabin?"

"Depends. Would you be in there with me?" She tilted her head back to look up at him.

He shook his head at her. "You don't really seem to be in the spirit of the game. You're supposed to be the captive. I'm the captor. The one in charge."

"Oh, please, I'm going to have to tie myself up at the rate you're going." She stuck her tongue out at him and felt her heart skip a beat when he came toward her and scooped her up in his arms.

"Make no mistake. I will be in charge, and you will be helpless in my power."

"I think you mean I'll be happy in your power." Sabrina cuddled into him, not at all embarrassed to be naked while he remained fully clothed. He might be taking her captive, but she was the one who had the prize. She had this impressive male specimen all to herself, and she couldn't wait to be the lucky one who took everything he wanted to give her.

"Bad girl."

"Gentleman."

"Wrong." Kane deposited her on her feet outside the door that had to be the head. "I'm a pirate, you're aboard my boat, and you will not get another chance to escape me."

A thrill ran through her at his words.

"When you're finished, go in there." He pointed to the cabin. "Wait for further instructions. Oh, and don't try to pick the lock on the trunk. Consider that Bluebeard's closet. If you find out what's in it, I'll have to kill you."

Kane delivered his instructions and his warning dead-pan, fondled her bare tush, and left her there. Sabrina watched him walk away, shook her head, and went to tidy up in the powder room before she officially became a pirate's captive.

The cabin was nice. Sabrina poked around it, enjoying the teakwood interior, the neat portholes that let in sunlight, the riot of color the patchwork quilt made as it covered the bed. She sat on it and gave a tentative bounce, testing the mattress. Firm, but not hard. Springy. She approved.

"Do that again."

She looked up to see Kane filling the doorway, watching her breasts bounce. She grinned at him. "Like that, you dirty old man?"

"Yes, and it's dirty old pirate to you." He crossed his arms and waited. Sabrina obligingly bounced her bare bottom on the mattress, jiggling her breasts for his viewing pleasure.

"Like the bed?"

"Yes." Sabrina threw herself back on it. "This is a great mattress."

"Glad you approve, because you'll be on your back on it quite a bit."

She rolled to her side and leaned up on one elbow. "Say 'Arrrr' for me again."

"Wench." Kane came to stand beside the bed. He stripped off his sweater, and Sabrina nearly drooled at the sight of that washboard stomach, those muscles, that chest.

"You are so ripped," she said in awe. "Can I touch?"

He gave her a disgruntled look. "I'm huge. You're tiny. I'm stripping. Shriek a little."

"Oh. Sorry." Sabrina hugged her arms protectively around herself and fell back with a sobbing gasp. "Oh, no! I've been captured by a really hot pirate, and he's taking off his clothes. Whatever does he plan to do to me? And do we have enough lube?"

"You really aren't ever serious." Kane undid his jeans and took them off.

"I can be, when the situation calls for it. Hey. Boxer briefs. Nice. I was betting on tighty whities."

"So glad you like my underwear, you shameless, brazen hussy." Kane kept them on as he joined her on the bed.

"Oh, damn." Sabrina bit her lip and sat up, feeling her playful bubble burst. "I'm not supposed to be brazen. I'm supposed to be innocent. I'm doing this all wrong, aren't I?"

"Depends." Kane stretched out full length and hooked an arm and a leg around her, pulling her against him. "Does it make you hot to imagine being innocent and untouched and being forcibly seduced by a wicked pirate who is sexually depraved and deprived?"

"Well, yes." Sabrina put her hand on his chest and traced the outline of some impressive muscles. "But we have this teasing thing going on, and I can't seem to stop. You make me want to be brazen and make you want me." She thought it over for a minute while she explored his amazing abs. "It's your fault. You kept trying to get rid of me, so I had to seduce you into letting me stay. If I'd acted like a shrinking maiden, you wouldn't have told me you wanted to make me take your cock in every hole."

"What a mouth you have." Kane pulled her on top of him, and she felt the hard, hot length of his erection through the thin fabric of his briefs.

She arched a brow at him. "And obviously you're offended by that. Mr. Woody says so."

"Mr. Woody?" Kane's lips twitched in a visible effort to keep from laughing.

"Your Johnson. Schlong. Pecker, penis, hard-on, cock," Sabrina recited. She stretched her body on his, feeling an endless expanse of warm male flesh and rippling muscles under her that made her want to rub all over him like a kitten in catnip.

"Watch it. I'm planning to kiss that mouth."

"Sorry. Do you prefer 'purple-helmeted warrior?' " Sabrina rocked her hips into him, slid up and down on him, and luxuriated in the way he felt against her bare skin. Intoxicating. And he was so enticingly engorged for her.

"Promise me you will never say that again." Kane caught her and imprisoned her in an iron grasp, holding her immobile.

"I went too far," Sabrina admitted. "You make me giddy. You're such a hunk, Kane. All this gorgeous male flesh, all bare, all for me. And your huge cock put me over the top. I lost my head."

"You're about to lose more."

"I can hardly wait."

"You're not supposed to sound so eager. At least, not until I've had my way with you a few times and you've become resigned to it."

"Resigned." Sabrina looked him in the eye, disbelief clear in her voice. "I can't do resigned. You make me drool. You make me wet."

"Pretend."

She collapsed on his chest in defeat. "Oh hell, Kane. I'm a lousy captive. Now I'll never experience the fantasy, and you'll find somebody else to use your woody on. Dammit."

"I want to use my woody on you."

"Oh." That was reassuring. Sabrina stayed where she was, enjoying being on top of Kane and feeling his thick shaft jutting into the curve of her belly with only the thin fabric of his briefs between them. "Maybe if I just don't talk."

"I like you talking." Kane toyed with her hair. "If I want you quiet, I have ways of keeping your mouth busy."

"You do, huh?"

"I do. There's kissing. You'll be quiet every time I kiss you except maybe for a few little moans and sighs and purrs."

Sabrina smiled against his bare chest. It was all too easy to imagine sighing and purring as his mouth plundered hers. His lips were so sexy. They'd felt so warm on her breast. And his tongue, the clever way he'd curled it around her nipple. The man had a very practiced oral technique. She was certain Kane knew how to use a kiss like a lethal weapon, devastating any woman he turned his lips loose on.

"There's giving you something to work your mouth on. I'm really going to enjoy feeding you my cock and watching your lush lips stretch around it. Your tongue will be so busy gliding up and down my shaft and over my head while you suck me off, you won't have a chance to make smart-ass remarks."

"Hmmm." Sabrina felt like lapping him up as his words painted a vivid picture. "Now?"

"Not now. Just letting you know I have strategies for handling you."

"Good to know."

"Come here. I'm going to kiss you, and it's going to take all your concentration."

Sabrina felt a thrill run through her at his words. She moved up his body to align their mouths. Kane cupped the back of her head with one large palm. She could feel the rhythm of his breathing and his heartbeat under her, the warmth of him. "I'm ready."

"No, you're not."

Her heart lurched at the blatant sexual promise in his voice, and then his mouth took hers and rational thought went away, taking her ability to form words with it.

Eleven

Kane kissed as though he meant to plunder her mouth and didn't plan to stop anytime soon. She'd been kissed before. She'd never been devoured with raw sexual intent. He stole her breath, ravished her tongue, bit and then sucked at her lower lip, letting it go when it was swollen and throbbing. He thrust his tongue between her lips in a graphic demonstration of what he intended to do with his cock. When he finally ended the bruising, claiming kiss, Sabrina was left dazed and dazzled and panting for air.

"Don't hold back," she managed to gasp out.

"I'm just getting started." His voice was low and hard, and Sabrina felt her inner muscles quiver as her sex clenched in reaction.

"I am such a lucky girl." She hadn't quite caught her breath when Kane rolled over with her, putting her on her back while he braced himself above her. The position was so aggressively male, so sexual. She could feel herself getting hotter by the minute in response. By the time Kane took her, she had no doubt she'd be so wet and ready for him that his size would be no problem at all.

Kane shifted position to plant one knee between her thighs, pushing against her sex. She let out a little moan and rocked her hips into him, loving the pressure against her vulva. She felt hot and swollen and so in need of something touching her there that she ached with it. The indirect pressure gave her some relief, but she wanted so much more. His hand on her. In her. His mouth taking her sex the way he'd devastated her lips.

Instead, he bent over her and sucked her nipple while he rode his knee between her thighs. Sabrina arched her back to thrust her breast farther into his mouth and push her sex harder against him. It felt so good. She was quivering, throbbing deep inside. His mouth drew on her, and it shot straight to her womb, making everything tighten. "Kane . . ."

She gasped out his name and dug her hands into his hair, finding the leather thong that tied it back and pulling it loose so it spilled free. He looked like a throwback to another age looming over her, hard and demanding and male. A man who was a stranger. Who wanted her and intended to take her, and she couldn't stop him. Sabrina let out a low whimper as her body went liquid and her temperature shot higher.

His lips burned over her breasts, drawing her other nipple into his mouth, flicking the sensitive nub with his tongue, and Sabrina nearly came off the bed. Oh God, she was going to come before he even got inside her. She could feel the orgasm building and drawing closer. His mouth was so wicked, so thorough, so very knowledgeable. He knew his way around a woman's body, and he used that knowledge to devastating effect. Her breasts ached, her nipples throbbed, and she ground her pelvis into his knee in a desperate effort to get more stimulation where she needed it.

"Kane," she managed to say, "I'm losing it. Oh God, I'm so close."

He didn't stop. He bit and licked and kissed and sucked her nipples by turns, making her buck against him as the frenzied need for relief built. The heat of his mouth on her sensitive flesh, the strength of his leg between hers, and the position of his body over hers made her feel fragile and female and about to be thoroughly sexually possessed.

She felt a frisson of fear mixed with a rush of lust. She wasn't in control here. He was. It was exactly what she wanted, and the reality of it had her momentarily on the edge of orgasm and panic both. Some deep female instinct told her to flee. The craving for sexual satisfaction told her to stay.

Kane rose onto his knees and stripped off his briefs, and the internal conflict intensified. He was so big, so engorged. A pearl of moisture gleamed on the head of his cock, and Sabrina unconsciously licked her lips with the urge to taste his pre-come.

"Should I feed you this?" Kane closed his hand around the base of his shaft and slanted a look at her.

"Yes. No. Kane . . ." She felt wild with lust and intensely aware of her vulnerability. Self-preservation told her to stop now before it was too late. Another drive had her parting her lips and rising up off the bed to taste him.

"You don't have to talk." Kane moved to kneel beside her. "Lick the head of my cock."

Sabrina half sat, turning her head toward him to offer her mouth. He brought his penis in line with her lips, the head just short of kissing distance. She let her tongue swirl over it, lapping up the glistening drop he'd spilled for her, tasting his masculine flavor.

"Very good. Now kiss it."

She brushed her lips against the velvety skin that was stretched taut as his cock swelled to full readiness. She opened her mouth to take as much of him inside as she could, re-laxing her throat, sucking and licking his shaft as he filled her mouth.

He thrust in and out, fucking her lips, coating her tongue with the taste and feel of him, and Sabrina realized dimly that she was still poised on the brink of shattering.

Giving him head wasn't a pause in the foreplay. It was making her even more excited, making her even hotter. She wanted his cock between her legs, wanted him to plunge into her and fill her. He was so big that it could actually hurt if he did it hard enough, fast enough, and some part of her wanted that. Wanted him to make her feel every inch of him taking her so thoroughly, so demandingly, that she couldn't stretch to accommodate him fast enough without a measure of erotic pain.

He pulled out of her mouth, and she made a sound of protest.

"On your back. Spread your legs wide. Show me your sexy bare pussy."

Sabrina melted into the mattress and opened her thighs as wide as she could push them apart. She watched through half-closed eyes as he moved between them, one hand on each thigh in a possessive hold. He slid his hands toward her center until his fingertips just brushed her labia. "I'm going to take you now."

Every nerve in her body screamed, *Yes!*

Kane guided his cock into position and lowered his body over hers. She could hear his harsh breathing and knew he was as lost to need as she was. Good. She wanted him to want this as intensely as she did, wanted his balls to ache with the need to fuck her.

"Hard," she managed to say through swollen lips. "Make it hard, Kane. Make it hurt a little."

"You want to hurt so good?" Kane asked as he settled himself on her.

"Yes." His body felt incredibly good on hers, the heat of his bare skin teasing her aching nipples, the crisp hair on his thighs rubbing against the smooth skin of hers, the implacable pressure of his cock against her slick and oh, so sensitive opening. "Please."

"You don't have to be polite." Kane drove into her, giving her all of him in one hard, demanding thrust.

"Kane." She hugged him to her with her arms and legs and dug her nails into his back. Her spine bowed and she arched into him, lost, taken. He withdrew and then plunged back in to the hilt before she could recover, before she could relax enough to make it easy, and her flesh resisted as he took her. It intensified every sensation. She'd never felt so tight, so utterly filled to capacity and beyond.

"More," she whispered, clinging to him. "Kane. I need—"

She couldn't say what she needed but sensed instinctively that he knew and could give it to her. He growled low in his throat, and the sound made her shudder and clench around him. He thrust hard and fast and deep, fucking her furiously, pushing all the way in until the head of his cock touched her cervix. The deep pressure was almost a pain as he forced the thick length of himself all the way into her again and again until she was too soft and slick to offer anything but surrender, welcoming his entry.

"That's right," he grated out as her body softened for him. "Take my cock. Take all of it."

"Kane." She whispered his name and raked him with her nails, needing more and unable to say what eluded her.

"I love fucking you hard," he growled out as he rode her. "I'm not going to stop. I'm going to fuck you until you can't walk and you can't do anything but lie there and spread your legs for me and take it."

His words hit her deep in her most erotic imaginings, and his cock plundered her while he had her trapped under his body, at his mercy. Sabrina felt her vaginal walls clamp down hard on his shaft, felt the wave that had been building sweep over her, and then she was drowning in sensation and a pleasure almost too intense to bear.

"Stay with me, kitten. I don't mind your claws." Kane slid his arms under her, holding her tight while he rocked into her. Sabrina whimpered and moaned and convulsed around him, then screamed when he throbbed deep inside her and spilled himself into her oversensitized inner flesh. She dug her nails into him again and ground her hips into his, shaking and helpless, racked with spasms of pleasure that seemed to have no end.

It seemed like hours later when she loosened her grip on him. "Sorry," Sabrina said. Her voice sounded low and gravelly, as if she'd been smoking, and that made her want to giggle because smoking was supposed to happen *after* sex.

"You didn't hurt me," Kane said. He lifted his head to look into her eyes, pure male satisfaction on his face. "You can purr for me or be a wildcat. Either way, I'm going to fuck you until I'm good and finished. For variety I'll fuck your soft little mouth, and then I'll fuck you in the ass while I finger-fuck you between the legs."

"Promises," Sabrina mumbled. Her tongue didn't seem to fit in her mouth, her mouth felt like the wrong shape, and her body was stretched to capacity with Kane still buried deep inside her, his body covering hers.

"Doing all right?" He frowned at her and levered his weight off of her. "Can you draw a complete breath?"

"No. Forgot how."

He pulled out of her, and she clutched at him. "No, don't go."

"I'm not going anywhere, but you need to breathe." Kane stretched out on his back and pulled her on top of him, arranging her on his long frame to his satisfaction. He cupped the back of her head and pressed it against his chest, her face turned to the side. "Breathe for me. Nice and slow. Deep breaths. Steady. Let yourself come back down, nice and easy."

Sabrina let out an unsteady laugh. "There's no coming back down from that. That thing you keep in your pants ought to be a registered weapon."

"I think 'love gun' is even worse than 'purple-helmeted warrior.' Don't go there," he warned her.

"Don't have to. You said it."

"Hell." She heard the realization in his voice and would

have smiled, but her mouth wasn't up to it yet. Every muscle in her body felt slack and spent.

Kane stroked her hair and her back, then wrapped his arms around her and rocked her gently from side to side. "Talk to me, Sabrina. I take back everything I said about your mouth. You make me nervous when you're this quiet. Did I hurt you? Do you need anything?"

"I need something. I don't know what." She cuddled into him and let his warmth and his clean masculine scent wrap around her like a protective cocoon. "You hurt me just right. I think I almost had a heart attack. Can you actually die from coming too hard?"

He let out an exaggerated sigh. "You're talking again, in complete sentences and words of more than one syllable. Now I know you're fine."

"I'm fine. I just can't move, and for a while there my lips didn't work."

"They worked when it mattered." Kane gave her a gentle squeeze. "Your oral skills are outstanding."

"Yours, too," she mumbled into his chest.

"I haven't given you oral sex yet. You might want to withhold judgment." His voice made a comforting rumble below her ear.

"I don't have to," she informed him, stretching lazily and feeling her bare body slide against his in a very interesting way. "The way you kiss told me everything I need to know. When you put that mouth between my thighs, I'm going to hit the stratosphere in about nine seconds." And the sensation of his skilled lips on her waxed-bare labia was something she wanted very much to experience.

"I love an easy woman."

"Doesn't get easier than a woman you're holding as your love prisoner."

Sabrina exerted herself to lift her head enough to grin at him. The sight of him stole her breath all over again. His black mane of hair spread out on the pillow, making his features look even harsher, more primitively male, than he looked with it neatly tied back. His muscles gleamed with a sheen of exertion, and every rippling line of his shoulders, chest, and arms made her want to touch him everywhere.

"You are so hot for an old guy," she informed him. "If this is your midlife crisis, feel free to chain me up and drip wax on my nipples. You're worth it."

Kane quirked a brow at her. "Feeling grateful, are we?"

"God, yes. An orgasm that intense should get a shrine erected in honor of the memory. Do you have anything to make a shrine with?" Sabrina traced the muscles of his upper arms with one finger, unable to resist the urge to touch and explore.

"Cocoa packets?"

Sabrina giggled and gripped his biceps with both hands. "Look at the muscles on you. What do you do for a living?"

"Can't tell you. I'd have to kill you." Kane's face gave nothing away, his voice equally bland.

"Huh. Back to Bluebeard's closet, are we?" Sabrina gave him a measuring look. "I can eliminate things I know you don't do. You're not in the military with that hair. You also don't work in corporate America."

"Why so curious?" He ran his hands up her back in a slow, massaging stroke that made her go limp. Sabrina collapsed on him again, enjoying the firm pressure along either side of her spinal column.

"I'm a woman. I'm curious."

"I thought you wanted anonymous sex with a perfect stranger. No last names, no real information about each other, except for what we wanted in bed." Kane worked his way up and down her back, and Sabrina found it very difficult to focus on the conversation. Lassitude spread through her, and her body felt heavy after the intensity of her physical response.

"Yes, but that doesn't mean I'm not curious about you." Sabrina nuzzled his chest and planted a random pattern of soft kisses on his bare skin. "Aren't you curious about me? What I do for a living?"

"You're a Mafia hit woman on vacation. You've just finished a job over the border in Canada, and you wanted some satisfaction after the action. Killing makes you want to commit a life-affirming act. Sex with a stranger means you don't risk any complications, anybody getting too close or finding out too much about you. You used the agency as the most efficient means of locating a suitable partner for your exotic tastes."

His voice was low and lazy as he rubbed her back. Sabrina shook with helpless giggles. When she could finally speak, she said, "Mafia hit woman? Killing makes me want to commit a life-affirming act? Why don't you sound more concerned about being in bed with a dangerous woman?"

"Well, you're only dangerous for a fee," Kane explained. "Nobody's hired you to hit me, and as long as I satisfy your base urges, I'm in no danger. You're always law-abiding when you're not on the job. It's one of the reasons you have no record and you've never been caught. You're smart."

"I like this explanation." Sabrina nipped at his pectoral

muscle with the sharp edge of her teeth. "I'm dangerous. Don't mess with me. I know forty ways to kill a man and a hundred ways to hide the body."

"I'm bigger than you," Kane pointed out. "And you're not done using me to get your kinky thrills, so I've got no worries."

"I like this fictional identity." She kissed her way up to his throat and scooted higher on his body to kiss his chin. "Makes me feel sexy. You're pretty good at this game. Maybe you should write a book."

"I'll keep that in mind." Kane rolled over with her, placing her underneath him again. His chest pressed against her nipples, making them harden in response. "Meanwhile, there's another game I'm interested in."

Twelve

Kane looked at the woman sprawling underneath him. The feel of her soft body cradling his aroused him all over again. Seeing her naked and flushed and thoroughly satisfied made him feel possessive and primitive. Sabrina might be temporary, but right now she was his, and he had her right where he wanted her. In his bed, on her back.

Research had never been so enjoyable. This plan was a stroke of genius.

"I think I know what you need," he informed her.

"Oh?" Her pink bow of a mouth curved in a half-smile, and her brown eyes sparkled. "A game of chess?"

"I had another game in mind."

She gave him an innocent look. "Hide the salami?"

He shook his head at her. "Were you born evil, or did your life as a hardened Mafia contract killer make you this way?"

"The old nature-versus-nurture question. Good one. That should keep us busy for a while. Or you could find a creative way to shut me up." Sabrina batted her eyelashes at him flirtatiously, and it was all he could do not to laugh.

"I was actually thinking you might want a quick shower."

"Oh." She let out a long sigh. "I guess you old guys have a longer recovery time, huh?"

"I deeply regret using our age difference as an objection." Kane shifted his position to let her feel the proof that he didn't need long to recover. He was hard and ready. He watched her eyes widen and then darken as he rocked his pelvis to stroke his cock along her passion-swollen labia. She was soft and slick. It would be so easy to slide inside her again.

"So you admit you're not too old for me." Sabrina gave him a smug look that changed to sexual hunger as he probed her opening with the blunt head of his penis.

"I'm exactly the right age for you," Kane said. "You need an experienced man who knows how to satisfy your cravings." He thrust into her slowly this time, waiting for her body to stretch around him and accept his intrusion, yielding to him as he pushed forward until he was balls deep in her tight, wet heat.

Sabrina made a soft humming sound, and he watched her face flush with pleasure. He stroked in and out with leisurely movements, careful to keep most of his weight balanced on his arms and knees. He didn't plan to finish this way, and not yet, but preparing her for what he wanted to do to her meant keeping her relaxed, open, sexually attuned to him. "Like me fucking you?" he asked her in a conversational tone.

"Very much." She smiled like a cat in cream, and Kane felt her vaginal walls tighten around his shaft.

"You're going to love taking my cock in your ass," he

said, thrusting deeper. Her inner muscles clenched harder at his explicit words. "You'll feel so stretched, so filled. And it will hurt, just a little. It'll hurt just right, the way you like it. The way you want it. I'll make you ready for it, and I'll make you feel so good while I'm pushing my big cock into that tight little hole. I'll stroke your pussy and rub your clit while I fuck your ass. You'll be squirming and making those little gasping sounds because it all feels so good and you love getting it two ways at once, by one man who knows what you like."

"Kane." Her eyes were glazed and glassy, her breathing accelerated with arousal. "And you complain about my mouth. You make it sound so damn hot. You make me hot talking like that."

"Anticipation is key." He thrust a little harder into her and then stopped, enjoying the feel of her tight sheath clasping his cock from head to base, her body under his and open to him. His to take. "I want you thinking about it. Wondering. Wanting it. When I take you like that, you need to be very ready. And you need to trust me to make you feel good."

"You do know what you're doing with your love gun." Sabrina gave him a wicked look from under her lashes. "You're making me feel very good right now."

"Love gun?" He pulled out of her, and she reached for him.

"Hey! I take it back."

"You wish you could take it back between your legs, but no more for you for now."

"Why? Because I made a stupid joke? You're punishing me?" She stared at him in open disbelief.

"No, because you were very tight the first time and we didn't go gently. You need recovery time. And if I don't stop now, I'll be tempted to keep going." He tried hard not to laugh at the look on her face or her accusation. "I won't punish you by withholding sex. That would kind of go against our purpose here."

Kane eased himself off her to lie beside her. He settled his hand on her belly and rubbed in gentle circles, soothing her.

Sabrina shot him dark looks and grumbled under her breath before saying, "I am not a child."

"That's obvious." Kane palmed one breast and squeezed gently. She looked slightly mollified. But she still had complaints.

"I can't believe you decided to stop. I would have told you if it was getting uncomfortable."

"No, you wouldn't have." Kane stroked his hand over her rib cage and down to cup her hip. "You would have kept going, riding the mattress while I rode you until you had another orgasm. Then later on you'd feel it."

He felt certain to his bones that she would've done exactly that and been sore afterward. He wanted to ravish her and cherish her at the same time, and neither desire felt in conflict. By the rules of their game, she was his to care for the same way she was his to take. His X-rated pirate treasure. Kane wanted to hoard her as much as he wanted to spend her, and the weekend allowed ample time for both.

A shower would help ease any sore muscles she might have from their vigorous activity, and then he'd find her some clothes to wear. Her jeans wouldn't feel very comfortable without underwear. He didn't want her chafing in sensitive places. And he really didn't like the thought of taking her out with nothing but Sabrina under her coat. He didn't want any accidental flashes of skin where any eyes but his could see. He also didn't want her to be cold or uncomfortable.

It occurred to him that he was thinking about his little sex kitten a shade too intimately. *Research,* he reminded himself. *Focus.*

"Come on." Kane stood up and took Sabrina's hands to pull her to her feet. "Shower time. I'll find some sweats for you to borrow, and then we'll go get a cheeseburger."

"Mmm, cheeseburgers. My mouth is watering," she said. "Can we skip the shower and just eat?"

"No." Kane pulled her body against his and kissed her hard on the lips. "You'll feel all sticky if you don't shower, and then I'll have to watch you squirming around in your seat instead of relaxing and enjoying your food. And I'll feel guilty because I'll know it's my fault your thighs are sticky."

"Okay. I don't want you feeling guilty. I'm still feeling grateful."

Sabrina kissed him back with enough intensity to make up for the brevity. She tasted sweet and eager, and she went to his head faster than whiskey. Kane ended the kiss and set her apart from him. "Go shower. I'll bring your clothes in."

Sabrina nodded and padded off, barefoot and naked, her heart-shaped ass swaying enticingly as she walked. Kane admired the view until she was out of sight and then went to search out clothes for her.

Sabrina stepped into the shower cubicle and turned it on just long enough to get wet. She'd spent enough time around boats to know the importance of conserving the water supply. With the water shut off again, she picked up the bar of soap that sat in the shower caddy and sniffed. Citrus.

She was hit with the memory of breathing a hint of this clean scent on Kane's luscious, muscle-bound body and felt a little dizzy. Or maybe that was just low blood sugar from too much physical activity and not enough breakfast that morning. That was it, she decided. She needed to eat. It couldn't be anything else, because she was *not* losing her head over Kane.

The very idea unnerved her and lent speed to her motions. She lathered herself with citrus foam in record time. A quick rinse and she was done. When she stepped back out of the shower, she found a neatly folded pile of clothes waiting for her. Kane had slipped in and out without disturbing her.

She felt briefly miffed that he hadn't even tried to cop a soap-slippery feel or offered to wash her back. Although probably he knew that would lead to more, and the more was what he was determined to hold off on while she recovered. Laughable thought. She was never going to recover. Her pirate would be indelibly imprinted on her body for the rest of her days. Not only was Kane funny and sexy, he did things to her body that should get him immortalized. He was thoughtful, too.

Sabrina picked up the briefs he'd brought her, stepped into them, and looked down, shaking her head. They were ridiculous on her. She took them off again and put on the light gray sweatpants, which weren't much better, but they had a tie at the waist she could use to bunch them up and keep them around her middle. Rolling up the cuffs made them safe to walk in without tripping. The matching giant sweatshirt dwarfed her, but she rolled the cuffs back on that, too, and then gave herself a critical look in the mirror.

Boyfriend-wear chic? It could pass. And she did have a postcoital glow that made up for any fashion shortcomings. Her body felt loose and liquid, her skin was soft and rosy, and when she moved she felt the swing in her hips that said, *I feel sexy.*

"You're hot, babe," she informed her reflection. She fluffed her shag haircut, which lent itself nicely to that *I've just gotten out of bed, where I had the greatest sex ever* look, and went to find Kane.

It occurred to her that she'd only explored the back of his body by way of gouging him with her nails in an orgasm-induced seizure. He might be sporting a tattoo she hadn't seen yet. She had an obligation to find out if he did. If he was going to lay claim to every part of her body, including one previously untouched by man, she was damn well going to know everything about his.

The thought of thoroughly exploring all of Kane's length and breadth and width at her leisure made her dizzy again. Sabrina gave her head a hard shake to clear it just as she entered the galley and found him there.

"And what are you saying no to?" Kane asked.

"Nothing. Just trying to focus. I think I'm light-headed from lack of protein because I keep having these brief swooning fits," she informed him.

"We can fix the lack of protein, but maybe you're swooning because you've discovered the joys of older men." He stood up and came over to take her by the hand, and just that innocent touch made her knees weak.

"Older men for sure," Sabrina said, trying not to topple into him and bury her nose in his mouthwatering muscles. "Can we forget the protein and go back to bed?"

"No." Kane grinned down at her and then tugged at the waistband of her borrowed sweats. "Are you wearing underwear now?"

"No." She gave him a bright, sunny smile. "I'm too sexy for your shorts."

"Can't really argue with that." He pulled her into his side, tucking her against him. "Ready to see the outside world?"

"No, but we need to eat, and visions of cheeseburgers are dancing in my head. We'll go, we'll eat, we'll come back to play another round of the pirate and the prisoner." She ducked out of his hold and got behind him to pull up his shirt.

"Checking to see if you drew blood?" Kane asked.

"No. Well, that, too, because I really am sorry about clawing you. But mostly I wanted to find out if you had a tattoo."

She viewed his uncovered back and sucked in her breath. The man had muscles everywhere. Faint scratch lines and half-moon-shaped nail marks did decorate his back, but she was relieved to see that he wasn't actually injured. No tattoo. That disappointed her. And fed her curiosity. Why did he have the boat, the long hair, the earring, and no tattoo?

"If you're trying to find a treasure map, you're looking in the wrong place," he informed her.

"Shows what you know." Sabrina ran her hand down the line of his spine and fondled his butt. "You have buns of steel. Your whole body is amazing. What do you do, spend three hours a day in the gym?"

"Keeping up a boat is hard work." Kane turned and caught her hands.

"Do you live on the boat?" she asked.

He paused, as if thinking over whether or not he should tell her before admitting, "Yes."

Sabrina arched her brows. "Curiouser and curiouser."

Who was Kane? She wasn't an idiot. This was a Carver yacht. Those did not come cheap, even older, previously owned models. He moored on Bainbridge, not Seattle, but there were an awful lot of people in the Greater Seattle area who'd made their money in computers and dot.coms and retired early. Was Kane one of them? The age bracket fit.

"It allows me to keep a low profile, as part of my role in the witness protection program," Kane said deadpan. "Only a post office address, a fake name, and a built-in escape plan if the Mob ever finds me. Which, unbeknownst to them, they have because their best hit woman is here, getting shagged raw by the man who turned state's evidence against a don. When they trace me through you, I'll hoist sail and escape, taking you with me as my prisoner."

"Wow." Sabrina blinked at him, awed. "Then what?"

"Then I'll have to keep you tied up and incapacitated with amazing sex day after day until I've convinced you not to kill me. A role-reversed but tastefully short of porno-graphic version of 'Scheherazade.' Still, can either we or our sex-addicted love survive when the Mob catches up to us?"

Sabrina giggled. "You're so good at this."

"I aim to entertain." Kane pulled her body against his

and kissed her, hard and fast. "Time to go feed you before I rip these pants off you and take you again."

She blinked and dug her hands into him to steady herself. "Yeah. Wouldn't want that."

"You want that, and you can have it. After I've fed you." Kane turned her toward the door and herded her to the deck and off the boat.

An hour and a half and one cheeseburger plus most of Kane's fries later, Sabrina had no further clues to the mystery of Kane and more questions. They were sitting side by side at an outdoor table at the restaurant they'd walked to, and she enjoyed the warmth of the pale winter sun on her face as she considered her angle of attack.

"I don't buy this witness protection explanation," she said, taking another sip of her calorie-and-fat-loaded strawberry milkshake, for once not caring that she'd have to pay for it later on the treadmill.

"Why not?"

"You have a Carver," Sabrina said, shooting him a triumphant look. "The government is not going to buy you one of those along with a new identity. Although if that's the kind of thing they do, it would explain the deficit."

"Federal funding is murky business." Kane reached for her shake. "Are you going to finish that? Some ruthless criminal stole all my French fries when I wasn't looking."

Sabrina passed him the calories. With his muscle mass, he could afford them. "You're dodging the hole in your cover story."

"In addition to being on the run from the Mob and

living a new life in the witness protection program, I won this boat in a poker game. When people get curious about me and ask what I do, I say I'm in salvage."

That sounded familiar, but she couldn't place why for a minute. Then it clicked. "You stole that from a book," she accused. "Travis McGee won *The Busted Flush* in a poker game, hence the name of the boat. And he says he's in salvage."

"Very good." Kane finished off her shake and pulled her into his lap. "Did I mention that women who read turn me on? Especially the ones who discuss books with me while not wearing any underwear?"

"Meet a lot of those, do you?" Sabrina parried, cuddling into him.

"It happens." His bland expression gave nothing away, but he had to be lying. Didn't he?

"Well, there's only one here right now," she said. "And we're done eating. I've recovered." She tried to look brave and martyred. "I will now fulfill my promise to sacrifice my innocent body to your bestial lusts."

"Innocent?" He gave her an outraged look and let go of hiding from the Mob to turn pirate in the blink of an eye. His ability to spin fiction and role-play amazed her. "What about that Spanish naval officer I pulled you off of when I captured your ship and took you as my booty?"

"He meant nothing to me," Sabrina assured him, slipping effortlessly into the pirate and prisoner fantasy.

"And that prince in Monaco?"

"His penis was much smaller than yours. Sex with him gave me no pleasure. I faked it every time."

"What about when my rival Black Jack carried you off

and held you prisoner on his island for three months before I could steal you back?"

"He was impotent." Sabrina kept a straight face with an effort. "He forced me to endure endless rounds of oral sex to compensate, but I always closed my eyes and thought of you."

"Impotent?" Kane considered this.

"On my honor, I swear it." She widened her eyes in innocent protestation.

"I will believe you, but only after I use your helpless body to satisfy my bestial lusts repeatedly."

"That's fair," she said.

Kane placed a twenty on the table to pay for their lunch, used the edge of the empty milkshake glass as a paperweight, and then stood up with her in his arms. "I've got you, my pretty, and you'll not escape paying the pirate's price."

"You should be fined for reckless use of alliteration in a public place," Sabrina said, subsiding into a fit of giggles.

"It could be worse. I could threaten you with my purple-helmeted warrior." He scowled at her in mock ferocity, and she clutched at his shoulders as she laughed until her stomach hurt.

When she finally caught her breath, she said, "Kane . . ."

"Yes, kitten?" He didn't pause, long legs eating up the ground as he carried her off.

"How do you do that so easily?" She'd never met anyone who invented worlds with words in an effortless flow the way he did.

"You're not hard to carry," he assured her. "And I'm not exactly a small guy."

"That's not what I meant." But he'd distracted her by drawing attention to his heavily muscled frame. There was a lot of Kane to be distracted by, and soon she was going to be seeing and touching and experiencing all of it. The thought made her melt into his arms.

Thirteen

"So those other men meant nothing to you." Kane set her on her feet on the deck when they reached his boat. She curled her fingers into the soft polar fleece jacket he wore and rubbed her body against his.

"Not a thing," she assured him.

"I'll just make sure. You will have entirely forgotten them by the time I'm done with you." His deep, growling voice made her shiver, and the intent look on his face told her the pirate role was firmly in place.

Sabrina was in heaven. Her breasts felt full and heavy, her nipples were aching, her belly felt tight, and her sex was slick and eager for his touch under the loose sweatpants.

"I think we'll start by making you forget all the oral sex any other man has ever given you." Kane gripped her waist and backed her toward the steps that led down inside, out of sight and into their private fantasy world.

"You're going to make me forget the three months I spent with Black Jack's face between my thighs?" She gave him a wide-eyed look. He caught the hem of her sweatshirt and stripped it off her, tossing it aside. Her nipples puckered as cool air hit her bare breasts.

"I'll make you forget his name, and then I'll make you forget yours." Kane picked her up and carried her to the galley, where he placed her on the edge of the table. His hands found the strings at her waist and untied them. Then he hooked his fingers into the soft, thick fabric and pulled them down her hips.

He pushed her down to lie back on the table with her hips on the edge and her legs dangling down toward the floor and tugged the sweatpants all the way off, leaving her naked. He planted his hands on her thighs and pushed them wide apart, then knelt in front of her. His hands slid under her ass, tilting her pelvis. Sabrina let her legs rest on his shoulders as he pulled her just off the edge of the table and brought her bare sex into contact with his mouth.

She closed her eyes to give the experience her full concentration. He kissed her as thoroughly between her legs as he'd kissed her mouth the first time. Exploring her with his lips, drawing her into his mouth to suck and release, tracing his tongue along the line of her labia before sliding it into her slick folds. He licked his way to the sensitive bud at the apex of her thighs, captured her clit with his teeth, and then sucked it, released it, ran his tongue around it, and sucked it again.

The warmth of his lips, the pressure of his tongue, the light scrape of his teeth, and the constantly changing pattern she couldn't predict made her tremble. She never knew when he would nip, lick, or thrust his tongue into her in a hard rush or a slow slide.

"Kane . . . ," Sabrina said on a sigh. Her hands curled into fists. She wanted to curl them into his hair, but she couldn't reach unless she pulled herself forward in an abdominal crunch. So she balled her fists by her side and rocked her hips into his mouth in silent encouragement.

She'd never been devoured before, as if oral sex were the cake and not the icing. As if tasting her thoroughly brought Kane as much satisfaction and pleasure as it was bringing her. He took his time, he was inventive and aggressive and seductive by turns, and his mouth destroyed her.

Her body went taut, her head moved restlessly from side to side, and she dug her nails into her palms as the need to move, to do something, racked her. She wanted more, she needed something just out of reach.

"Ready to purr?" Kane asked. He licked lazily at her clit, endless, slow laps of his tongue, and she shuddered.

"Yes."

He drew her clit into his mouth again, gradually increasing the suction. Then he alternated suction with his tongue moving over that sensitized bud, and the combination had her breathing hard and fast, rocking her pelvis in rhythm with him. The pressure built inside her as he increased the intensity of stimulation, and then she felt her inner muscles convulse.

"Kane." Sabrina nearly came off the table as her back bowed. He kept up the insistent pressure of his mouth and tongue on her as the orgasm shook her. When it ended, he released her clit and licked the length of her labia in long, slow strokes, bringing her down and making her ready for the next stage simultaneously.

"You are so hot," he murmured, licking at her as if she were his favorite flavor. "So wet and willing. So ready to be taken."

The explicit words made her shudder. He slid his hands out from under her and moved them up her torso to stop just at the undersides of her breasts. He traced the line they made as they mounded up from her rib cage, and she ached for more. His hands cupping her breasts, squeezing, touching her nipples.

He lapped at her one last time with his tongue, then stood between her open thighs. His hands moved up over her breasts, his palms rubbed lightly over her nipples, and the fabric of his jeans scraped against her soft, swollen sex. The contrast made her breath catch.

His hands stroked back down her body and then left her to unsnap and unzip his jeans. Sabrina watched as he shoved them down his hips, dragging his briefs with them. He kicked off his deck shoes and pulled them all the way off. His fleece jacket went next, followed by his T-shirt, and then he stood there in all his naked glory, and she had never seen anything she wanted more.

"Turn over, kitten."

Her sex clenched in anticipation and a little apprehension as she rolled over onto her belly. Sabrina scooted back until her feet rested on the floor, legs parted, her hips just against the table with her torso lying on it. Her nipples pressed into the cool surface, and she closed her eyes, turning her face to the side.

She felt deliciously exposed. Kane could see the bare curves of her ass and the soft flesh of her sex between her open legs. He could see how wet she was, how eager. And she wondered how he intended to take her next.

His hands cupped her butt, stroking her cheeks, massaging down to her thighs. His fingertips brushed her labia and then moved away, in circles that moved in and out, covering the curve of her ass and teasing her sex.

"Kane," she complained, arching her back to push her sex into his hand as he brushed it again.

"All in good time." He spread her ass cheeks, and Sabrina felt something cool dribble between them. He stroked a fingertip down the dividing line between the rounded globes and rubbed the cool liquid over her anus. She felt him apply more lubrication and then work it steadily into her ass with his finger.

The unfamiliar penetration felt strange, but not unwelcome. Kane's movements were careful, gentle, and the stimulation to her anus felt pleasurable. "Relax," he murmured as she tightened involuntarily when his finger pushed farther into her.

Sabrina let out a breath and consciously relaxed her muscles, opening to him. He worked his finger all the way in, drew it back, pushed in again, moving in and out in slow, gliding strokes. "Your ass feels so tight," he said, his voice low and rough with desire. "So hot around my finger. It's going to feel incredible around my cock."

She tightened up again at the thought, and his free hand massaged her butt to soothe and relax her before working down to cup her sex. Kane had one hand exploring her ass, the other rubbing against her mons, and the combination was mind-blowing. When he thrust a finger into her sheath in time with the one inserted into her anus, the sensation intensified. She sucked in a breath and pushed her hips back toward him, seeking more penetration.

"Ah, like that, do you?" Kane bent over her to kiss her

between her shoulder blades. "You're so sexy when you arch your back and invite me to pet you."

"I feel sexy," Sabrina answered. She did. She felt hot and aware of every nerve ending in her body. His fingers worked her in tandem penetration, and her hips rocked in rhythm.

"You're ready for more," Kane murmured. "You feel so empty, don't you? You want me to fill you here." He pushed in a second finger as he spoke, then a third, and Sabrina moaned as she felt herself being stretched and so pleasurably invaded.

Before she had time to adjust, he worked a second finger into her ass, opening her there, too. The twin digits in her anus scissored, stretching her delicate skin, pushing in more lubrication to make it easier for her to accept him.

"I want to fuck your sweet, hot ass," Kane said, kissing down the line of her spine. "I want you to take my cock here, like this." His fingers moved inside her, on both sides of the separating membrane, and Sabrina moaned in response. "I'm going to stroke and pet your soft little pussy with one hand while I make you ready with the other. I'll rub your clit and make you hotter and hotter, until you can't think of anything but my cock filling you and how hard I'm going to make you come."

That wasn't far off, Sabrina realized, lost in a haze of sensation. He rubbed his thumb around and over her clit, worked in and out of her sheath while his other hand steadily continued to prepare her ass, and it felt incredible. She didn't worry that he'd hurt her, unless it was in the most pleasurable way. She trusted him utterly. He was careful with her delicate tissue, making her ready by steady stages, and so focused on her response that she had no fears she would find anything but enjoyment in her role as her pirate's prisoner.

Kane gradually increased the pressure on her clit, his fingers moving faster as they worked in and out of her, and she felt another orgasm building.

"That's it," he said, approval and satisfaction in his voice. "Show me what you want."

She arched her back to offer him her ass. "I want you, Kane."

He withdrew from her, and Sabrina bit her lip, trying not to squirm with the need for more. She heard a soft tearing sound and realized he was opening a condom package. He moved into position behind her again, and she felt additional slick lubrication applied to her anus, imagined he was coating his latex-covered cock with more of the same, and closed her eyes as she felt him position the head of his cock.

"We'll take it slow, kitten," he promised her. The hand he'd used on her sex before returned to stroke her labia and her clit before opening her to penetrate her with two fingers together. It felt good, but it wasn't enough. She pushed her hips back at him, urging him to give her more, and breathed out again to relax as completely as possible as he slowly pressed forward and worked the head of his cock into her tight passage.

"I love touching you like this, fucking you with my hand while I fuck my cock into your ass," Kane growled behind her. "I want you to take more of me."

"Yes," she said in fervent agreement, feeling raw with need. "More, Kane." She felt him work the tip of a third finger into her, realized how impossibly tight she was with his cock pushing into her. Her sex convulsed around his fingers, and he groaned as he thrust deeper. Sabrina panted slightly, stretching to take him, feeling the orgasm approaching and wanting him all the way inside her when she came.

"Hurry," she said in a low, urgent voice. "Fuck me, Kane. Fuck me until I'm so full of you I can't take any more." She rocked under him, inviting him to press deeper, and he did, pushing steadily forward as she worked to take all of him. His fingers moved insistently inside her, and when he rubbed his thumb over her clit again, she felt her inner muscles clamp down and release, spasming as he filled her to capacity.

"I'm coming," she managed to gasp out, as if he could have any doubt.

"Oh yeah. Come for me." Kane moved back and forth in gentle thrusts, claiming her anal passage while his fingers played her sex. "Come for me while I fuck your hot little ass."

She felt his tempo build as the tremors continued to break over her. "Kane. More," she almost wailed.

He thrust a little harder, still careful but taking more of her. She felt his cock swell inside her and knew he was about to come, too. He twisted his fingers inside her, and her spine bowed with the intensity of her release as he thrust deeper and they came together in a rush.

Afterward, Sabrina clung to the table, panting. She felt Kane withdraw in a steady, gentle slide and move away from her.

She closed her eyes and rested there while he disposed of the condom and cleaned up before coming back to slide his arms under her. He lifted her limp, unresisting body into his arms and cradled her against his chest. His lips moved over her temple in a tender kiss. Then he carried her to the cabin, holding her as if she were fragile and precious.

Kane looked down at the woman in his arms, eyes closed, body limp, utterly spent. She was so small, so vulnerable, with her lashes resting against her cheeks and her body curled trustingly into his.

He lowered her onto the bed, pulled back the covers, settled her on her side between the sheets, and laid her head on a pillow. Then he stretched out beside her and spooned around her, drawing her into the curve of his body, his arms around her in a protective circle. He kissed the top of her head, and she let out a soft sigh.

"Sleepy?" Kane asked, his voice low.

"Mmm-hmm." She cuddled her back into his chest, and Kane held her closer. Her perfect, heart-shaped ass was pressed against his groin, and he loved the sensation of the soft flesh he'd just taken so pleasurably cradling his semihard cock.

"I loved doing that," he informed her.

"I loved it, too," she answered, her voice drowsy and thick with satisfaction. "It felt so intense, Kane. I felt so full of you."

"That was the idea." He stroked the silky skin of her side, wanting to soothe her after taking her so completely. She'd taken all of him, accommodating his desires, giving herself in an unaccustomed way, and he valued the trust she'd shown him. If he hadn't thoroughly prepared her, if he hadn't been careful of her size and inexperience and taken pains to arouse her fully, it wouldn't have been a pleasure for her at all. Just the opposite.

He wondered if she'd experiment with anal sex with

her next partner, and something raw and painful raked his insides at the thought of any other man having her. But it was bound to happen. They had a temporary agreement. When it ended, Sabrina would no longer be his.

Would another man be as careful with her, as conscious of the need to protect her delicate tissues from strain or injury? Would another man carry her to bed afterward and tuck her in to sleep with his body wrapped around hers, or would he take what he wanted and leave with no thought for how she might feel, what she might need in the aftermath of passion spent?

She's not yours to care about, Kane told himself. Obviously he needed reminding. She couldn't be his, because if they had a relationship, she might take issue with the fact that he'd initially picked her as a research subject. Not that she'd given him any indication that she wanted anything more from him than what they'd agreed to.

While he grappled with his thoughts, her breathing grew deep and even, telling him she'd slipped into sleep. Then he realized that he was cradling her as close as he could in a fiercely possessive hold, as if some imaginary rival like Black Jack might appear to rip her from his arms.

He was listening to the sounds of her breathing and feeling the rhythm of her heart and the rise and fall of her rib cage as if nothing else in the world could be more important. He was intensely aware of the fit and shape and feel of her body against his, the mysterious feminine scent that was uniquely Sabrina mingled with the fresh citrus fragrance of his soap making a heady perfume, the slight tickling sensation of her hair against his chest. Christ, he was mooning over her.

For the first time, the story of Ulysses memorizing the lines in Helen of Troy's hand didn't strike Kane as ridiculous. If he learned Sabrina's body so thoroughly, he would know her completely and recognize her anywhere, even a world and an endless passage of years away.

You have lost it, he informed himself. But there was no denying that she floated his boat, and he would launch it for her in any direction she desired, without hesitation.

It was impossible to spin fiction while flinching from inner truths, and this one hit home with a vengeance. He hadn't just wanted a fling to experience sexual freedom with a woman he didn't have to hold back or restrain himself with. He sure as hell hadn't wanted it simply to further his career, although that had provided a convenient excuse and a prod to action. There goes the book, he thought without regret. He could hardly stick to his original plan and fictionalize the experience.

What he'd really wanted was obvious to him now. He'd wanted a woman who matched him, in bed and out. A woman whose mind was nimble enough to follow his, whose sense of humor made him want to tickle it just for the pleasure of hearing her laugh, seeing the sparkle in her eyes. A woman who took everything he wanted to give with no holds barred and begged for more instead of mercy.

He had Sabrina here, now, but not on the terms he wanted. She could walk away at any time, and he would have no way of contacting her or finding her, except to send a message through the agency. Which she might or might not choose to respond to.

Kane was painfully aware that although he'd decided he wanted more from her than their agreed-on weekend of fantasy sex, there was no guarantee that Sabrina felt the same and no reason to assume she might. She could be sleeping off the intensity of her first experience with anal sex right now with no thought of anything but what a brilliant plan she'd come up with and maybe a sense of gratitude to him for making her weekend of playing pirate's prisoner an orgasm-filled reality.

Gratitude wasn't what he wanted from her, but there were worse beginning points to work from. A fulfilling sexual experience was obviously important to her, and she'd told him enough to make him believe that any long-term relationship she entered into would have to include the variety she craved.

What had she said? Kane frowned and searched his memory for the details of that first conversation this morning. She'd said she didn't want to be locked into a relationship that was based on nothing but games, and relationships with no room for games were too limited. It boiled down to the fact that she hadn't found a man who could appreciate the full expression of who she was, all sides of her. Not unlike his own reasons for remaining single.

Kane knew with bone-deep certainty that he could have that with Sabrina if she was willing. She was bright and quick, playful and sexy, adventurous and also balanced. She didn't take foolish risks, but she did like the thrill of riding the edge.

She'd pursued her goal of fantasy fulfillment in a way that was very telling to Kane. She hadn't trolled a bar for a likely candidate and picked up a stranger who was a complete unknown. She'd looked for a partner who was thoroughly and professionally screened to eliminate the dangers of acting out a scenario that would place her in a vulnerable position, and then she'd picked the candidate she'd found most attractive and felt most comfortable with.

He thought about the realities of being with Sabrina long-term. Would she be willing to live aboard *Rebecca*? He wasn't about to live on dry land again, although he could stay moored in one place during her work week. Weekends they could sail free.

He pictured Sabrina living with him while he worked to a deadline, hours when he wasn't free to concentrate on her and had no energy left at the end of the day to play. She was the type of woman he could imagine coping with the ebb and flow of his work life, amusing herself when he was busy and not feeling neglected if he got up in the middle of the night to write the scene that had just come to him.

Sabrina wasn't a clinging vine. She posed somewhat the opposite challenge for Kane. He'd have to make domestication with him attractive enough for her to consider it. He took some comfort in the knowledge that their sexual compatibility was proof that the Capture Agency's profiling and matching was worth every penny. They were both experienced enough to recognize what a rare thing that was.

All he had to do was use the remainder of their time together to show her what he had to offer, get her accustomed to associating him with pleasure, and keep her interested in having more.

And think of a way to explain Bluebeard's closet to her.

Fourteen

Sabrina floated up from sleep to find herself cocooned in Kane's embrace. His long, muscular body was wrapped around hers, his arms cradling her, her back tucked snugly against his broad chest, his penis cushioned by her butt. Their legs were tangled together, and she could feel his hands smoothing along her skin in gentle strokes.

"Ahoy there," she said to let him know she was awake. "Avast, ye sea-scurvy scalawag." Then she frowned and blinked her eyes open. "What's a scalawag? And what kind of word is that, anyway?"

"It's a noun," Kane informed her. He slid his hand up her rib cage to cup her breast. "You know. A person, place, or thing."

"Thank you." She rolled her eyes even though he couldn't see and was missing the effect. "I believe I learned what a noun is from *Schoolhouse Rock,* while watching Saturday morning cartoons."

"Which you remember like it was last week," he teased,

flicking her nipple with his fingertip to make it harden. "Because you're barely old enough to be out of school."

"Are we back to that?" Sabrina arched her back and pressed her bottom farther into his groin, rubbing his cock against her bare skin. "I'm old enough to bend over and take it up the ass from you." Then a sudden thought had her flipping around to face him. She poked a finger into his chest. "Do not tell me you're having guilt feelings over that. I wanted you to do it. I asked you to do it, and I was the one saying *more*."

"I remember." Kane covered her hand on his chest with one of his. "I don't regret it at all. Having you bend over and offer your ass to me was an erotic dream come true. Just thinking about it makes me hard and makes me want to fuck you again."

"Oh." Sabrina felt her determination dissolve, diffused by his answer. "Well . . . good." She ran a physical inventory and noted a distinct soreness, in spite of Kane's very careful preparation and penetration. "I don't think I can do that again this weekend, though."

"Fuck?" Kane's lips twitched with barely suppressed humor at her expression. "Or take it up the ass?"

"You are so crude, Sir Pirate." Sabrina slithered across the sheets to rub her nipples against his chest, loving the way they hardened and tightened from the stimulation. "But since you ask, my backside is definitely feeling the effects. The rest of me, however, is all yours to use at will."

"You like crude. If you wanted a gentleman, you wouldn't have asked for a pirate." Kane worked one hand between her thighs to ride just below her sex, not quite touching her.

"Lucky for me, I got both." Sabrina grinned at him and wiggled until his hand was right where she wanted it, snug against her mons. "Your gentlemanly streak almost won out over the pirate, too. It was a near thing. Fortunately for me, you really wanted to go pirate on my ass, so it wasn't too hard to persuade you."

"Medieval." Kane stroked his finger along her labia. "The term is, go medieval on your ass."

"Only if you have a thing for knights." She hooked her thigh over his to make it easier for him to plunder her. "I wanted a pirate. Besides, those suits of armor? How long would it take to get naked and bend me over? Medieval is so impractical."

Kane shook his head at her, trying visibly not to laugh. "The term implies beating the hell out of, not screwing into unconsciousness. Speaking of which, how was your nap?"

"Very nice, but I'm loving my wake-up call." Sabrina let out a throaty moan as Kane's fingers explored her with leisurely thoroughness, not parting or opening her, just stroking and pressing her into insanity or early senility. "And I know what going medieval means. That was word-play. Or something."

It was getting really difficult to concentrate, and her thoughts were turning too hazy with the fog of lust to keep up with Kane's razor wit.

"Foreplay?" Kane found her clit and put his fingertip against the sensitive bud with light pressure that was enough to make her squirm in reaction.

"I forget. What were we talking about?" She reached down to fit her hand around his shaft and found him thick and engorged. He felt so hard and smooth in her hand, his skin stretched tight, the head of him velvety and sensitive to her exploring fingers.

She couldn't get enough of touching him. She loved the sight and sound and scent of him, and the more she had, the more she wanted. A warning sounded in the distant recesses of her brain, but she ignored it and burrowed down in the bed until she could fit her lips around his cock and take him into her mouth.

"Kitten . . ." Kane slid his hands into her hair, cupping her head as he gently massaged her scalp. "I want to feel your lips wrapped around the base of my cock while you deep-throat me."

That was a challenge, but maybe . . . Sabrina adjusted her angle and relaxed her throat, stretching her mouth to take more of him until she was swallowing most of his cock. Not quite all, but as close as she was going to get. He let out a groan of pleasure, and Sabrina focused on gliding her mouth up and down on him, sucking and licking and delighting in the taste of him.

"Suck hard, baby." Kane rocked his hips into her, fucking her mouth, his movements carefully restrained to keep from crossing the line from participation to overriding the pace she was setting.

Deep-throating Kane wasn't easy, and Sabrina was very aware that one wrong move on his part would end the experiment abruptly. She relished the combination of sexual control and unrestrained passion between them.

She loved him with her tongue and lips and did her best to show him how sexy she found him, how intoxicatingly male, how much she appreciated him allowing her to direct this act as she tried to give him what he'd given her. An oral assault and a sensual pleasure unlike anything else.

"Do you want to swallow me?" Kane asked, his voice deep and rough with desire. "If you don't want me to come down your throat while you suck me off, you need to stop now, Sabrina."

She didn't want to stop. She tightened her lips around him, increased the pressure of her tongue along his shaft, took him deeper, and felt him throbbing as his orgasm began. She moved back a little and worked him with her mouth and tongue as he came in a liquid rush, let him fill her mouth, then released him to swallow before sucking all of him all the way back in, now able to take him fully as his size subsided slightly.

"I love your mouth on me." Kane stroked her hair as she laved him with her tongue, lapped at the sensitized head of his cock, explored the ridge below, and sucked his shaft up and down in long, lazy strokes. He was still hard, and Sabrina realized he wasn't going to need any recovery time before he was ready to go again, but it might take him a long time to come.

Her vaginal walls squeezed tight at the thought of riding him for as long as it took, and she slid her mouth free to explore the possibilities.

"Kane," Sabrina murmured, kissing his hard, sculpted belly. She crawled on top of him and sat up, straddling him. "You're so big," she said in awe. "It's like my own private pirate playground. I want to touch you and kiss you everywhere. And then I want to do it until my thighs chafe."

His lips twitched. "Do it?"

"Yes. *It.*" She grinned at him. "The horizontal mambo. The mattress dance."

"Don't be coy. Tell me what you really want." Kane reached up to cup her breasts with his big hands, and the sight of them fitting over her soft flesh struck her as incredibly erotic. She was soft and slight and feminine, he was big and heavily muscled, and his hands covered her breasts completely.

"I want you," she said simply, and the statement rang in her head like an echo. Oh yes, she did want him. She wanted to touch him and taste him, and she wanted to take him inside her and ride him in a long, lazy rhythm for the pure pleasure of having her body joined with his.

Sabrina rose, positioned herself over him, and reached down to guide his shaft into place. Then she sank down, closing her eyes and breathing out in a sigh as she sheathed him fully.

"You feel so good inside me, Kane," she said. It was such an understatement, it was almost ridiculous. Getting a massage felt good. Sunshine in the winter felt good. A light rain in the spring felt good. Kane inside her was as elemental and electric as it was grounding, and she craved it to the depths of her being. But she had no better words, so she focused on feeling the connection between them.

His hardness rising to take her where she was soft and giving. His strength supporting her. His warmth and his clean male scent with a hint of citrus enticing her. His arms moved around to circle her and pull her down to lie on his chest, her torso pressed into his. Kane's embrace promised comfort and a haven even as he plundered her, his uncompromising grip holding her securely where he wanted her and pistoning his hips into her, taking her hard.

"Slow," she whispered, feathering kisses over his chest. "I want it slow, Kane. I want to feel you filling me inch by inch. I want to wait for it and ache for it until you're all the way inside me again, and then I want to feel my body's need for yours when you pull out almost all the way."

"Sabrina." His arms tightened around her, crushing her against him, then loosened a little to allow her to draw a deep breath. "Take what you want."

So she rocked her pelvis as she rode him, slow and rhythmic, teasing both of them and drawing it out as long as she could stand it. And somewhere along the way, she felt herself beginning to tighten and felt the lazy rocking motion of their coming together building into the promise of fulfillment just ahead, like the end of a rainbow. She forced herself not to speed up, biting her lip as she struggled to hold on.

"So close," she whispered, panting a little as she tried to slow down, but it was sweeping over her and she couldn't hold it off. "Kane." She said his name as if it were an anchor and closed her eyes as pleasure surged and emotion broke her.

It seemed like a long time later, but in reality only a few seconds or a minute could have passed before she stirred on top of him. Sabrina could feel Kane's arms banded around her, one hand in her hair, stroking and caressing her, their bodies still joined together. Not for long, though. This moment couldn't last forever, as much as she might like to make time stop.

His heart thudded under her ear, a steady drumming sound that soothed her. His body felt solid and sure under hers, and she took in a deep breath, letting it all the way out in a sigh of satisfaction.

"Need to move?" Kane asked, his voice a deep rumble in her ear.

"Yes," she said in real regret. But she stayed a moment longer, savoring the feel of him and the fit of their bodies. Then she pushed herself to her knees in one fluid motion, climbed off, and stood beside the bed. She cocked her head to the side, looking at the picture Kane made lying there on his back, naked, semierect, his long black hair loose.

"Pirate," she said with a satisfied smile.

"As you requested." Kane looked back at her, letting his eyes wander over her naked body from head to toe in a leisurely sweep that told her he liked what he saw.

"I look good from the back, too," Sabrina said, and turned to walk away, swinging her hips for him to make her bottom bounce and sway. His low growl sent a delighted thrill through her.

A few minutes later, she stepped out of the shower and found Kane holding a towel for her. She let him wrap it around her, lifting her arms so he could tuck one end between her breasts. He slid his hand along the upper curve of her breasts when he finished in a teasing caress. Then he took her place.

Sabrina padded back to the galley, retrieved the borrowed sweats, dropped her towel, and dressed. Her motions felt liquid and lazy. She didn't think she could hurry if her life depended on it. Say if the fictional Mob caught up to them. Or Black Jack, the dreaded pirate rival. Or if she spotted a giant spider.

Kane came up behind her just as she finished and wrapped his arms around her waist to draw her back against his chest, his chin rubbing the top of her head. "You're all covered up."

"I thought you might need a break," she said in a voice of grave concern. "You're so much older. I'd hate to give you a heart attack."

"Kitten, you *are* a heart attack." Kane's voice was amused and affectionate as he cuddled her from behind. "I'll never be the same. Neither will my kitchen table."

"I like to leave my mark." Her lips curved in a smile as she ground her butt into him. She eyed the kitchen table and thought how useful it was to have all the furniture bolted to the floor. It prevented all sorts of potential awkward accidents.

"You've succeeded there." Kane turned her and slid a finger under her chin, tilting it up for his kiss. He bent his head to brush his lips over hers in a sweet, lingering movement, tasting her, nibbling at her lower lip, then probing with his tongue until she opened her mouth for him. He took the invitation to deepen the kiss and teased her with his tongue until she tangled hers with his.

When he finally released her mouth and lifted his head, Sabrina could feel her heart thundering and blood roaring in her ears. She clutched at his chest to keep from losing her balance, then realized she'd lost her inner balance somewhere along the way.

She may have left her mark on Kane, but the reverse was obviously true. Her pirate had taken more than her body, and she couldn't even say when that line had been crossed. Maybe it had started the moment she'd stepped onto his boat, when he'd tried to protect her from himself.

"You're very quiet," Kane said. He tugged her closer and wrapped his arms around her. She leaned into him.

"Thinking," Sabrina said. Although not very clearly or very well.

"That goes well with hot cocoa. Want some?" Kane rubbed the small of her back as he made the offer, and she felt tears sting at the backs of her eyes.

Tears. Because an incredibly sexy man with a great sense of humor who'd done things to her body that she'd fantasize over and remember fondly to her dying day was obviously something to cry about.

Don't be an idiot, Sabrina, she chided herself. She blinked furiously and waited to answer until she trusted herself to speak without her voice wavering.

"Thank you. I'd love a cup." Her voice sounded small to her ears, but it was the best she could do.

Fifteen

Sabrina sat on the cushioned seat with her legs drawn up and folded in a half lotus as she watched Kane work around the little stove. Watching Kane was a very worthwhile activity, even when he was doing something as simple as preparing twin mugs of hot chocolate. His hair was loose and damp with a hint of curl after the shower, and while he'd put his jeans back on, he'd left the button at the top undone, and he was bare-chested.

"Nice six-pack," she said as she admired the lines and planes of his sculpted body.

"When you're in hiding from the Mob, you stay in shape," Kane said, stirring the cocoa. "You never know when you'll have to run for your life."

He carried over the mugs and set hers in front of her. Sabrina curled her hands around it and looked up at him. "Tell me something real about you."

"Something real." Kane sat across from her and held out his hand. She freed one to place in his palm. His fingers closed around her, his hand so much larger that it covered hers entirely. "I don't go to the gym for bodybuilding. I'm not that vain. But I do lift weights three times a week. People who take care of their bodies live longer and have fewer health problems, fewer injuries. And it's good stress relief."

"It must be working for you," Sabrina said. "You're pretty much the direct opposite of stressed out."

"If I had any stress, you relieved it when you came aboard and took off all your clothes." Kane picked up his mug and sipped. His gaze held hers as he looked at her over the rim. The warmth in those deep blue eyes made Sabrina's heart trip. The loose hair and earring and bare chest made him look untamed and dangerous and so very desirable.

She broke eye contact and forced herself to focus on her cup. *Pick it up. Drink. Remember to swallow.* She managed to maintain a semblance of control until he relaxed his hand around hers and began to trace patterns on her palm with his fingers. Her heart rate doubled, and her hand holding the cup trembled. Sabrina set the hot chocolate back down, very carefully, and unfolded her legs to stand up. "I can't do this," she said.

"Drink?" Kane's hand was very still on the table, remaining there when she'd tugged hers free to get to her feet.

"Drink. Think. Have a conversation. Sit across from you." Sabrina waved her arms as she spoke, needing some physical outlet to express her chaotic internal state. Then she climbed onto his lap.

Kane wrapped one arm around her and hugged her close. "Are you having regrets, Sabrina?" His voice was very careful and even, but she could feel the tension in his body.

"No." Whatever else she felt, she was clear on that one. Kane had given her exactly what she wanted, and she couldn't regret that. The thought of missing out on this time with Kane, of another man fulfilling her fantasy, made her stomach hurt.

"I'm happy to hear that." His voice was still guarded and impossible to read, but Sabrina felt him relax slightly as he held her. So. Her pirate wanted her there as much as she wanted to be there. That was reassuring.

She burrowed into his big body and absorbed his warmth, took comfort in the security of his arm around her, and tried not to question why she needed that so badly.

"So you're not a big fan of cocoa," Kane said, making it a light, teasing statement.

"I like it." She shrugged. "I'm restless, I guess."

"There's nothing like the open water for that." Kane scooted her around to the side so he could cradle her lying back in the curve of his arm and look down into her eyes. "We could take *Rebecca* out. This pirate ship does not have to stay docked."

"That sounds good," Sabrina said. "And it'll make it so much harder for the Mob to catch up to us."

Kane bent his head to kiss the tip of her nose. "I'll check for weather updates and make ready. You can walk around, or read a book. Whatever you feel like doing." He nodded in the direction of her abandoned wool coat. "Put that on over the sweats if you come out, it'll be colder when we're under way."

"I have spent some time on the water," Sabrina assured him. "I do know to bundle up."

"You rode the ferry over with nothing under your coat, and you probably stood outside during the crossing." Kane frowned at her, and she couldn't help grinning back.

"Well, yes. But the view is so much better outside," Sabrina admitted.

"I'd say the view is spectacular inside." He touched her cheek, a light caress with the back of his hand, then set her on her feet and stood.

"Spectacular?" Sabrina asked, forcing her legs not to wobble underneath her.

"Definitely." Kane lifted the hem of her borrowed sweat-shirt to stroke her bare stomach. She sucked in a breath as that simple touch made her body tighten and react.

"I'll just get my deck shoes on," she managed to say through lips that felt swollen and awkward. Or maybe that was her tongue. Kane only had to look at her and she prac-tically swallowed it.

She bent down and fumbled around for the shoes she'd discarded along with her jeans what seemed like a lifetime ago. She heard his footsteps recede and sounds of something opening and closing, probably a drawer. Of course, he couldn't go outside bare-chested. He'd have to put some-thing on. It was kind of a shame to cover up a body that beautiful to look at.

But then looking led to touching. She hadn't even been able to stay on her side of the table with him sitting across from her. She'd had to climb into his lap. If they'd stayed there, she probably would have started working on the zip-per of his jeans.

She froze, one shoe in hand, contemplating what might have happened if she'd lowered that zipper. Which led to re-membering Kane naked and in her mouth. Kane hard behind her, working his way into her anal passage so very carefully. Kane under her, telling her to take what she wanted.

"Okay down there?"

She blinked up to see Kane standing over her, now wearing a sweater, his polar fleece, and deck shoes over thick socks in addition to his jeans. Which were now fastened all the way, no tempting top button left open.

"Fine," Sabrina said. Her voice only squeaked a little bit. "Just finding my shoes." She waved the one she'd found as proof that she was doing something besides sitting on the floor having hot flashes. She was too young for hot flashes.

"The other one is over there." He pointed.

"Okay. Thanks." She nodded, trying to look as if she could see anything in the room besides him. Which probably didn't come off, since she was staring up at him instead of looking in the direction he'd indicated. She clutched the found shoe tighter. "I'll just put this one on."

He looked as if he were on the verge of saying something, then thought better of it. "Okay, then. See you on deck."

She nodded and stayed there, clinging to her shoe as if keeping a grip on it would help her keep a grip on herself. *Deep breaths, Sabrina,* she told herself. *Put the shoe on. Find the other one.*

It wasn't so hard, if she kept her mind on the task and didn't allow it to go reveling in memories of sexual excess or drifting into moony imaginings starring Kane. She got both shoes on the right feet. Mission accomplished. Having something to focus on was good. Maybe she needed something else to focus on now, while Kane got ready to head out on the water. He'd mentioned reading. Which meant he had books somewhere.

Sabrina looked around the galley, and her eyes came to

rest on the cushions covering the kitchen bench seats. Of course, that would be storage. She walked over and lifted one up, opening the cabinet top to peer inside. Rope and assorted useful items and tools. No books. She did know where to find a life vest now, though. She dropped the lid and cushion back into place and poked through cupboards at random, exploring Kane's world.

He lived simply, she realized, but he didn't lack for comforts. The *Rebecca* was a self-contained little oasis. Everything was neatly stored and well kept. Kane ran a tight ship, it seemed. Literally.

Sabrina picked up her coat and put it on so she wouldn't forget it when she went on deck. In her current distracted state, that was possible. Then she wandered into the cabin and threw herself onto the bed. The crazy quilt was bright and colorful, the mattress inviting, and being on Kane's bed was like being near him. She stretched out on her belly and thought that if she was the kitten he called her, this was where she'd choose to curl up. It felt good to be there.

How was it going to feel when the date was over and she went home? How would it feel to never be near him again? Her stomach twisted, and she knew the answer. She didn't want it to be over. She didn't want this to be the only time she was welcome in Kane's bed.

She wanted to be with him out of bed, too. He made her laugh. He made her mind race to keep up with his. He made her feel good just by being around him. She wanted more from him than amazing sex, although it was amazing. And addictive. If she'd really been a hit woman like the identity he'd invented for her, and he'd kept her tied up and distracted with sex to convince her not to kill him, it wouldn't have taken very many days before she'd have wanted Kane to live forever.

The date had to come to an end. They couldn't live the pirate fantasy, but maybe they could try reality. Which meant taking the very risk she'd wanted to avoid when she chose the agency. Opening herself up to rejection.

She wanted a chance to know the real him. She already knew what kind of lover he was, and that told her a lot about his character and personality. He was protective and passionate, giving as well as demanding, very careful about how he used his size and strength. What else? Kane was smart and creative and quick, good at thinking on his feet.

And he lived on a boat. Retired navy? Possible. There were a lot of navy people in the area. If Kane had joined up just out of high school or college, he could have put in his twenty years and retired by forty-two. It would explain why he felt comfortable making his home at sea, although it was hard to believe any man could spend that many years in the navy and never get a tattoo. The long hair, well, after years of military haircuts, a natural rebel like Kane would probably want to grow it long.

That thought made her frown, and she rolled onto her back, considering his personality in terms of the military. They really didn't run to nonconformists. Probably not navy, then. His creative drive and intelligence made her first theory, that he'd made his money in computers and retired early, much more likely.

At least she knew for sure Kane liked her. It showed in the way he looked at her and smiled at her. The little things he did. If he'd only wanted sex, he didn't have to cuddle her or joke with her or touch her in nonsexual ways. So much of the physical contact between them had simply been touch, being close to each other.

Hopeful signs. Buy signals, in sales talk. So she'd sell him on the idea of moving from anonymous sex partners to something more. While she was at it, she could sell herself on the idea that she wasn't free-falling with the ground rushing up at her.

Her stomach plummeted. *Think of something else.* Sabrina closed her eyes and savored the fulfillment of a long-held fantasy. She'd been taken by a pirate, cherished and ravished and satisfied. Her lips curved in a smile as she remembered just how thoroughly Kane had satisfied her. The smile widened as she thought about their exchange over Kane's imaginary rivals for her affection and her explanation for her fidelity during her captivity by Black Jack.

Something about that struck her as familiar and stirred in her memory. Something from a book? The smile faded as she concentrated. Kane had lifted his explanation about the boat from the Travis McGee mysteries. Had Black Jack come from a similar source?

Then her eyes flew open as it struck her. *Pirate's Prize.* The historical romance that had planted the seed of her favorite fantasy, the desire for a man to take her and make her his. In it, one of the plot twists that had divided the lovers was . . . the pirate rival who had stolen the heroine from under the hero's nose. And held her on his private island. For three months.

What were the odds that Kane would invent details of his imaginary mock foe that so exactly paralleled a novel he'd never read or heard of? That would take one hell of a coincidence. And men did read romance novels.

Some even wrote them.

"Oh. My. God," Sabrina breathed. *Rebecca.* If she was right, she knew who Kane was, and she knew whom the yacht was named after. The answer was in Bluebeard's closet. She'd stake her entire shoe collection and her Nordstrom card on it.

Sabrina leaped off the bed and went to the trunk. She tried the lid. Locked. But there would be a key, and organized, shipshape Kane would put it in a logical spot. She found it in the first drawer she tried in the little desk cubby that housed a laptop and fitted it into the lock with shaking hands.

The key turned and the lock opened. She lifted the lid and looked inside and drew in a sharp breath. Paperbacks stacked wide and deep filled the trunk, emblazoned with the author's name: Rebecca Kane.

The truth had been under her nose from the very first, and she hadn't seen it. Hidden in plain view. She remembered telling him he should write a book and wanted to groan out loud.

Kane was Rebecca. And at least one other person, she noted, seeing a stack of men's adventure novels under the name Kane Woods.

It explained a lot. His ability to spin stories out of thin air on a moment's notice or pull from other fictional sources. How he lived on a boat. He hadn't retired early, he just worked from home. As a writer, he could live anywhere. If he had an adventurous streak, having a portable home probably held a lot of appeal. Any time he got bored, he could pull up anchor and go someplace else, taking his home and his work with him.

Sabrina noted a thick stack of manuscript pages on top of the paperbacks. A new book? And which of his alter egos had written it?

It was under the Kane Woods name. Which, she realized, might actually be his real name. There was a page of notes paper-clipped to the top of the manuscript, and she read them with a sickening sense of disbelief.

A lot more than the mystery of Kane had been locked in this trunk. The mystery of why he'd gone to the Capture Agency was here, too, in the handwritten notes detailing a conversation with his agent. Sex scenes were uninspired because Kane was holding back. He had to break out. Experiment with and research fantasy material. And evidently, he'd wanted to be the hero from *Pirate's Prize* as much as she'd longed to find herself in the role of heroine. Except that he wasn't the hero of her erotic and romantic imaginings. He hadn't arranged this date with her for the sake of having hot, kinky sex. He hadn't done it for the same reasons she'd done it. He'd done it to further his career. And he'd picked her because the kind of woman he needed wasn't the kind he'd get involved with.

I am a research subject, Sabrina thought numbly. A guinea pig. And she'd not only let Kane use her, she'd encouraged him to. He'd known exactly how to romance her because he was a damn professional. And while he pretended to romance her, Kane had planned to use everything they'd done together in his book. She imagined a scene starring herself bent over the kitchen table, her most private erotic memories stolen and made public.

She felt sick. Dropping the manuscript, she lurched to

her feet and half ran, half staggered to the door and made her way up to the deck. Good, they were still docked.

Sabrina ran for the ladder and the pier, and then she was off the boat and running back to the ferry terminal before Kane saw her and noticed she was gone.

Sixteen

Sabrina was halfway back to Seattle before she realized she'd run away in his sweats and left her jeans behind. It was pure luck that she'd had her coat on with her wallet and keys in the pocket when she bolted. She'd at least been spared the humiliation of having to go back for those items. No way would she go back for her pants. Kane could keep them.

She thought of him finding her gone with only her jeans left behind. He didn't know her full name, her address, where she worked, who her friends were. And unlike the Prince in "Cinderella," he could hardly go all through the Greater Seattle area trying to find the ass that would fit those jeans.

Not that he would have any trouble recognizing her ass, being so intimately familiar with it. Hysterical laughter bubbled up in her chest, and she fought it grimly down. She stayed outside for the full half-hour ferry crossing, breathing in great gulps of sea air, staying near the rail in case she needed to throw up.

When the ferry docked, she made her way off, found

her car in the parking lot, and drove home on autopilot. She stabbed the security button on her apartment building's door too hard and damaged her nail tip in the process. Now her day was perfect. Sabrina made her way into the lobby, to the elevator, and finally home. Once inside, she locked the door behind her. Then she stood there, frozen, lost, with no idea what to do next. She felt like a stranger to the self who had left that morning full of excited anticipation.

Finally, she gave herself a mental shake. She couldn't just stand there like a statue until the next morning. *Do something. Start small.* Sabrina held up her hand to inspect the damage. The broken nail would have to be dealt with. That gave her something concrete to fix, and she desperately needed to fix something in her shattered state.

"I broke a nail," she said out loud. And then, to her horror, she burst into tears.

When everything was ready to move *Rebecca* out into open water, Kane went to find Sabrina. She hadn't come to join him, and she wasn't in the galley. The cabin was empty, too, but something was out of place. The trunk was open.

Sabrina. Somehow she'd figured it out, and she'd unlocked the trunk to be sure. But why hadn't she come to talk to him about it? He didn't think the discovery that he was so in touch with his feminine side that he'd given it a name and a career would be a turnoff to Sabrina. A big surprise, sure. Maybe a little difficult to understand. But after the hours they'd spent in bed, she couldn't have any doubts about his masculinity.

She hadn't come to talk to him about his alter ego, though, and she wasn't here. Kane retraced his steps and saw her jeans still lying on the floor. He picked them up and folded them neatly, then walked back to the cabin with them and put them in a drawer. Then he opened the drawer again and took them back out to check the pockets for clues to her identity. A receipt with her name on it, an address, anything.

His search came up empty.

Kane held the pants while he mentally shuffled the puzzle pieces around, trying to make them form a picture. The trunk was open. Sabrina was gone. She knew who he was, so she'd left? It didn't make sense. He checked the label on her jeans and shook his head. Gloria Vanderbilt. She'd want them back. He refolded them and put them away for a second time.

Then he walked back over to the trunk and saw his last manuscript with the notes on top. How would it have looked to Sabrina?

She couldn't have known that his intentions had changed. He hadn't had a chance to tell her. Instead, she'd found this and thought the worst. It had upset her. Enough, maybe, to make her leave him without a word.

Kane locked the trunk again and put away the key. Sabrina might be upset right now, but she'd cool down and then they'd talk about this. He'd call the agency first thing Monday morning and find out how to get in touch with her again. This wasn't over.

"So how did your date go?"

Rachel was glowing, Sabrina noted with a mix of envy and tired sadness. "Not as well as yours obviously did," she said. She plopped herself into the chair that faced Rachel's desk, her back to the windows and their city view.

"He didn't run, too, did he?" Rachel asked, her eyes going wide.

"No." Sabrina extended one leg to inspect her shoe. Navy was probably a mistake on a day like today. She should have gone for color, pizzazz. Pink. She made a note to stop by Nordstrom during her lunch hour. "I did."

"Oh." Rachel blinked at her in surprise. "I suppose you had your reasons." Then she sat forward, her face drawing in visible concern. "Did he want to do something really strange or scary in bed? Because if he did, I think you should complain to the agency. It should go in his profile."

"Nothing strange or scary," Sabrina said. "Unusual, maybe a little kinky, but nothing he wanted in bed went beyond what I wanted."

"Okaaay." Rachel drew out the word while she reached for her coffee cup. "Let's recap. You asked the man in your last relationship to do something kinky and he bolted. So you went to an unusual dating agency to find a more adventurous partner. You got an agency match. You met, you talked, you liked him. You made a date. Were the two of you sexually compatible?" Her voice softened in sympathy. "Was it lousy, Sabrina? After you went to all that trouble?"

"It wasn't lousy." Sabrina took off her shoe and sat back, turning the pump in her hands. "I don't know why I wore navy blue today. What was I thinking? It's dark and depressing."

Rachel drank her coffee and then set the mug back down. "Enough twenty questions. Spill. What went wrong?"

"He didn't want me." Sabrina's voice cracked, and she blinked furiously. Dammit, she was not going to cry again. She could live with crying once. She had silk tips, not acrylic.

A broken nail was worth shedding a tear over. But she wasn't going to sit here in the Opal Life Insurance Agency's Seattle branch office crying over Kane, Rebecca, or whoever the hell he was. Maybe his real name was George. She didn't know, and he'd never told her.

Tell me something real, she'd said to him, and he'd told her he lifted weights three times a week. That was significant personal information there.

"Didn't want you?" Rachel shook her head. "That can't be right, Sabrina. You were his most compatible match. He was there for the same reason you were. And, hello, have you looked in a mirror lately? Unless he's gay, insane, or impossible to please, he wanted you."

"He wasn't there for the same reason I was." Sabrina's voice came out so small, she winced at the sound. She put her shoe back on, concentrating on the task with fierce determination. "Enough pity party. You're right. Somewhere out there is a man who wants me. Just because my first agency date didn't work out, that's no reason to abandon the plan. I'll set up a time to meet the next man on the list."

Sabrina scrubbed at her eyes and stood up. She'd make the call. Right after she fixed her mascara. Then she'd find some shoes that didn't make her feel as though she were on her way to a funeral.

"Right," Rachel said to Sabrina's back as she left.

"What do you mean, you can't give out personal information?" Kane asked, incredulous. It was Monday, and he was standing in the office suite that housed the Capture Agency, because he'd decided he had a better chance of success if he showed up in person. It was a lot easier to put somebody off on the phone than it was if they were standing in front of you. "You told me she liked skydiving, kinky sex, and wanted to be held captive on a boat. I know what birth control method she uses and how many sex partners she's had. That's pretty damn personal."

"Personal *contact* information," the man behind the desk informed Kane. He was better dressed than anybody Kane had ever seen outside the pages of a magazine. He wondered if Sabrina had met him. She'd love him. The thought depressed Kane, so he shoved it away and focused on the problem at hand. Namely, getting Mr. Fashion Plate to cough up Sabrina's phone number, address, or e-mail account. Anything he could use.

"Is there any rule against giving her mine?" Kane asked. "No, never mind. She knows where to find me. I need to find her. Look, can't you at least call her and ask if she'll talk to me?"

"We take client privacy very seriously," the man, whose nameplate said he was Mark, informed him. He waved an imperious hand, heading off Kane's next protest before he'd gotten further than opening his mouth. "This doesn't mean that we won't convey a message. Do you have a message you'd like to send? A request for a follow-up date?"

"A message." Kane tugged at his earring. "Sure. Do you have paper?"

Mark passed him a "While You Were Out" message slip and a pen.

"Something bigger," Kane said. "There's not enough space in that form."

Mark picked up a full legal pad and handed it to him. "Will this suffice?"

"Yeah. Probably. I think." Kane took the pad and pen. "Is there a conference room I can use?"

"I'll show you." Mark stood and walked around the desk to guide him in the right direction.

Two hours later, Mark reappeared. "I thought you might like some coffee," he said. He set the cup on the conference table.

Kane looked up, then looked around him at the profusion of balled-up pages he'd started, scratched out, and discarded before trying again. "Thanks."

"Not going well?" Mark asked.

"You could say that." He picked up the coffee and took a sip. "I tried a sonnet. That was bad. Iambic pentameter comes across as either smug or desperate. I tried letters, but they were either too polite or too forceful. I tried writing an allegory, but that was too subtle."

"Well, that certainly covers all the bases. I'd say the 'put it in writing' approach isn't going to work," Mark said. "Why don't you just capture her?"

"What?" Kane nearly spilled his coffee. "You're going to tell me where she is?"

"She's here. And I believe you both need the opportunity to work things out face-to-face."

Kane was on his feet and nearly through the door before he realized he had no idea which way to go. He stopped and turned back to Mark.

"Where do I find her?" Kane asked.

"Down the hall, third door on the left." Kane was in

motion before Mark finished talking, a pirate bent on re-
claiming his prize.

Sabrina stood in front of a framed watercolor painting of a
sailboat on the water while she waited for Mark to come
back to finish discussing the end of her term as an agency
client. The painting was bright and full of life and color and
sunshine. Just looking at it made her feel better. So did her
decision to remove her profile from the client database. The
truth was, she didn't want to try another agency match.
Dating somebody else struck her as a colossally bad idea. It
also made her stomach lurch.

She'd be better off forgetting about men, pirates, and
her sex life and taking some advanced sailing and navigation
lessons. She could buy her own boat and then run up her own
damn Jolly Roger if she felt like it. Read romance novels.
Drink lots of rum and pineapple juice. Sing all the verses of
"Sixteen Men on a Dead Man's Chest" to the tune of
"Hark! The Herald Angels Sing."

She looked down at her shoes. Lovely pink leather lace-
up pumps with a four-inch heel. Much better than dark, dull
navy. Men were unpredictable, but Nordstrom never let her
down. She couldn't wear them on her future sailboat, of
course, but if ever there was a day when she needed a little
pink to cheer her up, it was today. Maybe she could find a pair
of canvas deck shoes in pink for her new life on the high seas.

The door opened and closed behind her. Without turning around, Sabrina said, "I'm glad I've decided to give up
men."

"Killing them? Or sleeping with them?" a deep voice
that was not Mark's answered her.

All the air left her body, and she felt light-headed. When she recovered enough to answer a beat later, she said, "Sleeping with them. I think killing them is probably okay as long as I only do it for the money and I'm careful not to get caught."

"In case you were thinking of killing me, I have to tell you that I'm prepared to keep you tied up at sea, having multiple orgasms, until you reconsider."

Dammit. She could feel herself weakening, softening toward him, wanting him to tell her it was all a mistake and then sweep her off her well-shod feet before he bent her over some convenient and well-supported surface.

Sabrina sighed. "Why are you here, Kane?"

"Because I had to find you. Why did you leave?" He moved up behind her and wrapped his arms around her, pulling her back against his body. "I was planning to tell you about Rebecca, but you'd be surprised how hard that is to work into a conversation."

"Forget Rebecca. You should have told me I was research." The pain hit her in the solar plexus all over again. "You shouldn't have let me think you wanted me, wanted the fantasy with me, when all you wanted was a book."

Kane was silent for a minute. Finally he said, "I don't mean to be slow, but I can't imagine what I did to make you think I didn't want you. I told you I wanted you. If that wasn't enough, consider the sex. I promise you, any guy past the age of eighteen who performs like that with a woman is seriously interested."

"Nothing you did," she admitted. "It was in your notes."

"My notes said I didn't want you?"

He knew exactly what his notes said. Sabrina was sorely

tempted to drive her brand-new four-inch heel into the top of his foot. He was wearing canvas deck shoes. No protection at all from a dangerous woman bent on vengeance. "No, your notes said you were doing research. I only came into the picture because I was convenient." And disposable.

"I didn't expect you to take that well," Kane said. "Although I could point out that you were out of line to open the lock in the first place, and you should have asked me about it after you did. But you were already upset before you opened the trunk. Is there maybe some other reason you reacted so badly, and my notes gave you a good excuse?"

Oh, hell. He was right. If she hadn't been braced for rejection already, she would have confronted him instead of bolting. He couldn't have known the weekend would turn into more than either of them had planned when he'd made those damn notes. He hadn't even met her then.

"Yes," Sabrina said. "The last man I was in a relationship with ditched me when I asked him to meet my sexual needs. I came to the Capture Agency because I was determined to avoid another disappointment or rejection."

"So it hit you in a sore spot." Kane hugged her close and rocked her gently from side to side. "I'm sorry. And amazed. He ditched you?"

"Yes." She grimaced. "I told him what I wanted in bed, and I never saw him again."

She felt his body shake with silent laughter. "Well, hell, kitten, you probably made him feel inadequate. He couldn't handle you. Lucky for you, you've caught the eye of a notorious pirate, and nothing will stop him from carrying you off to have his wicked way with you."

"Nothing?" Sabrina felt a faint stirring of hope.

"Nothing." Kane swept her up into his arms, then paused to look at her shoes. "Those are interesting. Can you wear them without panty hose?"

Sabrina felt her heart skip and her body stir to life. "Why do you ask?"

"I'd like to bend you over my kitchen table wearing those and nothing else. I think they'd put you at the perfect angle." He gave her a heated look, and Sabrina melted. Then she put a hand on his chest to stop him.

"Wait a minute. You still haven't explained."

"You want an explanation?" Kane looked around, spotted a chair, and sat with her in his lap. "Okay. Yes, I intended to use the fulfillment of my fantasy to fuel my fiction. That does not mean I didn't want you or didn't want the fantasy. Although once I had you, I realized it was never about sex or a fantasy, and it sure as hell didn't have anything to do with my career."

"That sounds promising," Sabrina said. "Go on."

He touched her cheek. "I thought I wanted the perfect stranger for the ultimate sexual fantasy encounter, but you made me realize what I really wanted was the perfect partner. I had you, but only for a short time. So I was planning to get you hooked before bringing up touchy subjects like who I was, what I did for a living, and the original reason I became a client of the Capture Agency."

Looked at from his perspective, it made sense. It wasn't fair to blame him for her own oversensitivity or the fact that her feelings had become so deeply involved in what was supposed to be purely sexual.

"You've gotten all quiet again. Do you have anything to tell me? Like why you're here?" Kane asked.

Yes, he was bound to wonder about that. And he deserved the truth. Sabrina took a deep breath. "I was mad. And hurt. At first I thought if you didn't want me, maybe somebody else on my match list would. It didn't take long for me to realize I didn't want that at all, though. By the time I got here, I'd come to my senses. I asked to be removed from the client database. Mark had gone to get the paperwork when you came in."

She looked up into his eyes and gave a little shrug. "You've ruined me for all other men. I don't want anybody else. The thought of being with another man makes me want to throw up, and the thought of never being with you again makes me feel cold and sad."

A look of wonder broke over his face. "You're in love with me."

Damn his perceptiveness. "Well, if I am, it's your own fault." Sabrina tapped his chest with her index finger and its newly repaired nail tip. "You romanced me with your back rubs and cuddling, calling me kitten. You seduced me with world-class orgasms and the most amazing sex I've ever had. And you made me laugh. We had so much fun, and it felt so good to be with you, in bed as well as out. Did you think that would make me hate you?"

"So I get all the credit." Kane looked pleased. "I'm pretty good at being a pirate. I stole your body and your heart. I made you love me against your will."

She scowled at him "You don't have to sound so proud of yourself, Rebecca. And what about you? Do you love me? And is Kane even your real name?"

Kane hugged her close and worked his fingers into her hair to cup the back of her head. "Kane Woods is my real name. And Rebecca isn't my only alter ego. There's a guy named Keith who writes science fiction in the bottom of the trunk."

Sabrina groaned. "I'm in love with a man who has more personalities than Sybil."

"Pen names are not personalities. They're marketing tools." He touched the base of her throat and traced a line down, coming to rest with his hand in the valley between her breasts. "To answer the rest of your questions in reverse order, yes, I love you. And as a romance writer, I am proud of myself. I romanced you like a pro. This is even better than *Pirate's Prize*."

"I know. I loved that book," Sabrina admitted. She shifted in his lap, twisting from the waist to encourage his hand to explore more interesting territory. "It's why I wanted a pirate to take me and make me his."

Kane smiled at her and moved to cover one breast with his hand. The warmth of his touch spread through her body, as welcome as the sun coming out from behind the clouds. "So you're a romantic. I notice you're not making a lot of noisy protests about how love at first sight is ridiculous."

"I'm a romantic," she agreed. "I also jump out of airplanes and ski very fast down dangerous mountains in my free time. There's nothing wrong with a little risk as long as the equipment is sound." She wiggled in his lap, feeling his erection pressing into her hip. "I've tested your equipment thoroughly. It's sound."

"Maybe you should test it again." Kane gave her a solemn look and rubbed his thumb over her nipple. "I should definitely test yours."

"Yes. Yes, you should," Sabrina agreed. She did her best to keep her face straight, but she could feel her lips curving in a smile. Her nipple was hardening under his thumb, and she could feel the rest of her body softening and growing ready for him to take.

Kane slid one hand up under her skirt, and she opened her thighs to let him pet her sex. He stroked and pressed lightly into her. Sabrina arched her back and moaned as the hand manipulating her nipple and the one between her legs worked in tandem.

"What about you?" she managed to ask before she lost the ability to think, much less form sentences. "Love at first sight doesn't bother you?"

"Not at all. It's efficient. When you get to be my age, you don't want to waste time. Speaking of which, it's time to carry you back to my ship," Kane said, his voice rough with desire. He stopped touching her to cradle her in his arms as he stood.

"Pirate," Sabrina said in a throaty murmur.

"That's right." He looked big and dangerous and blatantly possessive as his eyes held hers. "And now you're mine."

And she was.

Ex Marks the Spot

Seventeen

Emma Michaels halted in the doorway to Rachel's office, frozen in place by a conversation that had nothing to do with business and was all about pleasure. Forbidden, erotic fantasies and a way to fulfill them through a unique dating agency. The Capture Agency, specializing in matching up the men and women who wanted to experience capture and bondage sexual encounters.

She was riveted, imagining a man holding her captive. A forceful stranger bent on seduction and determined to have her. The very idea of being the focus of a man's attention when she was so tired of settling for the crumbs that came her way thrilled her. And the promise of sexual fulfillment made heat rush through her body.

How long had it been since a man had wanted her, really wanted her? Emma felt a twist of pain at the thought of how different it had been in the early days with Gage. It wasn't fair to judge a mature relationship by the heady, hormonal rush of teenage years, but there had been a time when they couldn't keep their hands off each other. And then slowly other things had begun to take precedence. Education. Career.

Time had moved on, and sex had ceased to be a thing of impulse and become something that happened when time and energy permitted. They'd both become more skilled, more experienced with each other over the years, but Emma longed for the time when leaving one button undone on her shirt was enough to drive Gage wild and guaranteed that he would undo all the rest.

Although as it turned out, it wasn't just his career that was now absorbing all of Gage's drive and energy. Emma wondered if his assistant left buttons undone and enticed Gage to finish the job in his office, behind a closed door, after hours when everybody else had gone home and his wife waited with more than dinner growing cold.

She didn't know what hurt more, that she'd lost her husband's interest or that he'd found another outlet for it. She'd never been exciting. She'd been the classic good girl, shy, innocent, and utterly unprepared when she'd drawn the attention of the high school's star football player.

Emma knew Gage hadn't been a virgin when he'd persuaded her to go all the way in the back of his car, and she'd also known that she wasn't sophisticated and had no idea how to please him. She'd tried, but she'd worried about how she measured up. And she'd worried about the fact that no matter what she did, she always seemed to be ten pounds overweight with curves that no amount of dieting affected.

It hadn't seemed to matter at first. Gage had always wanted her, always seemed to find her naked body a thrill. And then, well, they'd grown up, she supposed. Work and responsibilities and other things began to take precedence.

Gage was less interested in spontaneous sex outside the bedroom and then less interested in bed, too. Finally, the gradual habit of working late and business travel had eroded the time they spent together. Even before she'd found out her husband was cheating on her, she'd begun to believe she was losing him.

Infidelity was the last straw, however. Emma had packed some clothes and moved into a hotel, and a month later she was still there, in limbo, unable to move forward or go back. She couldn't bring herself to call a lawyer, and Gage hadn't, either. She also couldn't resign herself to remaining in a marriage that was so much less than what she'd wanted, to taking last place in her husband's list of priorities.

Sixteen years together. So much time. Her whole adult life. From high school sweethearts to lovers to college students and newlyweds to thirtysomething professionals. How was it possible that after so much time it was over? How was it possible that she'd been blind for so long? That was another good question.

She didn't stir Gage's fantasies anymore. But maybe she could stir a stranger for one night. A stranger who wouldn't care if her body was unfashionably shaped or that she wasn't eighteen anymore because he'd have no basis for comparison with her younger self.

The idea held so much appeal, not just because she longed to feel sexual pleasure again, but because it might be the action that would help her get unstuck from this awful place she found herself in. She knew she couldn't continue to simply avoid decisions about the future, but whenever she tried the grief overwhelmed her.

Signing up to have kinky sex with a strange man was

something that shy and well-behaved Emma Michaels would never do. But being well behaved hadn't kept her husband's interest, hadn't kept her marriage together. She was heartily sick of the good-girl role she'd always been stuck in, and it was time to break out. Do something wild and wicked. Throw away her goody two-shoes and trade them in for fishnet stockings and what Sabrina would call "come fuck me" shoes.

"Satisfaction guaranteed," Emma heard, and something inside her turned and clicked like a lock in a key.

"Or a full refund?" As she asked the question, both Rachel and Sabrina turned to look at her.

"Um, Emma, I'm not sure—" Rachel broke off mid-sentence, and Emma could just imagine the cool blonde's mind racing as she tried to figure out how much Emma had overheard. "Thing is, it's a dating agency, Emma."

"For people who want to act out captor and captive fantasies. I heard."

Rachel blinked. "I don't think your husband would approve of you signing up."

"I don't think it's any of his business if I want to date. He lost the right to disapprove when he slept with his assistant," Emma said. The blunt words coming out of her mouth shocked her but also gave her a sense of relief. There. It was out in the open. She was a failure in bed, a failure at marriage, and now the women she worked with knew the truth. It felt much better than coming and going each day pretending that nothing had changed and her world hadn't collapsed in the space of an instant.

Rachel and Sabrina looked at each other, then back at her. The concern on their faces made Emma sorry she hadn't said anything sooner. They cared, and by keeping her problems buried, she'd kept herself isolated instead of reaching out for the support she needed.

"I'm sorry," Rachel said, her voice soft with sympathy. "But Em, you don't need to be hasty. You've never been with anybody else, and this might not be the best time for you to jump in at the deep end of the dating pool. You could start smaller, take a baby step."

Emma felt herself flinch at the word *baby*. No chance of that now. She'd always wanted children, but she'd waited and waited, let Gage put her off with arguments and sound logic, all the reasons why it wasn't the right time for a baby. And the years had passed, and now she knew he would never give her the child she wanted. She could almost hate him for that, and herself even more, for all those wasted years.

"No, thank you. I'm done waiting. I'm done asking for permission instead of asking for what I want. I may have failed in bed and in my marriage, but I don't have to fail myself. I don't have to repeat my mistakes." Emma took a deep breath and got a firm grip on herself. This was not the time to break down. She'd have more than enough opportunities for that later. She struggled to put her impulse into a logical explanation.

"The fantasy date would be like a practice partner. I can explore what I really want, find out where I went wrong. Then maybe the next time around, if there is a next time, I can get it right."

Sabrina nodded. "That's not bad thinking. Have a fling under very clear and very safe circumstances. No misunder- standings, no complications."

Emma set her chin in a determined line. "Exactly." Her stomach churned with nerves, but after this there would be no going back to her old self, her old life, the patterns and habits that were so obviously not working and needed to be changed.

"Well, I guess it's unanimous," Rachel said. "Here's to our fantasies, and the men who will fulfill them." She raised an imaginary glass in a toast, and the other two women followed suit.

Gage Michaels thought the shock of his life had come a month earlier, when his wife informed him over the phone that she was staying in a hotel for a cooling-off period. Whatever the hell that meant.

He refused to believe it meant she wanted a divorce, because he hadn't been served papers, and besides, the idea was ridiculous. Emma, gone for good? No. Emma was his, they belonged together, and she belonged at home.

He'd given her a week to come to her senses. Then he'd tried to call her. She wasn't ready to talk to him, she'd said. He'd tried to see her. She didn't want to see him. He'd been patient, given her space, but enough was enough. Whatever her reasons, she owed him an explanation, and then she was coming home with him.

Tension tightened his muscles, and Gage rubbed at the back of his neck in irritation. Under his frustration and impatience with the current situation, an icy sensation had crept into his gut, and he didn't like it one bit.

They'd had some disagreements over the years. That was bound to happen to any couple, especially a couple that more or less grew up together. But in sixteen years, there had never been a serious disagreement. Never this silence and separation.

The ice inside him cracked and expanded and whispered that maybe Emma simply didn't want him anymore. He wasn't the high school's star quarterback now, he was a businessman. He'd channeled the same drive to succeed into work that he'd put into winning on the field, but was it possible Emma wasn't as impressed with his wins in the business world as she'd been when he'd thrown a touchdown pass?

Sixteen years, and it seemed like yesterday that he'd finally gotten the attention of quiet, studious Emma Walker. Her soft green eyes had glowed with admiration when they met his. Buoyed by the win and his part in it, Gage had gotten up the nerve to ask her out. Emma, the girl who was out of his league, a rich girl, smart, an honor student, while he distinguished himself in sports. To his disbelief and never-ending satisfaction, she'd said yes.

Later, she'd said yes to so much more.

Yes to his suggestion that they take a drive. Yes when he'd blurted out that he wanted to kiss her. And if he lived to be a hundred, he'd never forget Emma saying yes the night he did his fumbling, hormone-crazed teenage best to seduce her in the back of his car, knowing all the while that it wasn't good enough for her. It wasn't what she deserved.

As the years went by, Gage had driven himself to achieve, to succeed, to give Emma everything she ought to have. He'd never wanted her to feel she'd given up the life she should have had by marrying him. He'd never wanted her to regret choosing him instead of somebody else.

Now he stood just inside the reception area of Opal Life

Insurance, listening as Emma declared her intentions to have sex with a practice partner. Because she thought she'd failed with him. Because she believed he was having an affair.

Gage wasn't sure which statement bothered him more, that she thought he'd cheated on her or that it could possibly be her fault if he had. There was no question how he felt about Emma having sex with another man. It would happen over his dead body.

He'd wanted to know why Emma left, what was bothering her. Well, now he knew. The next step would be deciding what to do with that information. Until he'd had time to think it over, confronting Emma here was probably not the best idea. So Gage quietly went back out the way he'd come in.

Going home to the house that felt far too empty without her didn't appeal, so he drove back to his office. The route was familiar enough to make the trip almost automatic, leaving him free to think. Once the initial shock subsided, one fact emerged: Emma never would have believed he would betray her without convincing evidence. Something or somebody had convinced her. Since his assistant was the one Emma believed he'd betrayed her with, Gage had a few questions for Tanya Wells.

He found her still at her desk, long nails clicking on the keyboard as she typed. "Good, you're still here," he said.

Tanya looked up at him and smiled. "Finishing up that report you needed for Monday's meeting."

"That can wait. I want to ask you something."

"Oh?" Brows arched, she hit "save" and swiveled toward him. Her eyes darkened, and he noted with detachment that she was displaying a fair amount of cleavage to him. The signs were there, now that he was looking for them. Why hadn't he noticed sooner that his assistant had a more than business interest in him?

"Did you want to talk over dinner?" Tanya asked him, lips curving in a suggestive smile.

"I don't want to keep you from your plans," Gage said. "I just wondered if you might know why my wife believes I'm sleeping with you. I hadn't said anything to give her the idea that I was interested in another woman. Somebody helped me out there."

"She believes it because I told her," Tanya said, not missing a beat. "I did it for you. She was holding you back, Gage. She didn't support your goals. She didn't like you working evenings and weekends. Remember the Monroe account? She wanted you to reschedule the trip to Denver."

"That would be because you scheduled the Denver trip so that it fell on her birthday," Gage said in a mild tone.

"The timing was critical." Her mouth hardened into a mutinous line.

"No, it wasn't. It could have been scheduled any other time that month. You created a conflict deliberately, and I was too busy and too blind to notice." He studied her for a minute, looking for any sign that she understood and regretted the harm she'd done. He saw only sullen determination. "You're fired."

"What?" Shock froze her for a few moments. Then her eyes narrowed, and anger twisted her face into a very unattractive expression. "You can't do that to me."

"I can, actually." Gage slid his hands into his pockets so he wouldn't be tempted to throw her out bodily. "I'm the boss. I get to choose who I work with. An executive assistant occupies a position of trust. You stabbed me in the back, and I wouldn't trust you to order lunch now. I also have a few problems with your ethics. So, you're fired. I'll give you ten minutes to pack up your personal items and get out."

Her mouth opened and closed a few times. Then she stood up and without a word began yanking open drawers, pulling out her purse and the other items that personalized her work space. It didn't take her ten minutes—it took approximately three, and then she was gone, slamming the door behind her.

Which removed at least one obstacle. Getting Emma back was going to be a greater challenge than he'd expected. And he had a deadline to work with now. Emma was determined to have a blind date assigned to her from that dating agency. Allowing his wife space was one thing; letting her date another man for the purpose of experimenting with sex was not going to happen.

But what if *he* was Emma's agency date?

Gage considered the plan and turned it around in his mind, examining it for strengths and weaknesses. The more he pondered it, the more he saw that it offered several advantages. If he captured Emma, they would have dedicated time alone together. A perfect opportunity to work things out, give him time to convince Emma she had nothing to worry about from Tanya and that there was nothing wrong with their sex life, either.

Although he had to admit that the opportunity to spice up their familiar lovemaking had appeal all on its own. Clearly, Emma had fantasies he'd never imagined she entertained. He found that intriguing, and imagining Emma delivered to him, his willing captive for all the sensual pleasure he wanted to lavish on her luscious body, made his cock harden.

This could be an opportunity for more than straightening out the misunderstanding and hurt between them. If Emma wanted more in the bedroom, Gage was very willing to accommodate her. Sexual games, toys, props . . . there was a world of possibilities to explore. Who knew what might be to Emma's taste?

He was going to give them both the opportunity to find out. And then Emma was coming home for good. The decision made, he wasted no time in putting it into action.

Eighteen

Two weeks later, Emma let the driver help her out of the limo that had been sent to bring her to the hotel where her captor waited. Everything had been planned by her mystery date, from the location of their rendezvous to how she would arrive and what she should wear. The clothes had been delivered the day before. When Emma had tried them on, she'd been sure they wouldn't fit or would look ridiculous.

Everything had fit. And she didn't look laughable. She'd stared at herself in the mirror, wondering who this stranger was staring back at her.

A white silk corset that laced tightly in the back and pushed up her breasts, emphasizing her cleavage, was the first item she'd put on. Next came a wisp of a thong in matching white silk and then sheer thigh-high stockings designed to stay up without garters. White shoes with high heels that made her legs look longer and more elegant than she would have thought possible. And over it, a faux fur coat in dark mink that made her pale skin look luminescent and contrasted boldly with her strawberry blond hair.

She looked exotic. She looked, Emma realized, like a very expensive plaything bought for an evening of pleasure. Her round ass was bare against the coat's silk lining, and the lingerie felt like very fragile protection. The generous curves of her breast, hips, and bottom were not so much covered by the garments as put on display. The corset showed much more than cleavage; it left her dark rose aureoles exposed and her nipples barely concealed. And her sex was clearly visible through the thin fabric of the thong.

The man who had chosen this outfit for her to wear wanted to see her body gift-wrapped in a way that was more enticing than full nudity. The thong would provide no protection at all. He could stroke her covered sex with as little impediment as if she were bare to his touch, and it would be easy for him to press a silk-covered finger into her if he chose. He could touch the upper curves of her breasts, lift them free of the corset to see her nipples if he wanted to. He could have her walk around in the privacy of their hotel suite, swaying on high heels, while he watched her bare backside bounce and shimmy.

Given the amount of thought he'd put into the details she knew about, Emma could only wonder what else he had planned for her. That had kept her awake the night before and inspired more than a few fantasies. Now she was about to find out. The final item she'd been instructed to wear was to be put on after she'd come to the reserved suite. She'd been given a silk blindfold, and she was to tie it over her eyes before knocking.

A tremor ran through her at the thought of being seen in her barely dressed state by a man she couldn't see at all. Although in a way, it was a relief. It made what she was doing less real, made him less real. A fantasy figure.

Emma checked in at the front desk, conscious all the while of her state of undress and certain that somebody suspected. Her nipples made stiff little points against the tight silk of her corset. She was so aware of her body and her almost nudity that it seemed impossible everybody around her wasn't aware of it, too.

She felt herself blushing as she took the card key that would open the room where a man waited for her and walked as fast as she dared in her high heels to the elevator. She breathed a sigh of relief when the doors slid closed, encapsulating her in privacy and solitude, safe from curious or lascivious stares.

When the doors opened on the penthouse floor, Emma tightened her grip on the card, walked to the door, and slid the card into the reader slot. The door unlocked with an audible click. She glanced around to make sure she wouldn't be seen and tied the blindfold over her eyes. Then she knocked on the door before pushing it open.

Silence greeted her. Emma took a few steps in, feeling her way, then stopped. She'd come in far enough for the door to shut behind her, and the sound it made when it closed almost made her jump. She hesitated, not sure if she should wait or come in, half-afraid of tripping over something in the unfamiliar setting and in the unaccustomed height of her heels.

She felt a finger brush her cheek and drew in a sharp breath. Her heartbeat sped up, and fine tremors ran through her. She felt hands move to the front of her coat and slowly undo the buttons that held it closed, one by one, all the way down. Then she heard the man move behind her. He gripped the coat and slid it off her shoulders, down her arms, then used it to trap her lower arms in the sleeves as he pulled her back against him.

A whisper breathed near her ear. "How lovely."

A hand came to rest just below her throat, then slid lower to rest on the bare upper curves of her breasts. It was a possessive touch, one full of intent, and Emma swallowed hard as she realized that he could touch or take anything he wanted. And he would.

His hand moved, fingertips gliding along the outline of her corset, almost touching her nipples, then sliding lower to touch her through the silk.

"So hard," he whispered as he rubbed his palm over one tight bud. Her breasts felt swollen inside the tight silk, and it seemed to enhance the sensation of his hand moving over her breast, stroking lightly over her nipples by turns. Then his hand moved slowly down to cup her belly, and Emma almost shuddered. It felt so good to be held, to be touched. And at the same time, it was almost more than she could bear. Her body knew the touch of one man's hands. Sex and Gage were inextricably entwined in her mind. Would she even know how to respond to another man?

"Wait," she said through stiff lips.

The hand on her belly pressed in, gentle, steady pressure exerted until her body was nestled into his. "Second thoughts?" The low whisper was punctuated by a soft kiss in the hollow below her ear.

Second, third, fourth, fifth—they collided in her brain

until she was almost dizzy. Or maybe that was from his breath tickling the nape of her neck, his hand rubbing slow circles over her belly, massaging her into relaxing in his hold. "I don't know if I can do this," Emma admitted. "I've never . . . that is, I've only . . ." Her voice trailed off into uncertainty.

"You've never done anything like this." A soft whisper, a kiss on the curve of her shoulder that slid over her skin like silk. "I won't hurt you."

"I might not be any good," Emma said baldly. "I might disappoint you."

"Let me worry about that." His lips feathered along the line of her neck. "Tonight, you are my captive. I arranged for you to be delivered to me, blindfolded and gift-wrapped. And I have plans for you, lovely Emma. Plans for your pleasure and mine."

His whisper was as seductive as his words. Emma leaned back against him as his hand moved up to cup her breast and hold the weight of it before squeezing the soft mound of flesh in his firm grip. The room looked dim through her blindfold, as if the blinds had been drawn and the lights turned off or lowered before she arrived. She was being touched and held by a faceless, voiceless stranger, a phantom lover. It seemed she'd stepped through a doorway into a dream.

"First, I want to remove this coat. And then I want you to sit with me by the fire."

So that was the source of the low light in the room. Emma thought of being nearly naked in the soft glow of firelight while a stranger enjoyed the sight of her body displayed as he'd wanted it. A shiver ran through her. She didn't resist when he let the coat drop to the carpet and took her hand to lead her where he wanted her.

He put his hands on her shoulders and pushed down lightly, indicating that she was to sit. Emma lowered herself until she felt a couch cushioning her naked bottom. She touched the fabric, exploring with her hands. Velvet. The brush of velvet against her bare skin was a pleasure in itself. The silk she wore caressed her breasts and her sex, and the fragile stockings whispered when her thighs brushed together.

He moved in front of her and placed his hands on her knees, letting her adjust to his touch before he used his hold to open her legs. He pushed her knees wide apart, then gently stroked up the insides of her thighs, sliding back down before he touched the silk between her legs.

His hands on her felt warm, strong, knowledgeable. She felt him bend forward, felt a puff of warm air against her sex through the thin silk, and drew in a sharp breath at the sensation. His lips touched the fabric, lightly tracing the outline of her labia. His tongue probed for the sensitive bud nestled in its protective hood of flesh. The silk seemed to amplify the touch of his lips and tongue. Emma felt her breathing quicken and her belly tighten in response. Then he lifted his head and straightened. His hands stayed on her thighs, warm and sure, squeezing lightly, then stroking up her hips.

"I will have you," the low whisper in the near dark told her. "But not yet. When I do take you, sweet Emma, you will be ready for me, and you will not disappoint either of us."

Those hands moved up her hips along her rib cage, then cupped her breast in a possessive hold. His thumbs stroked over her nipples, and Emma sighed as the warmth of his touch and the cool silk combined to tantalize her nerve endings with the promise of pleasure to come.

When he released her and moved away, she missed his touch immediately. She heard sounds and strained to identify them. A light scrape of glass against ice, a muted pop, then a fluid sound. Champagne? She could hear him moving around, his footfalls partially muffled by the thick carpet. Two glasses were placed on a table near her. And something else, a more solid-sounding object.

Emma felt the couch cushion sink beside her, followed by the warm press of his thigh against hers. Then a sliding sound, like a lid being lifted off a dish. A moment later, something pressed against her lips. "Open," whispered her mystery seducer. "You'll like it."

She parted her lips and felt something firm and cool sliding between them. The shape was not quite round. A strawberry? She bit down tentatively and felt the burst of sweet flavor on her tongue with the bite of citrus. Yes, a strawberry.

Emma savored the taste, surprised at what a sensual experience it was to be fed while blindfolded, having to depend on her hearing and sense of touch and taste to feel her way through this dream world.

The rim of a glass touched her lips next, and Emma sipped, ready for the effervescent bubbles that danced in her mouth and washed the berry down.

A second strawberry came dipped in champagne. She could taste the wine mixed with the fruit, her tongue alive to the subtle difference in flavor. Another sip of champagne tickled her throat.

"Open wide," he whispered to her. Something different

this time? Emma opened her mouth wider as instructed and felt another berry pressed between her lips. This time, the sides were smooth and hard, and she felt the difference before the dark, rich chocolate the berry had been dipped in melted on her tongue.

"Mmm," she sighed when her mouth was empty. The taste of chocolate lingered, and the next cool sip of champagne mixed with it in a burst of flavor.

She heard the glass settle back on the table and felt something small and firm wedge into the cleft between her full breasts. "My turn," she heard him whisper, then his head lowered to take the strawberry he'd placed in her cleavage.

Champagne swirled in her head, silk and velvet whispered against her skin, the remembered bite of strawberries, and the smooth slide of dark chocolate all seduced her senses while he ate the fruit between her breasts and kissed each warm, exposed curve in turn.

"I like the taste of berries," she heard, then felt his fingers take the edge of the silk corset and fold down the fabric to expose her nipples. He moved beside her, doing something, and she didn't know what until his fingers brushed the hard, tight buds he'd bared with something warm and not quite liquid.

"I especially like them dipped in chocolate," he murmured as his head came down. His mouth closed over her nipple, drawing it in, lapping at it with his tongue, sucking until she heard a low moan and realized with a shock that it had come from her. He gave both nipples equal treatment, and by the time he'd had his chocolate-dipped berry treat, her stomach muscles were quivering and the wisp of silk between her legs was damp.

Her nipples felt swollen and red like the berries he'd called them, ripe and ready. She felt as exotic as dark chocolate, as bubbly as champagne, as sensual and beautiful as the silk she wore.

"Lie back," her lover whispered, and then guided her body down to lie on the couch. He lifted one leg and bent it at the knee, then let her foot rest on the floor. The other leg extended straight. Then he slipped off her shoes by turns and sat at the far end of the couch, where he lifted her stocking-clad foot into his lap.

Emma closed her eyes under the blindfold and gave herself up to sensation. Warm hands stroked from her foot up her calf to her knee and back down. Light pressure, gliding along her skin in a slow exploration, finding the sensitive hollow behind her knee, paying attention to the shape of her ankles. He touched her as if all of her interested him equally, not just the obvious places. He didn't speak, and neither did she. The silence felt light rather than leaden, easy, without the awkwardness she'd expected.

When he finished with her first leg, he let her foot rest in his lap while he picked up the other. Emma drifted in a soft cloud of sensual stimulation, all of it so smooth and gentle that it slid under her defenses. How could she brace herself against a whisper, against the touch of silk and velvet on bare skin, the sweet and distinctly different tastes and textures of berry, chocolate, and sparkling wine?

If he'd stripped her at the door, she would have frozen. But skilled hands on her body that gave her pleasure while making no attempt to rush her or remove anything more than her coat and shoes lulled her and let her give herself up to the moment. It wasn't sex. It was sensual and erotic and enticing. It was irresistible. And Emma had no idea until he lavished it on her how she craved it. The heady blend of sensory delights and the knowledge that she was dressed and delivered for a night of seduction played on her imagination.

She was in the hands of a man who could do anything he wished with her. She'd given him permission in advance, agreed to be his for a night with only the assurance that he was a compatible match who'd fulfilled all the agency requirements and had passed the in-depth screening. He'd wanted complete anonymity, and she'd agreed because the more a stranger he was to her, the more unreal the encounter was, the easier she found it to follow through.

Emma could feel cool air against her belly and her upper thighs where her skin was completely exposed. Her nipples were bared to him with the corset folded back, and even though he wasn't touching her there, the knowledge that he could look or touch at will kept her body in a state of erotic suspense.

She felt him move and wasn't sure what he planned next. When chilled liquid pooled in her navel, she gasped— then sighed as she felt his tongue lap up the champagne, his mouth on her belly warm and wicked. The skin around her navel proved surprisingly sensitive. His mouth exploring her there had her body drawing tight in response, her breasts swelling against their silk prison, her sex growing warm and slick and aching for attention.

It shocked her that she could respond so readily to a stranger. Then again, physical needs were physical needs, and hers had been neglected for far too long. And the masculine attention he lavished on her was a healing balm to her spirit and her feminine confidence. Proof that her body was desirable, in spite of everything. . . .

"Where did you go?" The low whisper reached her ears, and Emma realized she'd stiffened during her mental wandering. She'd started to think about what she was doing, about Gage, and why she was here about to have sex with a strange man. He'd noticed the tension in her body and stopped.

"I was thinking," Emma admitted. "You're not what I expected."

"What did you expect?" She felt the couch dip as he shifted position, sitting back. His hands rested on her legs, a light touch, not moving away from her but halting his seduction. Or maybe shifting course, Emma thought. A man who listened to her, that was every bit as seductive as one who fed her strawberries and champagne and touched her as if he had all the time in the world for preliminaries. Or as if the preliminaries were enough in themselves.

"I didn't expect you to be so patient, for starters," Emma said. "And I didn't expect to like having you touch me." Maybe it was the blindfold, the fact that he was a stranger, or the champagne. Or all three combined. But she found it easy to be honest without hedging or trying to be diplomatic.

"You expected it to be like eating your vegetables? An unpleasant thing to endure? Something to do quickly and get it over with?" His voice sounded almost choked.

Dammit, was he laughing at her? Emma was tempted to rip off the blindfold and find out. "No," she said. "But you didn't have to feed me strawberries or sit with me while I relaxed with you. And I thought it would be harder. You know from my profile I've had limited experience. Limited to one partner, to be specific. I thought it would feel strange or wrong or just uncomfortable, but I like having you touch me. I didn't expect that."

"I'm glad." He bent and placed a kiss just above her knee. "I want you to enjoy yourself, Emma."

"Shouldn't I know your name if you know mine?" Emma relaxed into the couch again as she asked the question. She didn't know if she wanted to know his real name, but could she continue to think of him as a phantom, a dream lover? She ought to call him something—he had gone to so much trouble for her, he deserved to be given a name, if only in her own mind.

"What would you like to call me?" He asked the question in a soft voice before brushing a kiss above her opposite knee, giving each leg equal time.

"I don't know," Emma admitted. It was problematic. John Doe was too generic, too pragmatic. The Phantom was too dramatic. "Adam?"

The first man. That seemed appropriately symbolic. The first man in her new life, and if tonight wasn't all about the fruit of forbidden knowledge, what was? Following the story further, she intended to fall with him and to find her way back to her old life barred forever afterward. The myth fit the man.

"Adam." He kissed her thigh, a warm brush of lips she felt through the thin membrane of her stockings as if they weren't there. "I like it."

"I do, too," she said.

Adam sat back and lifted her feet out of his lap, settling them on the floor, and then reached forward to take her hand and tug her up to a sitting position. "Come sit in my lap, Emma."

She let him guide her, his hands giving her cues as he helped her change position until he had her where he wanted her. He settled her on his thighs, with her bare bottom snug against his cock, while he sat with his back to the armrest, his legs stretched out on the cushions.

Emma could feel the soft fabric of his pants and the hard bulge of his penis underneath and drew in an unsteady breath. Adam might be taking his time, but there was no question what he wanted from her, what he would have in the end. When he chose, he would strip away the frail protection of her thong and guide the head of his penis between her legs, spread open for him, and thrust inside her.

His arms came around her shoulders to keep her close. She felt his fingers play along her collarbone before dipping down to explore the upper curves of her breasts and the hollow between. Then he captured her nipples between the thumb and forefinger of each hand, pinching the tight buds with gradually increasing pressure until she gasped.

"Right there, hmm?" Adam kissed the back of her neck and the curve of her shoulder as he kept the pressure on her nipples steady. The stimulation made her squirm in his lap, grinding her bare butt against his cock, as she felt the reaction in her lower body. Her womb tightened, her vaginal muscles squeezed together, and her sex swelled in invitation.

"Lean forward." He released her nipples, and Emma bent forward from the waist, feeling slightly bewildered. What was he doing? Then she felt his hands move to the tight lacing of her corset and understood before she felt him work the tied ribbons loose.

Nineteen

Gage undid the ribbons on Emma's corset, keeping his hands steady with an effort. She looked like the embodiment of every fantasy he'd ever had in the outfit he'd chosen for her. The rose of her nipples had been visible through the thin silk corset, and he could see her labia through the matching thong. He could also see the damp patch on the silk that told him how much she was enjoying their game.

With her bare ass cradling his cock, he didn't know how long he could wait. But tonight was important for too many reasons to rush. How long had it been since he'd taken the time to seduce his wife? When he had last even considered taking her away for a weekend devoted to simply being alone together, talking, laughing, and making love?

She shouldn't have felt that she had to turn to a stranger to feel like a woman. She should never have believed he could find another woman as beautiful, as entrancing, as desirable, as she was to him. In sixteen years, she'd never had a rival. From the moment she'd agreed to be his, he had never wanted anything more than to keep her.

During the preparation for this reunion with his wife, Gage had realized that despite his initial reaction that nothing was lacking between them in the bedroom, one vital thing was. He'd invested too much of his drive and energy into fulfilling his fifteen-year plan, working to create the financial security Emma and their future children deserved. He'd stepped up his pace to achieve his goals faster because the lack of children bothered his wife more every year, and he didn't want to ask her to wait again the next time she brought it up.

The irony didn't escape him. In his efforts to make Emma's world financially secure, he'd taken away the time and energy and attention she needed to feel emotionally secure. To the point that she'd believed it when that bitch Tanya told her vicious lies. They were here now because he'd been too focused on the future to see the present and to realize that he was hurting the one woman he wanted only to please.

It was a mistake that had nearly cost him everything, and Gage didn't intend to ever repeat it. Money mattered as a means to provide for his family. But Emma's love was priceless. His priorities had seemed right at the time, but now the truth was clear. He should have spent less time worrying about impressing her with his performance in business and making his career and his portfolio secure and more time showing her how desirable she was to him, how much he wanted her, how she was anything but a failure as a wife or a lover.

The ribbons felt fragile in his hands as he unlaced the corset, spread the sides wide, and let it fall forward. The naked line of her back was beautiful, and Gage showed her with his hands and lips how much every part of her body deserved to be worshipped.

He loved the way she shivered at his touch, the gooseflesh that danced over her skin, the soft sighs she made, the way she arched into his touch to invite more. When he had paid homage to her back and shoulders and neck, Gage put his hands on her waist and signaled her to lean back against his chest. From this position he could see her full breasts, the slight rounding of her belly, her upper half naked and her lower half clad in so little that it was more invitation than protection.

The gas fireplace lit the room with a soft glow and made her skin gleam with a pearly luminescence. Her redhead's fair skin had always captivated him. The full curves of her breasts, the rosy crests of her nipples, and the soft curls between her rounded thighs always made him want to touch her. He knew Emma had fussed with dieting on and off over the years, but he couldn't imagine why. She looked like a woman, not a girl. And he wanted a woman in his bed. This woman. His woman.

He slid his hands up her rib cage to cup her breasts, holding the full weight of them in his palms. He squeezed gently to relieve the aching pressure he knew she was feeling, and she moaned and arched into his hands in response.

Gage held Emma in his lap, in his arms, filling his hands with her, and knew that it wasn't going to be enough for him for much longer. It had been too long, and he needed her too much. But he was going to make the experience as perfect for her as he could. So he focused his attention on pleasuring her with his hands, stroking and touching her sensitive breasts, stimulating her nipples, letting his hands rove down to touch the soft skin of her belly and toy with the edge of her thong.

"I want to take that off you, too," he whispered. He could see the fevered flush on her skin that told him how ready she was for more.

"Yes, Adam," Emma whispered back.

Gage couldn't give her his real name, not yet. But he wondered if she even knew what it meant that she'd chosen to call her fantasy lover Adam. He was her first man, and if he had anything to say about it, he would be her only and her last. On some level, did she suspect the truth?

He slid his hand down farther, touching her mons through the thin silk. Emma moved her thighs apart in a clear request for him to continue. He could feel the heat of her through the flimsy fabric, the slick dampness that signaled her arousal. It was an effort not to fist his hand into the silk and pull until it tore free and bared her for him to take.

Her hips rocked to press her sex into his palm. Gage stroked her through the fabric, then slid a finger under the edge of the material to touch her directly.

"Yes," Emma moaned. Her head fell back against his shoulder, and she arched her back before tilting her pelvis forward. He inserted the tip of his finger between her labia, opening her to his touch, exploring her. He felt her shudder in his arms, felt the liquid invitation in her sex before he slowly penetrated her with his finger.

His cock throbbed and his balls were drawn tight with the need to make her his and find his release inside her body. Gage clenched his jaw and fought for control, then withdrew his hand from her thong and returned both hands to her shoulders.

"Not on the couch," he said in a low voice. "I want to unwrap my present on the bed."

He felt Emma quiver at his words, and it made him smile. "Do you like that? Do you like being my present? Knowing that you've been selected and gift-wrapped and delivered to me to do with as I please?"

"Yes." Emma's voice was husky with passion. "It excites me. It makes me feel sexy and desirable and wanton."

"Maybe you're a natural submissive, Emma." The possibility had occurred to him in the very enjoyable and eye-opening course of his research and preparation for tonight. There was no question about his natural desire to dominate, and instead of directing it to their mutual pleasure in the realm of sexual play, he'd channeled that drive into other areas. Ones that had led to less pleasurable results.

He felt her stiffen. "I don't want to be told what to do." Then she shook her head. "I didn't mean it that way. I like what we're doing, I like that you're in charge and I've given up control to you. But I don't want to be told what to do outside of sex."

"Sexually submissive, Emma." He kept his voice soft, not wanting her to recognize it if he spoke normally. "It excites you to be on my lap while I touch you, to know that every inch of your luscious body is mine. To know that I can do anything I want to, with you and to you, and that I fully intend to."

"Oh." Her voice sounded thoughtful. "Submissive in bed. Not like a doormat in a relationship. Like a very sexy game." Her lips curved. "A secret."

"Yes." He stroked a hand over her breast again because he couldn't stop himself from touching her. "A very sexy game, and a very exciting secret. I could play with your breasts for hours, or simply tell you to leave them bare, and you'd never know if I was going to touch you or just look. I could have you walk around in these very sexy thigh-high stockings and high heels and nothing else, and you would wonder if I was going to bend you over a piece of furniture and have you, or make you touch yourself for me while I watched, or simply spread your legs to show me your pussy. And all that time, the anticipation and the suspense would make you hotter and hotter."

A shudder went through her, and he knew if he touched the silk between her thighs, he would find it clinging damply.

"You like that, Emma." He let his hand slide down to grip the thong she wore. "Should we find out how much?"

She didn't answer, and he inserted his hand under the white silk thong and slid it down to cup her sex, letting his fingers discover just how much hotter and wetter she was now than she'd been minutes ago.

"You like that a lot." Gage felt a primitive surge of satisfaction at the proof of her arousal. "And now you're going to walk with me to the bedroom, knowing that this very wet piece of silk between your thighs is going to come off."

"Adam." Her voice sounded hoarse.

"Hmm?" Gage separated her slick folds and inserted the tip of a finger into her, making her gasp.

"Wait a minute."

Was she having second thoughts? Gage removed his hand from her thong and wrapped both arms around her, hugging her to him. "Problem?"

Emma let out a shaky breath. "I knew that was coming.

I mean, I know why I came here, and I intend to go through with it. Can I just have a minute?"

She could have until the end of time, as long as she spent the passage of years with him. But Gage couldn't say that, so instead he reached over to pick up her fluted glass. He placed the stem in her hand and guided the rim to her lips. "Why don't you finish your champagne?"

She nodded and sipped. Gage added a splash to his champagne flute and sipped along with her. He stroked her arm idly as he held her and wondered if she felt what he did. There was a certain contentment in sharing a quiet moment between lovers. Something they hadn't done together in far too long. Emma was half-naked, in his arms, in his lap, soon to be in bed with him. He wanted her to want that as much as he did, and while he fully intended to stake his claim on her, he wasn't going to rush her.

"More?" Gage asked when he noticed her glass was empty. Emma shook her head and held out the fluted glass for him to take. He placed it back on the table, then set his beside it.

"You're being very patient," Emma said in a soft voice.

"You're worth waiting for, Emma."

She laughed, a shaky sound. "I hope you think so afterwards."

"Why so lacking in confidence?" Gage was genuinely curious about that. Had he done something to make her feel this way? Had he failed to say or do something she needed to know that she was never a disappointment to him?

"I told you I was inexperienced." She shrugged. "My husband wasn't. When we first got together, I mean. High school. He played football, he dated cheerleaders. Had sex with cheerleaders. I was shy and quiet and, well, it seems like I've always had an extra ten pounds I couldn't get rid of. I knew I didn't look like what he was used to. I didn't know how to perform. It's not like you learn how to be a good sex partner in sex ed."

She sounded disgruntled, as if she would have signed up for training in Sexual Techniques 101 if she hadn't been unjustly denied the opportunity. Gage bit the inside of his lip to keep from laughing. And did she really think some bubble-headed cheerleader from the past had given him something she failed to? How could she not know that being with the woman he loved, knowing she wanted *him,* surpassed anything else?

"You aren't too heavy." Gage cupped her breasts in his hand, luxuriating in their fullness. "You are just right."

"Thank you." She sighed. "Anyway, I didn't compare well to cheerleaders in high school. I can't even compare to how I used to look in high school now. The seventeen-year-old me didn't have cellulite."

"Emma." Gage squeezed her breasts gently to get her attention. "Do you think your not being seventeen means I don't want to have sex with you? That would make you underage. I'm not interested in getting arrested."

"Oh." She lifted one hand and placed it on his thigh, and he almost held his breath as she touched him voluntarily for the first time. "I didn't think of that."

"Age and weight have nothing to do with what makes a woman sexy." Gage released his hold on her breasts so he could stroke his hands over them. "Cellulite doesn't prevent you from feeling pleasure when you're touched or having an orgasm. Instead of worrying about how you think you look, why don't you focus on how you feel?"

"Feel." Emma sighed and turned her head sideways to rub her cheek against the fabric of his shirt. "I can do that. I think."

"How does this feel?" Gage asked the question in a soft whisper as he moved his hands up and down her torso, touching the curve of her belly, the valley between her breasts, the hollow of her collarbone, and the sides of her breasts.

"Good." She drew in a deep breath and let it out slowly. "Okay. You wanted me in the bedroom?"

"Yes. I want you in the bedroom." And everywhere else, but he left that unsaid. Gage turned with her on his lap and helped her stand. She felt around with her feet to locate her shoes and stepped into them with his support. Then he stood behind her, his hands playing along her waist for a moment. "Ready?"

She nodded. He was tall enough to see the pulse fluttering at her throat and knew nerves were riding her. That could heighten her pleasure if she didn't freeze up. He'd have to go carefully. Gage moved beside her and tucked her against his side with one arm, using the pressure of his arm and the steadying support of his body to guide her blindfolded to their waiting bed.

Emma walked with Adam and couldn't help noticing how he shortened his stride to match his step with hers, taking slow steps so she wouldn't stumble in her heels trying to keep up. Thoughtful. Adam seemed determined to defy all her expectations.

Not that she'd really known what to expect. But she

hadn't expected to be pampered, treated with consideration, gentleness, patience. Then again, she knew very well the amount of trouble he'd gone through for tonight. Would anyone go to those lengths and fail to value the results? Adam hadn't gotten her easily, and it made a certain sense that he didn't treat her casually. Emma liked him for treating her and their night together as if he intended to thoroughly enjoy his present to himself.

"You're smiling."

The whispered words were easy to follow. Emma realized that at some point she'd adjusted to the low conversation, matching his volume, and wondered if their soft voices were a psychological cue to relax, making him seem less threatening, less a stranger. "I was thinking how odd it feels to be a present. But I'm glad you're enjoying your gift."

"I'm very much going to enjoy unwrapping you."

Adam turned her and then backed her up to the bed. Emma felt the mattress against the backs of her legs and sat down. There was a rustling sound, and then she felt his hand on her ankle and realized he'd knelt in front of her. He lifted her foot and slipped off her shoe, then removed its mate. His hands went to the top of her stocking next, and she held her breath as he rolled it down, inch by inch, until her leg was bare. The second stocking followed, and then his hands hooked into the fabric of her thong.

"Stand up, Emma."

Right. She could do that. She got to her feet and felt them sink into the carpet's deep plush. She felt unsteady and knew it had nothing to do with the champagne or being blindfolded. It had everything to do with standing in front of a man who was about to take away the last thing shielding her body, leaving her naked.

He did it slowly, sliding the silk down her legs, taking the opportunity to stroke her thighs and calves and finally her ankles in the process. "Put your hand on my shoulder and step out."

Emma reached out and found his shoulder with her hand. She let it rest on him for balance while she stepped free of the thong.

"Feet apart."

She closed her eyes and let her breath go. Then she slid her feet to shoulder width. The stance made it easier to stay upright, but then he touched her, and the feel of his hands on the insides of her thighs nearly made her legs collapse.

"So soft," she heard him murmur. The hands moved higher until they framed her sex. She knew Adam was looking at her *there,* and she wanted to sink into the carpet. It seemed too intimate, too personal. *And what did you expect, Emma? That sex wouldn't be intimate or personal?*

Adam's hands covered her like a fig leaf, cupped her, stroked her, petted her. He explored her plumped labia, opened her to test her readiness, and found her slick and welcoming for the finger he used to penetrate her. The way he was going to penetrate her. She started breathing faster and felt her legs shaking in reaction.

"On the bed, Emma." He thrust in and out of her with his finger, both hands on her sex, preparing her to take all of him. She half fell, half sat on the bed when he released her, then moved farther up onto the mattress and listened to the rustling fabric sounds that told her he was undressing. It seemed to take forever, the time stretching out as she sat there in an agony of suspense, but in reality it could only have been a few minutes before he joined her.

Emma felt the warmth of his bare skin as it came in contact with hers. His hands closed on her waist and slid her farther up the bed, then pushed her down to lie on her back in a submissive position before taking her wrists and stretching them over her head. Adam held her pinned to the mattress while his legs separated hers. Then he settled over her, hard, naked. His cock rode between her thighs, the head probing at her opening.

The reality of it overwhelmed her. What was she doing? She was lying naked under a man who was about to fuck her. And while her body might be saying *yes,* the rest of her burst abruptly into panicked *no.* Tremors racked her, and she could hear herself breathing in gasps. Not enough air in the room, she couldn't breathe, couldn't—

"No. Stop." Her voice came out thin and reedy, her throat too tight to shriek. "I can't. I can't."

"Emma?" Adam froze above her for a long moment, as motionless as if he'd turned to stone. Then he released her hands and rolled to the side, pulling her into his arms. Emma curled into a ball, shaking and unable to stop the tears that spilled out.

"I can't. I'm sorry. I'm sorry," she whispered, the words forced out past sobs.

"Shhh." He curled his body around hers, then reached down to pull the covers up over them to give her more warmth. "No need to be sorry."

She half laughed in response to that, shaking her head. "Don't tell me you're not disappointed when your hard-on is pressing into me."

"I'm a grown man. I can handle being hard and being told no," she heard him murmur. "I can also take myself in hand if it comes to that."

She caught her breath as a picture formed in her mind of his strong hand closing around his own shaft, stroking up and down, pumping himself into his fist. "Can I watch if you do?" she asked him.

"So you do still have an interest in me and my cock." Adam's arms hugged her close as he rocked his hips into her, letting her feel how hard he was. "I was in a position to know that your body was very interested a few minutes ago. Can you tell me what changed your mind? Was it being pinned? Did that scare you?"

Emma shook her head. "You didn't scare me. And the way you held me down, that was sexy. I just . . . couldn't. I'm sorry. I thought I could do it, I thought I could go through with it. I *wanted* to go through with it. I didn't mean to be a tease, and I didn't want to disappoint you. I didn't want to disappoint myself."

"Disappoint yourself?" He rubbed her arm as if trying to encourage her circulation, her body's ability to warm itself, as he shared his body heat with her. "What did you expect of yourself, Emma?"

"That I could perform, for starters," she muttered. She rubbed at her eyes through the blindfold. "I didn't expect to turn into a porn star or anything, but I thought I could at least manage the basics."

"And why couldn't you?" He stopped rubbing her arm to touch her cheek.

She drew in a shuddering breath. "Physically I was ready. Emotionally, mentally, I'm not. I can't separate myself in my mind, I can't separate you . . ." Her voice trailed off, then she tried again. "I wanted to call you by the wrong name."

"I see." He followed the line of her jaw, then touched the hollow behind her ear.

"I'm sorry," she said again.

"Do you love him?" The question was spoken as quietly as everything else Adam had said to her, but it seemed overly loud in her own mind. That was the real question, wasn't it? Not whether Gage had stopped loving her, but whether she could shut him out of her heart, cut him out of her life, find a way to make her body forget the lover who had been her first and only.

She set aside the hurt, the betrayal, and the confusion she'd felt over the growing distance between them and her frustration and helplessness as she couldn't seem to stop it from happening, and what was left was a well of sadness that seemed to have no bottom.

"I want to stop," she whispered back, "but I can't. I don't know how. How do you stop loving someone who doesn't want you?"

Twenty

Gage closed his eyes at the pain in his wife's voice and wondered how he could have screwed up so badly that loving him hurt her. It was a relief to know he hadn't lost her, but the damage went deep. Finding his way back to her was like feeling his way through a minefield. Where could they go next that wouldn't prove a fatal misstep?

He held her close for a minute longer and then bent to kiss her shoulder. "Stay here," he whispered. "I'll be back."

He rolled out of bed and tucked the covers back around her, retrieved the champagne from the ice bucket and re-filled their glasses, then carried them into the bathroom with the bottle. He set the chilled wine on the counter and stopped up the sunken jetted tub before turning on the water to fill it.

They might not have much to celebrate right now, but the alcohol might relax Emma. Sitting with him in the warm water, feeling the soothing hydromassage, might not lead to underwater lovemaking, but he'd settle for making her feel comfortable and keeping her close.

It didn't take long to fill the tub. When it was ready, he shut off the water, turned on the jets, and went to get Emma. She'd stayed where he'd left her, curled into a ball, only the bright strawberry blond of her hair showing above the covers. Gage folded them back and took her hand in his. "Come with me."

She sat up and scooted to the edge of the bed, letting her feet find the floor before she tried to stand. Gage led her to the bathroom and switched off the lights so the room was illuminated by the moon and stars that shone through the skylight.

He settled her in the water up to her chin, set the champagne bottle within reach of the tub, and climbed in to join her with a delicate stem in each hand. Beautiful and fragile, the glasses seemed to represent the current state of their marriage all too well. Gage handed Emma her fluted glass and touched the rim of his to hers. "Cheers."

"You're an odd man, Adam." Emma sipped the wine and tilted her head at him. "I could understand champagne before the seduction, but after it failed?"

"Maybe I'm gearing up to try again," he murmured, leaning close to her ear. "Maybe I'm hoping to get you drunk." He kissed the hollow behind her ear because he couldn't help himself and added, "Maybe I just don't want you to go."

"So you're using a jetted tub and champagne to tempt me to stay?" She smiled over the rim of her glass. "Effective."

Gage settled one arm around her shoulders and drew her close to his side. He tipped his head back to look through the skylight and wondered what Emma would think of the starscape overhead. It was dim in here. If he slipped off her blindfold, would she stay watching the stars with him? Or would she see too well in the low light?

Emma might have suspicions about his identity already, but she didn't know for certain. Gage wasn't sure what she would do when all doubt was erased. Would she be glad to see her husband and not a mysterious stranger?

"You've gotten quiet," Emma said softly.

"Looking at the stars," he answered in matching tones. "Would you like to look at them, too?"

"You can see them?" She tipped her head back as if trying to see through the silk that covered her eyes.

"There's a skylight above the tub." He stroked the upper slope of her breast and watched her reaction to a touch that was more sexual than simple closeness. She didn't move away. "I could take off your blindfold if you like."

"Would I be able to see you?"

Gage looked down at her. She was dimly visible in the low light, the shape of her, the curves of her breasts. But her features were softened. He could still tell it was Emma, but if she expected a stranger, would she fail to recognize him in the partial dark? "A little," he answered.

She finished her champagne and set the glass on the tile behind them. "Then I'd like you to take it off, please."

Gage placed his glass by hers to free his hands, undid the knot at the back of her head, and pulled the silk free, letting it fall between their empty glasses. "There." He slid his arm back around her and took it as a positive sign that she didn't object to that, either.

Emma looked at him, then up at the stars. "Beautiful."

"Like you." He moved his hand down to cup her breast.

"You haven't given up," she said.

"No." He gave her breast a gentle squeeze, then toyed with her nipple.

"I did tell you I couldn't go through with it," Emma reminded him.

"You said no to actual sex. That leaves some room to maneuver," Gage pointed out. "Foreplay. Manual stimulation. Hands. Mouths."

"I don't know."

Gage pulled her onto his lap, facing away from him. It was a position that made it very easy for him to touch her, and he communicated his intent by placing one hand over her breast and the other low on her belly, his fingertips brushing her pubic curls. She hesitated a moment or two and then opened her thighs enough to let him settle his hand fully over her sex.

"I'll make it easy for you," he whispered into her ear. "You belong to me, and I refuse to let you go. I have you naked for my pleasure. I'm going to touch you the way I want to. I'm going to fill you with my hands the way I want to fill you with my cock. And do you know what else, Emma?" He squeezed her mons, then ground his hand against her soft flesh. "I'm going to make you like it. I'm going to make you come."

He felt her shudder in his arms. Her breathing accelerated, but she didn't move away from him or protest. She stayed still, and when he worked a finger into her, he found her hot and tight and so slick that he felt equal parts triumph and lust rush through him.

He wanted to scoot her forward on his legs, position his cock, and thrust into her while he pulled her back down, filling her with every hard inch of his shaft. And then he wanted her to ride him, her round ass slapping against him as she took him, bouncing in his lap as he penetrated her again and again.

Since he couldn't do that, Gage told her what he wanted to do to her in explicit detail while he reached around to find her clit with one hand. He stroked the sensitive nub while he added a second finger to the one buried in her wet heat. His hands established a rhythm that he gradually increased until her hips began to rock in time. Her head fell back on his shoulder as she rode his fingers, giving in to him, to the pleasure of the moment and her need.

"That's it," he grated out in a harsh whisper. Her pelvis rocked into his hand faster, her movements growing frenzied. "You want to come, don't you? You feel so hot, so wet, and it feels so good having my hands between your thighs."

"Yes." Her voice sounded choked.

"Then come for me, Emma. Come for my fingers or I'll fuck you."

The erotic threat made her moan, and Gage felt her grow even slicker as he plunged his fingers rhythmically into her. "I'll do it," he whispered. She was so close. He had her right on the edge, and he was determined to push her over. "I'll fill you with my cock again and again while I bounce your beautiful ass up and down on my lap."

She made a low sound, and then he felt her body go tight as her back arched and her hips bucked. Her inner muscles clamped down on his invading finger as she broke and came for him.

Gage kept his hands where they were as she shuddered and finally grew still. "Wow," she said finally.

"Wow is good. I like wow." He kissed her shoulder as she relaxed back against him.

"It sounded so sexy. Like a lap dance, but the real thing."

Gage thumbed her nipple and wondered how much longer he could continue this conversation without having to stop and give himself some relief. "You can dance on my pole, too."

She laughed, a soft sound magnified just slightly by the water. "You want me."

"I think you can feel just how much." No point in being subtle when the hard ridge of his cock was pressed against her.

"I want it like that," Emma said. She wiggled in his lap, pressing the soft flesh of her ass into him. "Please."

It might be a mistake. But he'd been without her for too long and wanted her too badly. And she'd asked him for it. He could deny himself, but he was powerless to deny her.

"Please," she said again, and that settled it. Gage placed his hands on her hips, raised her up, and angled her slightly forward. That let him guide her slick opening to the head of his cock. He closed his eyes and pulled her downward as he thrust up simultaneously, seating himself fully inside her welcoming flesh as he held her on his lap.

"Oh." She made a sound of half surprise, half pleasure, and Gage fought the urge to come instantly as her inner muscles squeezed around his cock.

"This won't last long," he informed her. Emma was hot and slick around him, his balls were aching, and he didn't think he'd ever been so hard. Her round ass felt soft and giving as she squirmed in his lap.

He used his grip on her to help her ride him as he rocked his hips into her, and she rocked with him in a rhythm that made his heart thunder. The water added buoyancy and softened his strokes. She arched her back to take him deeper, grinding her bottom into his lap, and Gage reached around her to search out her clit. He stroked the sensitive nub while he drove into her. Emma was breathing hard and making little sounds that told him just how much she liked this position.

"You love bouncing up and down in my lap, getting fucked good and hard, don't you?"

"Yes," she moaned in response. "Yes, God, yes. Don't stop."

"I won't stop." He thrust harder. "I'm going to make you come for me again, and then I'm going to empty my balls into you."

He felt her inner muscles fluttering, and the knowledge that she was on the verge of orgasm triggered his. He held her tight as he pumped himself into her while she came with him.

"That felt so good." Her voice was a soft sigh in the semidarkness. Her head lolled back on his shoulder. "I may not be able to move again, though. I won't be able to walk back to bed."

"I'll help you." He cupped his hands over her breasts, loving the shape and feel of them.

"Mmm. I like that." She sprawled in his lap looking utterly abandoned, her legs spread, her back arching to push her breasts into his hands.

"I do, too." Gage stayed inside her, holding her, and wished he could freeze this moment in time. What did it mean that she'd said yes to him after looking at him in the starlight? What sort of change of heart had she had? How could he build on this fragile connection to repair the damage to their marriage?

After a few minutes, Emma sighed and shifted in his lap. "I guess we should climb out before we turn into prunes."

"True." Gage shifted her forward and withdrew from her, then helped her to her feet. They climbed out of the sunken tub together. He pulled down thick towels and handed one to her. Emma took it and dried herself off, then wrapped it around her body sarong style. Gage dried off and decided to let her set the tone. He wrapped the towel around his waist before he reached for her hand. He led her to the bedroom, and they climbed into bed together.

"Do you feel more comfortable with the towels?" Gage asked. "Or do you trust me not to ravish you against your will if we take them off?"

"I suppose we'll get the sheets damp if we don't." Which answered the question only indirectly, but Gage watched as she unwrapped herself, tugged the towel free, and then looked around as if uncertain what to do with it.

"I'll hang them up." He took it from her and kept his own towel around his waist until he reached the bathroom. Then he hung them to dry and walked back to her naked.

The bedroom was dim, too. The curtains were open, so the only illumination came from the moon and the city lights outside. Light enough that she could see. Dark enough that she could pretend he was a stranger named Adam if she wanted to avoid dealing with too much at once.

Gage knew that the two of them sharing a bed tonight was a long ways from reconciliation, but a part of him had relaxed with the knowledge that he could still make her · want him.

"I missed you," she said when he rejoined her in the bed. Gage drew her into his arms and settled her head on his shoulder.

"I missed you, too," he murmured, not sure if she meant the past weeks apart, the gradual distance over the years, or the time it had taken him to hang towels to dry. For him, it was true for all three.

"Tell me something." Her voice was soft, a little uncertain.

Gage gave her a reassuring squeeze. "Anything."

"How was it? For you? In the tub?"

"Life altering." That was the plain truth, although maybe not how she needed to hear him say that she'd pleased him. He tried again. "Nothing else compares. How was it for you?" He knew she'd enjoyed herself, but how did she feel otherwise?

"The same, but not the same." She traced a pattern over his heart with her fingers. "Like the first time all over again, but different."

The first time had been in the backseat of a base-model compact car. This time he had a luxury penthouse suite to offer her, with all the romantic touches he hadn't been able to give her then. He'd wanted to give her more, had known full well how much more she deserved, and he'd burned with the need to be able to give her everything.

"Better?" Gage asked.

"Different." She stretched against him, and he felt his body react to the slide of her breasts and her bare legs. "I think we should try it in bed next."

Her hand moved down his chest, followed the faint trail of hair that arrowed down to his groin, and touched his rapidly hardening shaft. Her soft hand closed around him and moved up and down in a testing stroke that undid him.

"Emma . . ." He rolled her onto her back and brought his head down to kiss her for the first time in over a month. He'd been careful not to do that when she was blindfolded, certain it would give the game away too soon. He'd taught her to kiss him, coaxed her into giving him her tongue in the first of many sessions in his car, where they'd gradually progressed from deep kissing to petting to the first time she'd let him unzip her jeans and touch her through her panties.

And now he needed to kiss her while he made love to her this time.

Emma's lips parted for his, and the taste of her filled his senses. He filled his hands with her, wild to touch all of her, to claim what was his. Her hand tightened around his shaft, and she continued to work him from base to head, and he cupped her mons in return, stimulating her with the palm of his hand, rubbing a slow circle over the sensitive nub of her clit in an indirect touch that made her moan into his mouth.

She was hot and ready and his. Gage caught her wrists again and pulled them above her head, pinning her down while he settled his body over hers. He wedged his knee between her legs and broke the kiss to say, "Spread wide for me."

Emma shifted under him, opening her thighs, making a cradle for him with her hips. He teased her with his shaft, riding it along her slick labia while she moaned and arched up under him in reaction.

"Want that?" He stroked himself against her slick sex once more. "Do you want my cock inside you again, Emma?"

"Yes." She rocked her hips into him, trying to get more of him.

He positioned his head at her opening and thrust in, slowly, drawing it out, making her wait for it. She felt so good under him, wrapped around him, enclosing him in her tight sheath. When he'd pushed his way in as far as he could go, he ground his pelvis against hers, making her feel the pressure deep inside. "Like that?"

"Yes," she whispered.

"I'm glad, because you're mine, Emma." He held her down and took her in a steady, driving rhythm. "And I will never let you go."

He kept his pace just slow enough that it would keep her from peaking too quickly. He wanted it to build until the intensity overwhelmed her. He took her mouth while he took her body, and when he felt her trembling on the brink, he increased his pace and altered the angle to press deep inside against the sweet spot that would send her off every time.

Emma arched up under him as the orgasm hit. "Gage!"

He felt his cock jerk inside her as he began to spill himself into her depths while her inner muscles clenched around his shaft and milked him dry.

Twenty-One

Emma floated back to earth in stages and knew she'd landed when she felt herself stiffen. Now she would have to face reality and repercussions and decisions.

"I love you," he breathed against her ear, still covering her with his body. "I wanted you from the first moment I saw you, and I'll love you until the day I die."

She felt tears spill from her eyes and hated herself for the weakness. "You have an odd way of showing it."

"I've made mistakes." He raised his head to look down at her face, dimly visible in the glow of city lights. "Although cheating on you wasn't one of them. I fired Tanya when I found out what she'd done."

Emma felt her stomach clench at the sound of that name. "You're saying she lied?"

"Yes, Emma. She lied." Gage rested his forehead against hers. "But if I hadn't already screwed up, you never would have believed her, so as convenient as it would be to blame our separation on her, it wouldn't be honest. I thought I was doing the right things to be the husband you needed.

Maybe instead of creating and following my own master plan all these years, I should have made one with you."

Gage, admitting he was at fault? Emma tried to take it in, tried to reconcile the patient, seductive stranger who'd met her at the door with the proud, stubborn man she lived with.

"I'm glad," she said finally. "That you didn't cheat. Because I don't think I could have ever gotten past that."

"You had sex with me thinking I cheated."

Emma closed her eyes. He would point that out. "Yes, I did. It happens all the time. Sex with the ex. It's comfortable and familiar, and people find the habit hard to break." And she could understand why now. Ex marks the spot, she thought, remembering how he'd known exactly where to find the sensitive point inside her to bring her off. The kind of knowledge that only came with deep familiarity.

"So you were willing to sleep with me but not sure you wanted to live with me again?" His voice sounded hard, and Emma forced herself not to flinch.

"I didn't know," she answered honestly. "I knew if you'd slept around on me, nothing would ever be the same between us. I knew I still loved you, but I didn't know if I could forgive you."

"You planned to cheat on me," Gage said.

"I couldn't do it." She swallowed, feeling a hard lump in her throat. "Whatever our problems, I couldn't take that step. And I thought I was losing my mind, because I felt like I was with you. Then I realized I wanted to be with you."

"I'm glad you wanted to be with me." He freed her hands and levered himself off her, lay beside her, and pulled her back into his arms. "Although I didn't mind giving you

Adam if that was what you needed to believe that you're a beautiful, desirable woman."

She sighed and burrowed into him. "I'm not sure I'm ready to talk about all this right now." The past and the future both seemed fraught with difficulties, but in this moment, here and now, they had a fragile truce. They were together and talking, and sex had reestablished one bond they'd always shared. As infrequent as sex had become in their too busy and too separate lives, Gage had always made certain it was good for her. Which was probably why she'd missed it so much when he didn't have the time or energy.

"Tired?" Gage stroked her hair as he held her.

She nodded, rubbing her cheek against his skin in the process. "Very." She felt emotionally drained as well as physically spent. She wanted nothing more than to close her eyes and rest. "I haven't slept well for weeks," she admitted a few minutes later.

"Me either." She felt his arms tighten around her. "I kept reaching for you at night and then realizing all over again that you weren't there." His lips brushed her hair. "I want you back, Emma. I want you home with me where you belong."

It was good to know where she stood, at least. Gage still wanted her. Enough to have planned this elaborate charade and to seduce her by steps and stages. It didn't erase the past or the way she'd felt all the nights she'd waited for him to come home, but knowing he did still want her soothed her bruised spirit.

He drew the covers up around her shoulders, and Emma relaxed with the warmth of his body and the blankets cocooning her. She'd missed this the most. Going to bed with Gage wasn't just about sex, it was the warmth and closeness and security she felt when she curled up with him at night. They had more to deal with, she knew that. But not now. She closed her eyes and let sleep steal over her, weighing her body down.

She woke to a series of light kisses on her forehead, nose, and cheeks. Emma blinked her eyes open and focused on her husband's face close to hers. So familiar, yet in some ways it was like seeing him for the first time.

She remembered the high school Gage very well, too good-looking in his letter jacket with his blond hair long on the top, brown eyes that followed her and made her belly flutter, an athletic build that had enticed her younger self and hadn't been lost in adulthood. Instead, he'd filled out a little more in his twenties, gained another inch or two in height. The hair was worn in a much more conservative style now, but his eyes still made butterflies dance in her tummy, because she knew exactly what it meant when he looked at her that way now.

"Good morning," she said. Then she noticed that the light in the room came from a bedside lamp. "Or is it still night?"

"Early morning." Gage stretched out on top of her, his legs and arms on either side of her body making a loving cage over her with the covers between them. "Room service has delivered. I was hungry. I thought you might be, too."

Her stomach growled at the mention of food, and he grinned at her. "Thought so."

Her appetite was back, apparently. In the past few weeks, it had deserted her for the most part. Not that the scales reflected any difference, Emma thought with an inner sigh.

"I don't have anything to wear," she said as the fact dawned on her.

"Yes, you do." Gage kissed the corner of her mouth, then teased her lips with his. "I love the outfit you wore last night, but I have something else for you to put on this morning."

Emma considered the implications of that. "We're playing dress-up?"

"We're playing, but dressing you is only part of it." Gage rocked his pelvis into hers in a blatant demonstration of one way he wanted to play with her. "I had you delivered to me, and I have this suite for the weekend. Consider it your golden cage and me the holder of the key. You, luscious Emma, are my captive. You will wear the clothes I picked for you to wear, and we will play with the toys I bought for us because this game is far from over and I play to win."

Her lips formed an "oh" as she realized he intended to continue to be her captor while she remained his plaything.

"Nod and I'll let you up." Gage smiled at her. "If you have doubts, the food will get cold while I rip off those covers and have you for breakfast instead."

Heat curled in her belly, and Emma woke all the way up without any help from caffeine. Her body's response told her that physically, at least, she wanted very much to continue what they'd started last night. How did she feel in her mind, in her heart? Cautious. Interested. Hopeful. "It's a nice cage," she said.

His face turned serious. "I thought it was an improvement over the backseat of a car."

"That had its own charm," Emma said thoughtfully. "I felt like such a bad girl, letting you go all the way with me in the back of your car. And there was the risk of getting caught. And the thrill of knowing you wanted me so much that you'd take me anywhere you could get me alone." She stretched under him, luxuriating in the feel of his body on hers. "Of course, we're older now. Stiffer joints, less flexible. More serious consequences if we get caught in the act. I think car sex is probably doomed to remain in the nostalgic past."

Gage looked at her in silence for a minute. "You're serious. Your first time was in a car and you liked it?"

"Well, it was kind of uncomfortable because it was the first time, but you're pretty good with your hands." Emma gave him a smile wide with remembered satisfaction. "As I recall, you got me there twice before you did the deed, and it all went pretty well."

And after that, as her body quickly grew accustomed to his, sex had been anything but uncomfortable, no matter how cramped the car was.

He shook his head. "Emma, I felt like the biggest loser and the biggest winner on the planet at the same time. You said yes to me, and I wasn't about to stop. I wanted you too much. But I knew you deserved better, and I swore I'd make it up to you by making sure you had better in the future." Gage levered himself up and moved to sit beside her. "At least tell me you like the scene of your present seduction."

"I like it very much. What I've seen and felt of it, anyway." She smoothed her hand over the mattress. "Um, you mentioned something to wear?"

"I did." Gage stood and gestured toward the window

with one hand. Emma turned her head to look and saw a chair with something peach colored draped over it.

She sat up and hesitated a moment before throwing back the covers. Gage had seen her naked enough times to make modesty ridiculous.

He watched her stand up with blatant interest and reached out to pet her pubic curls. "Spread your legs, Emma."

"I thought I was getting dressed," she said. She felt proud of herself for not stuttering.

"First you're going to spread your legs."

She drew in a sharp breath as she felt a rush of heat that had nothing to do with embarrassment and shifted her feet apart, opening her thighs in the process. He palmed her sex and stroked her labia, squeezed her mons, toyed with the soft folds at his fingertips.

"I love to touch your pussy, Emma." He held her eyes while he moved his hand between her legs. "I always have. The first time you let me touch you through your panties, I almost came in my shorts. Getting my hands and my mouth on you makes me hard every time. You can get dressed, but whenever I want to touch your pussy, or see it, or have it, I'm going to tell you to spread your legs. And you'll do it because you belong to me and because it makes you hot."

Words failed her entirely, but she did manage a nod. Having her husband order her to spread her legs affected her like nothing she'd ever imagined. He'd said something the night before about domination and submission in the bedroom. Was this what he'd meant?

He stroked his hand over her in a final caress. "Get dressed. I'll wait for you out in the living room."

Emma nodded again and stayed frozen in place with her

legs apart, watching him walk away until he was out of sight. Then she blinked a few times in an effort to focus. Dressing. He'd picked something for her to wear, and if it was anything like last night's outfit, it would be something they'd both enjoy.

The peach fabric turned out to be a dress with long sleeves and an A-line skirt that came midway down her calves and buttoned all the way from hem to neck in front. The scooped neck was low, and Emma thought she detected a pattern in Gage's clothing choices. He liked displaying her breasts.

She held the dress to her front and looked down at it, realizing that in spite of the deceptively conservative style, the low neck and all those buttons, not to mention the skirt, meant easy access to any part of her Gage wanted, without taking it off. She looked at the chair's cushion to see if there was anything else, like underwear. Or if he intended her to be completely bare underneath.

A bra in matching peach lace sat there. Emma picked it up and saw that the see-through lace cups would hide absolutely nothing. The low cut of the bra meant her breasts would be exposed nearly to the nipple again. Where had he found this stuff? Not in a typical department store lingerie selection, that was certain.

There was another scrap of peek-a-boo peach lace under the bra. It took her a minute to understand what it was, and when she did, she wondered why he'd bothered with anything. It formed a lacy frame for her sex while it left her crotch bare. He wouldn't even have a thin barrier of silk or lace to bar him from looking or touching. Or taking.

She sucked in a breath as she realized that he could simply lift her skirt and have her at any time, any way he wanted. She crumpled the lace in her hands and thought, My husband wants me to wear crotchless panties and spread my legs whenever he tells me to.

"I should have left two years ago," Emma whispered to the empty room. How stupid she had been, letting it go on for so long, being patient and understanding instead of complaining, feeling quietly wounded instead of throwing something at his head when he'd come home from Denver after being away on business while she turned thirty-three without him.

Gage had admitted he'd made mistakes. She had to take some of the blame for the state of their marriage, too. He'd ignored her needs, but she'd let him do it. She hadn't demanded better, had settled for silence and distance, and why?

Because I was always afraid he'd leave me. The realization hit her like a blow to the stomach. She almost doubled over from it. Shy, quiet high school Emma had been out of her depth with the popular and good-looking football hero, amazed at her luck that he'd noticed her, stunned into disbelief that he wanted her. Hadn't she grown up at all in sixteen years? Was she still full of adolescent insecurity on the inside? Or just trapped in the patterns of old habits she'd long since outgrown? She'd felt trapped, and she'd come here in an attempt to break free.

Well, it looked as though Gage wanted to break free, too, while holding her captive and refusing to let her go. Crotchless panties. Spreading her legs on command.

Breakfast could be really interesting.

Emma stepped into the X-rated underwear first, then put on the rest of the getup.

"Hussy," Emma said to herself, and grinned. She felt pretty and feminine and brazen and sexual.

A quick search in the bathroom produced a comb. Emma smoothed out her hair and then took a good look at herself in the mirror. The signs of strain in her face had relaxed. She looked younger, happier. Pretty. Even sexy, with her cleavage shown off by the low neck of the dress with the visible edge of her lace bra hinting at what lay underneath. The peach color complimented her fair skin and hair, and knowing that she was bare at the crotch underneath made her feel she had a naughty secret. The knowledge glimmered in her eyes, giving them a sparkle she hadn't seen in a while.

She retraced her steps from the night before, this time seeing what her feet had touched, the thick plush carpet that stretched ahead, high ceilings overhead, recessed lighting, beautiful original paintings hung on softly tinted walls. The penthouse. He'd spared no expense. She was willing to bet they'd been drinking Dom Pérignon last night, too.

Emma padded barefoot through the suite, making her way to the man who waited for her at a table for two.

"Very nice." Gage gave her an approving look, then stood up to hold out her chair for her. He seated her and placed an unhurried kiss on her cleavage before returning to his chair.

"I like your choices," Emma admitted. "Nothing I would have chosen for myself, but I like it all." Everything had fit comfortably and made her look better than she'd realized she could. She'd always felt she was reasonably attractive, but she'd never really thought of herself as sexy. Gage's choices made her feel sensual and displayed her assets to advantage.

"You don't seem to see yourself the way I do." Gage poured coffee into her cup, then refilled his. "I'm not saying I want you to show off your beautiful breasts in public, because I'm a little too territorial to want other men drooling over them. But I like seeing you dressed like this for me. Showing me what a sexy woman you are, and showing off those full curves I love to fill my hands with."

"I guess maybe I see myself as a size twelve in a size six world," Emma said. "Have seen," she corrected as she added sugar to her coffee and stirred. "I have to admit that I look good in your naughty undies, and my weight isn't unhealthy. Curvy doesn't mean fat. Also, I've realized recently just how much time I've spent trying to lose ten pounds without any progress. Now I'm asking myself if I want to waste any more of my life dieting or if I'd rather enjoy myself at the weight my body wants to be."

"Hallelujah," Gage said. "You're beautiful, Em. No, you aren't thin as a rail, and since I don't see the appeal of that, I'm not sorry. I like to think I'd love the woman you are no matter your shape, but I'm very partial to the shape you have. And I hate seeing you unhappy. Every time you try a new diet, you're miserable."

"I've tried a lot of them in the last year," Emma said, thinking about it. Had she stepped up her efforts in an attempt to regain her husband's interest? And if so, why hadn't she known that all she really needed to do was start wearing lower-cut things around the house and flashing a little bit? She'd assumed she didn't have the equipment to recapture his attention. She hadn't tried to seduce him. Maybe it was time she learned how.

Twenty-Two

"Your nipples are nice and hard," Gage said in a conversational tone as he lifted the covers off their plates. "I like to see them poking through the fabric of your dress like that. Are your legs spread, Emma?"

"No." She looked into his eyes and felt her heart skip. "Do you want them to be?"

"Yes."

Let the games begin, Emma thought, and opened her thighs under the table.

"Is the skirt keeping you from spreading your legs as far as possible?"

It was. She nodded and wondered what he'd say about that.

"Hmm." Gage considered her across the table. "We'll have to do something about that. In the meantime, keep your legs open. I want you to think about the fact that we're sitting here having breakfast together while you have your legs spread and you're wearing crotchless panties."

She dropped her fork with a clatter and nearly knocked over her cup retrieving it.

He smiled at her. "How's your breakfast, darling?"

Emma looked down at her plate as she realized she had no idea what was on it. Strawberry crepes. One of her favorite choices for a leisurely breakfast out. "Is there a hidden message in all these strawberries?" She gave him a curious look. "The strawberries last night. Crepes this morning. Just wondering."

"You love strawberry crepes. You love chocolate-dipped strawberries. And they go well with champagne." Gage reached over to touch her hand. "Maybe I'm hoping that if I offer you all the things you love, you'll associate them with me."

"Good strategy." Emma forked up a bite and let the blend of fruit, cream, and crepe delight her taste buds. "That shouldn't surprise me. You're very shrewd and an excellent strategist."

"You think so?" Gage looked genuinely surprised, and Emma blinked at him.

"Yes. You're always thinking ahead and looking for the advantage. You played football that way. Smart. Looking for your opening, thinking ahead of your opponents." She frowned. "Not that I want you to see me as an opponent."

"You thought I played smart." Gage rubbed his thumb against the back of her hand. "You didn't just think I looked sexy?"

"Well, that, too. Those tight pants. The shoulder pads." She grinned at him. "But I always knew you were smart, Gage. It doesn't surprise me at all that you've succeeded in business. You know how to pick your opportunities, how to go after what you want and get it."

"I want you." His eyes turned dark.

She licked a stray dab of whipped cream off her lip and then realized what an invitation it would look like. She froze, her eyes wide, not sure what to do next.

"You look nervous, Emma." Gage's lips tilted just a little in an almost smile. "Like maybe you've realized you're alone with a very powerful man and I don't even have to get you naked to have you."

Her heart rate and respiration shot up, and Emma wondered if she was going to hyperventilate before he even touched her.

"I will have you," he added.

Her sex clenched in reaction, and she felt her breasts swelling in their lacy confines. Heat spread through her as she thought about how easily accessible she was to him.

"But not just now. Finish your breakfast."

He sat back and went on eating while Emma thought about pouring ice water down her dress to cool off.

"Right," she croaked, and drank her coffee to alleviate the dryness in her throat. "I'll just ignore the fact that you told me to sit with my legs spread as far as they could go and my crotch is bare and I have no idea what you plan to do to me next or whether it'll be in five minutes or five hours. No problem."

"I'm glad you're enjoying yourself."

"If it's five hours, I'll be enjoying myself the manual way," Emma heard herself say, and it shocked them both. Him probably more than her, she decided.

Well, what did he expect? He'd gotten her hooked on

great sex at an impressionable age, gotten her accustomed to having it on a regular basis, and then expected her to not miss it when the last two years she'd been lucky if it happened once a month? She'd stopped waiting around for him after the first several months of frustration and started enjoying herself in the bathtub when she got home after a long day at work.

"Have you been pleasuring yourself while I worked late, Emma?" Gage asked.

"Yes." *You're not going to feel guilty about that,* she told herself sternly. "You were busy. I had needs." Beyond not feeling guilty, she needed to work on not feeling stupid. Why hadn't she demanded that he meet those needs a little more often? Why had she assumed a lack of interest on his part instead of something else, like market pressures and downsizing and increased workload?

"I'm sorry," she said a minute later.

"For masturbating? Why?"

"Not for masturbating." Emma felt herself blushing as she said the word and thought, This is one unforgettable breakfast conversation. "For assuming you had lost interest. For not saying something. For not meeting you at the door stark naked and demanding to be taken."

"You would have been," Gage assured her. "Right in the foyer. Possibly even before I got the door shut."

She thought about what that would have felt like, greeting him naked and demanding her conjugal rights, then getting thoroughly fucked in the entryway as a result. He probably wouldn't have even undressed, just unzipped his pants and bent her over that little table before giving it to her without any preliminaries. . . .

She dropped her fork again.

"Emma?"

She waved a hand in reassurance. "I'm okay. Just a little, you know, hot." And dumb, but wasn't hindsight twenty-twenty? She could wise up. It wasn't too late. At least, she didn't think it was. They were talking, really talking. If they could do that, if they could learn from their mistakes and not repeat them, she might find herself meeting him naked at the door in the not too distant future and getting a glorious Gage-induced orgasm as a result.

"I like you hot." Gage smiled at her and Emma thought, So do I.

She was beginning to realize that she had more than she'd credited herself with. Wasn't sexy mostly in the mind? It was that sense of confidence and knowing you had a man's eye that put a swing in your step. Her body hadn't changed in the last twenty-four hours, but the way she thought about it and saw it was changing. With the change in perspective came the recognition that she had feminine wiles and the power to use them.

When they finished eating, Gage picked up a small box she hadn't noticed sitting on the table. Given the distractions he'd provided, that wasn't surprising, Emma thought. She would probably have overlooked anything short of a three-ring circus.

"I have a present for you," he informed her.

His last present had been crotchless panties. She remembered that he'd mentioned playing with toys. What exactly did he have planned for their mutual pleasure?

He opened the box and lifted out what looked like two balls about the size of Ping-Pong balls on a string. They made a rolling sound when he moved them. Emma was in-trigued. "What are those?"

"Pleasure balls." He smiled at her. "A ball bearing inside each ball rolls with movement. Which produces vibrations."

Oh. My. Emma could feel her eyes widening as she imag-ined the sensation deep inside from the two balls rubbing against each other, rotating, vibrating.

Gage came around to her chair, pulled it back from the table, and turned it a little to the side so it faced away from the table. Then he knelt in front of her and lifted her skirt with one hand, sliding it up her thighs until her lacy almost panties were visible. She held her breath as she watched him put his hand between her legs, exploring the area open to him.

"You'll have to wear these more often," he said, stroking her sex. "Especially with dresses."

"Something to think about," Emma said. Her voice sounded hoarse. His touch felt so incredibly good. He teased her with light touches, gentle petting, indirect stimulation, making her want more. Then he pressed one of the balls against her opening, pushing it slowly inside her.

It felt surprisingly good. She'd thought it might be cold or hard, but it wasn't. The second ball followed the first until just the end of the string remained visible. For retrieval, Emma thought. She tightened her inner muscles around the balls and felt a very pleasurable sensation as they rubbed together.

"Do you like your present?" Gage asked. He kept his hand cupped over her sex, stroking her intimately.

"It's certainly novel." She tightened her muscles again and smiled at him. "If doctors handed these out during annual physicals, women everywhere would start finding time to do their Kegel exercises."

"Your health is important," Gage said with a solemn expression. Emma bit her lip to keep from laughing, then almost moaned as another jolt of sensation hit her when she shifted in her seat.

"Thank you," she said when she trusted herself to speak. "I'm glad my husband is so concerned about my health."

"I do actually have a purpose for this beyond pleasure," Gage said. "Although I'm not sure this is the time to talk about it."

His face blanked, and Emma wondered what he was thinking. Tension crept under her skin, and her first reaction was to say nothing. But that was the old trap she was determined to break out of. Not saying anything, waiting, had led to misery and finally a total breakdown of all communication between them.

Well, you have a pair of balls now, Emma. Speak up. "I'd like to know what you had in mind."

"I know now isn't the time, and I'm not going to pressure you about this." His expression was serious, his hand on her gentle. "But you do know that keeping those muscles in tone can help prevent problems in labor and delivery?"

Her breath stopped. Her heart nearly stopped. "I thought you didn't want children, Gage. Every time I brought it up—"

"I want children, Emma. I just didn't want them too soon." He stood up and smoothed her skirt down over her thighs and held out his hand to her. She took it, and he pulled her to her feet. The balls inside her shifted as her position changed, producing a very enjoyable inner massage. He drew her hand to his chest and placed it there with his covering it. "I had a fifteen-year plan when we got married."

"And they were on it? And you never mentioned this? Why?"

"It seemed like the right thing at the time." He gave her a half-smile. "I felt like I had to prove myself to you, and to your family. I was the guy from the wrong side of the tracks. My father was a dockworker. Yours was a doctor. It was important to me to be able to take care of you and our future children, that they would have everything you had. And before you say it doesn't matter, I grew up without those advantages, Emma. I know what it's like. I wanted a better life for my family. For myself. And I didn't want you to ever regret marrying me, to wake up some morning and realize what you'd given up by choosing me instead of a guy from your country club."

For a moment, Emma could only stare at him in dumbstruck silence. When she found her voice, she said, "And this is why you wanted to wait to start a family? Why you've been working all these evenings and weekends and acting like you were either having an affair or married to your career?"

He winced. "In a word, yes."

She moved forward until her body brushed against his, their not quite joined hands in between them. She laid her head on his shoulder and said, "It would have been nice if you'd told me about your master plan and why it was so important to you."

Gage touched her waist with his free hand, holding her lightly. "I screwed up, Emma. I never meant to hurt you, and I can't tell you how sorry I am."

"I'm sorry, too," she said softly. "We didn't talk enough, drifted away from each other, and I let it happen. I should have confronted you, told you I wasn't happy with the demands your career was putting on you and the lack of time and energy it left over for us." She rubbed her cheek against his shoulder and sighed.

"We're talking now."

"Yes, we are." Emma smiled into his shoulder. "Better late than never. Speaking of which, tell me why you brought up having kids now."

"I didn't bring it up as a way to try to save our marriage by having a baby, if that's what you're thinking," Gage said. "I wanted you to know why I've been working so hard, why I've been away so much, and that it won't be like that anymore."

She rested against him and tried to take it all in. Could he be different? He was here with her now, not away on business. He'd gone to some effort to arrange this reunion and to give them time and privacy in a neutral, romantic setting to reconnect, physically and emotionally. That was telling. But it wasn't enough for him to change. She had to be different, too. Could she break out of old patterns of behavior and old habits of thinking?

Wearing crotchless panties and walking around with pleasure balls inserted inside her, giving her an internal vibrating massage that had her body humming, that was a good start. So was speaking up, being honest, telling Gage how she felt and what she wanted.

"You said something last night," Emma said. "About me having submissive tendencies and playing sexy games."

"I did." His hand traveled up from her waist to brush the side of her breast. "It's in my nature to be dominant, but that doesn't have to mean dominating in the wrong ways. I can see the damage I did by acting without discussing my plans or priorities with you. I think those tendencies can be channeled in a different direction, with more mutually pleasurable results."

"Like telling me to spread my legs whenever you want me to." Which, she'd discovered in no time flat, was a huge turn-on.

And maybe the start of a new way to live together again, this time making it work in a way that made them both happy. Broken patterns discarded. New ones established. Re-creating themselves and the life they shared, in a marriage that would serve who they were now and allow them to continue to grow together with a love that had deepened over time.

It was certainly worth trying. She'd wanted to find out what she really needed in bed. She hadn't wanted to feel like a sexual failure who couldn't hold her husband's attention. Here was her golden opportunity to explore the realm of sensual possibilities, not with a stranger, but with the man who loved her.

Twenty-Three

"I didn't think there was anything wrong with our sex life before," Gage said. "But I have to admit, doing a little thinking and researching the possibilities has made me see that we both might enjoy a little variety. It might also allow us to better express who we are in ways that better serve our mutual goals."

"Mutual goals." Emma smiled and shook her head. "It's not business, Gage."

"No. It's pleasure." His hand moved on her breast, and she shivered. The movement made the balls inside her shift, and she almost moaned. "Something I very much want to give you, Emma."

"You always have," she reminded him. "I didn't know how lucky I was, the first time."

"I love you." He kissed her forehead. "I wanted to make it good for you, then and now and always. I knew exactly how lucky I was when you said yes to me."

"I love you, too." She felt her nipples hardening and tightened her inner muscles, making the balls shift and vibrate again. "Your present is really growing on me. Unusual, un-expected, but very enjoyable."

"The open-concept underwear? Or the balls vibrating inside you?" Gage asked.

"I meant the balls, but both, really." She tipped up her head to brush her lips against his. "I kind of like knowing you could do anything to me under this dress, without tak-ing anything off. For some reason, being naked under my clothes is a lot more interesting than just naked."

"I like knowing I could do anything to you without re-moving any of your clothes, too." Gage let his hand rove down to her hip, then began to bunch up the fabric of her dress until he could reach under the hem. His fingers stroked her mons. "Open your legs for me, Emma. I want to touch you."

She shifted her feet apart and closed her eyes to focus on the sensation as his fingers caressed her, circled her clit, stroked over it, and provided a very enjoyable external counterpart to the vibrating massage inside.

"You feel so slick and soft there, Emma." He probed at her opening, slid a finger along her labia. "So very touch-able. So inviting. Such a perfect fit for my cock."

Her inner muscles tightened again in response to his verbal seduction, and she moaned in pleasure.

"You're going to do a lot of that," he promised. "I'm going to make you sigh and moan, and I'm going to make you come, over and over."

She didn't think that would be difficult at all. She was fully aroused, stimulated from the inside and the outside simultaneously.

"Gage . . ."

"Yes, Emma?"

"Why didn't you ever suggest anything different before? You never brought home a sex toy or asked me to wear crotchless panties or meet you at a hotel blindfolded and wearing nothing but lingerie under my coat." It was hard to think with his hand on her sex and his present massaging the inside of her sheath. Harder to talk. But if he had these kinds of ideas, why hadn't she seen any hint of them before?

"Until I overheard you at your office talking about signing up to be held captive as a man's sexual plaything so you could explore the possibilities, I never thought you'd want anything like this." Gage pinched her clit very gently, and Emma sucked in her breath at the exquisite pressure. She tightened her inner muscles again to intensify her pleasure, and her knees threatened to buckle.

"Maybe we were both trapped by my good-girl role," Emma said. Her voice came out a little breathy, but at least she wasn't panting and moaning. Yet. "Be honest. If you thought I was a naughty nympho, would you have spent so much time dedicated to your plan and your goals, or would you have spent a little more time playing bedroom games with me?"

"I never thought of it as trapped." He released her clit and stroked her labia with slow deliberation, tantalizing her. "But I admit, if I'd been at the office thinking of you walking around the house wearing crotchless panties with a pair of pleasure balls warming you up for me, it would have been a lot harder to stay late instead of going home."

And now he wanted to show her what kind of husband he could be in the future. What kind of lover. She was very much interested in experiencing that. It was also time for her to find out what kind of wife and lover she could be to him.

"Make it up to me," she suggested. "Show me how you can use your dominating tendencies for good."

He loosened his grip on her and looked down at her. "Unbutton your dress from the hem up to your waist."

Emma bent and began to undo the buttons. They were small and there were a lot of them, so it took a few minutes. She did the last few standing upright, slowing down as she undid the buttons that covered her pelvic region until she reached the one just above her naval and stopped.

"Very good. Now spread the sides apart."

She did, showing off her barely there underwear in the process.

"And now, Emma, I want you to stand with your feet apart."

Making a mental note to buy more dresses with buttons, Emma moved her feet apart and felt the vibration inside her mix with anticipation.

Gage stood back to look at the picture she made, then walked around to stand behind her. He put a hand over her mons, and she rocked her pelvis forward to press her sex into his palm.

"Did you like it when I ordered you to undo your dress so I could see your pussy, Emma?" His voice was low and seductive as he spoke near her ear.

"Yes."

"Do you like me touching your pussy, too?" He separated her labia and inserted his fingertip just inside her.

"Yes." She had to swallow before she could answer.

He toyed with her, sliding his fingertip back out,

stroking and petting her sex. His free hand touched her side and moved up her rib cage until he just touched the beginning swell of her breast. She felt her breath catch and her belly flutter.

Gage moved his hands simultaneously up and down her body until they met at her waist and began to finish the job of unbuttoning her, slowly, one button at a time, his hands brushing her breasts in a tantalizing almost caress. When he finished, he slid her open dress off her shoulders, leaving her in the lacy underwear he'd selected for her that left nothing to the imagination.

He ran his hands over her breasts, exploring the curves and the valley between, rubbing his palms over her nipples while she sighed and luxuriated in the pleasure of his touch. "This seems a little tight," he murmured. His hands moved to her back, where he undid the hooks.

Once he had her bra unfastened, he peeled that off her, too. She heard him open something behind her, and then he brought a small open jar around in front of her. He waved it under her nose, and she inhaled a familiar scent.

"What's that?" Emma asked.

"Taste and see."

He dipped his fingertip in the jar's contents and spread the silky cream along her lower lip first, then her upper. She felt them react, puffing slightly. She licked her lip and smiled at what seemed to be the trademark of their wicked weekend. "Strawberry."

It tasted good, and it made her lips feel kiss-swollen and pleasantly tingly. Gage spread the cream over her nipples, and Emma gasped as it magnified every sensation. She felt them swelling and hardening as they reacted to the balm. "That's interesting," she said in a hoarse voice.

Gage set aside the jar, recapped it, and came around to face her. "Walk to the bedroom for me, Emma. Feel those balls moving and massaging inside you as you walk. Feel your lips and nipples tingling, and think about what else I'm going to do to you when I get you on that bed."

She could so easily imagine what he might have planned for her. He'd close his mouth over her nipples to enjoy a strawberry-flavored treat. The light suction combined with wet heat on that sensitive part of her, already swollen and stimulated by the silky cream, would make her groan with pleasure. He'd use his hands on her sex, touching and testing, searching out the nub of her clitoris to stroke and rub it while she squeezed her inner muscles around the balls.

And when he removed them, they'd stimulate her all the way out before he filled her with himself. His cock would be hard and ready, and she'd be so prepared that he'd slide into her with no resistance at all. . . .

She was breathing faster, and the bed seemed very, very far away.

Emma walked to the bedroom, feeling as if every step were foreplay. Her nipples throbbed, her lips felt unbelievably sensitive, and the shifting vibrations inside her were enough to make her unsteady. Would she be able to make it to the bed?

"Nice ass, Emma," she heard Gage say behind her. Knowing he was watching her walk as he followed her added another level of stimulation. "I loved bouncing it on my lap last night while I fucked you."

She stumbled and he caught her arm, steadying her. He smoothed a fall of strawberry blond hair back from her face. "I missed fucking you, Emma. You missed it, too, didn't you?"

"Yes."

He kept a light hold on her arm in case she needed the support as they continued forward. Almost there. She went ahead of him through the doorway and stopped when they reached the bed.

"Now I want you on the bed." Gage let go of her and watched as she sat down. "Scoot forward a little and spread your legs."

Emma shifted so that she sat with her sex at the edge of the mattress and opened her thighs.

"You look delicious sitting there with your nipples so hard and rosy, showing me your pussy." Gage was stripping as he talked, and Emma watched him, loving the sight of his bare chest, his flat stomach, lean hips, muscled legs. When he pulled down his briefs, she looked at his jutting erection and licked her lips once more.

"Want a taste, Emma?" Gage stepped forward, naked, and circled the base of his cock with his hand. He wove his fingers into her hair and guided her head down as he fed her the swollen head of his penis. She circled him with her tongue and felt him grow even harder, felt the silky cream slicked over her lips heighten the experience of his warm flesh sliding between them.

"That's enough." He pulled out of her mouth and knelt on the floor between her spread legs. "My turn."

She shut her eyes as he closed his mouth over her clit and let her head fall back, giving herself up to the pleasure of the moment.

He used suction and then his tongue to stimulate the little nub he'd captured with his mouth before moving down to taste more of her. His tongue parted her labia, swirled inside, lapped at her, thrust into her. He devoured her as if hungry for the taste of her. Her nipples were swollen into hard, aching points, her sheath was pleasured by the massaging balls, and the addition of his mouth on her sex stole her breath.

Emma sank onto the bed, unable to stay upright, lifting her hips to offer more of herself to him. He drew hard on her clit one last time, then let his mouth roam up her belly. He kissed her navel and swirled his tongue into it, followed the line of her rib cage up, and finally closed his mouth over one hard nipple and sucked.

She moaned and arched up into him, loving the feel of his lips on her. The strawberry cream magnified the sensation of his mouth and tongue tugging at her nipple, and it built her already excited state to fevered need.

"Gage," Emma whispered, digging her hands into his hair. "I want you so much."

"Good." He raised his head to look at her, his eyes dark with desire. "Want me the way I want you. Ache for me. Burn for me."

"I do." She let her eyes drift closed as he claimed her other breast, tugging at her nipple and making the need shoot directly to her sex. Her inner muscles gripped and released the balls, a tantalizing taste of what was to come and a sharp reminder of how she ached to be filled by him.

Gage worked his way around her breasts, touching and tasting, then back down her belly and hips. When his hands found her sex, she moaned and arched into him. He caught the string and drew the balls back out, slowly, teasing her with the pressure. As the last one slid out, he closed his mouth over her clit, making her cry out. "Gage!"

"Emma." He kissed her between her legs and stood up. "I want you doggie style. Move up onto your knees for me."

Changing position seemed like an impossible feat, but she had powerful motivation. Emma scooted up farther onto the bed, turned onto her hands and knees, and waited. She felt the mattress shift as Gage came behind her, felt his hands close over the rounded curves of her ass, felt the head of his cock press against her entry as he positioned himself.

"I love this part." He rocked his hips back and forth, teasing her but not entering her. "When you're so hot for me, so ready, and when I fill you, that first slide when you open for me and wrap around my cock, there's almost nothing better." He thrust into her in a slow, steady stroke, filling her inch by inch.

Gage rode her from behind, making each thrust hard and deep, making her breasts bounce with the rhythm, which added another layer of sensation. It felt so good to take him all the way inside, to feel him press home and push against the sensitive spot in her sheath with each stroke. She gripped his shaft with her inner muscles and felt a wave of heat and need building faster.

"Just like that," she heard him say from behind her, his voice thick with satisfaction. "Come for me, Emma." He increased the tempo, taking her harder, deeper, making the rush of pleasure build until the need for release was so urgent, it was explosive when it hit.

She collapsed onto her stomach with him driving deep

into her, her inner muscles convulsing around his cock, feeling him pouring himself into her while she took it all. Gage covered her back with his body, holding himself balanced on his arms and legs so he didn't crush her into the mattress, still buried deep inside her while she quivered and shook with the aftermath.

"Come home with me, Emma," Gage said. His voice was soft and persuasive. He moved against her, stroking her from the inside, surrounding her body with his on the outside.

She was already home, Emma thought as she sprawled under him. His body on hers, inside hers. Gage, loving her. This was home. "You're home to me," she told him.

"Em." His arms tightened against her, squeezing her. "I've missed you so much. You're my heart."

She felt both ravished and protected, desired and loved, and knew that all the pieces had fallen into place where they belonged, put back together in a new order.

Twenty-Four

"I can't believe you want me to get you pregnant in the backseat of my car." Gage held the car's rear door for Emma as she climbed in, then followed her and closed it behind them.

"It's a Mercedes," Emma said, trying not to laugh. She scooted over to make room for him. "That makes it classy."

"The last time I had you in the backseat of a car, I made very sure *not* to get you pregnant. This just seems wrong."

"It seems right to me." Emma was wearing the peach dress and the accompanying undergarments he'd bought her to wear that wicked weekend. She drew up the skirt and straddled his lap, facing him. "We've come full circle."

"At least this time we won't have to worry about getting caught in the act," Gage said. "Unless you accidentally hit the garage door opener button at the wrong time."

"It'll never happen." She smiled at him. "And if it does, the windows will be all steamed up. Nobody will see a thing."

"You're really enjoying yourself, aren't you?" He put his hands on her hips and pulled her body into his. "Bad Emma."

"Very." Emma rubbed her breasts against his chest, loving the feel of his body against hers. "I'm also fertile. Off the pill for a month, ovulating, and did I mention I'm wearing crotchless panties underneath this dress?"

"That makes it easy." Gage squeezed her hips and slid his hands around to cup her ass. "All I have to do is unzip my jeans to get inside you."

"I want you inside me." Emma rocked into him, feeling a rush of heat from the contact and the thrill of anticipation. Since the night she'd been delivered to his hotel room gift-wrapped for pleasure, they hadn't spent a night apart.

She'd waited to be sure they were solidly back together, that the changes they'd made stuck and they didn't fall back into old habits. Gage had proven true to his word, cutting down to a reasonable work week with infrequent travel. She'd never felt tempted to go back to being too polite, too restrained, too understanding, too undemanding. When they played sexy games and she followed Gage's dominating lead, she was anything but restrained and didn't hesitate to make her desires known. And he satisfied them all.

As time went on, she grew confident that the new, improved Emma was here to stay. After three months, she'd stopped taking oral contraceptives. And now it was time to take the next step in their relationship, starting the family they'd both wanted for so long.

"If you want me inside you, unbutton the top of your dress to your waist and show me what's underneath," Gage said. "I want to see your breasts swelling out of those little bra cups and your hard, rosy nipples peeking through the sheer lace."

"You want to see what I have before you decide if you'll have me?" Emma undid the top button, then the next, working her way down until the dress gaped open to reveal glimpses of lace and the round swells of her breasts.

"I'll have you. I just love it when you show off for me." Gage gave her a sexy grin. "Your body is so hot. Lush and feminine. I love your full breasts and your round ass and that tiny waist in between. I love it when you show me what you have because I love knowing it's all mine."

"Like this?" Emma parted the top of her dress, exposing a lot of creamy flesh that the sheer lace did nothing to hide.

"Yeah, like that." He reached up to toy with her nipples through the flimsy lace covering them. He tugged at them, stroked them, rubbed and pinched by turns, making Emma gasp and squirm in his lap. "I like this position, Emma. I can play with your breasts and touch your clit while I fuck you."

His graphic words sent a thrill through her. Sex in the back of the car seemed so clandestine. Doing it with her clothes on and those X-rated panties that were nothing but an open invitation added to the sense of forbidden pleasure.

"Are you getting hot and wet for me?" Gage filled his hands with her breasts and gave them a light squeeze. "Is that why you're squirming like that, Emma?"

"Yes." She let her lids fall half-closed as she arched her back to press herself into his hands.

"I like making you hot." He kneaded her curves and thumbed her nipples, making them tighten even more in response. "I like watching you get that look in your eyes that tells me how much you want it. I like making you moan and deciding how many times I'm going to make you come for me."

"Such a sexual control freak," Emma said, sighing.

"You love it," Gage said with a knowing smile.

"I love you," Emma said. She felt her body going tight and the liquid response in her lower half and knew this was going to be very good.

"I love you, Emma. My lover. My wife." He cupped one hand at the back of her head and pulled her into his kiss. His mouth took hers with fierce possessiveness, claiming her lips, then softening to coax her tongue into twining with his.

Emma fell into the kiss, letting him seduce her as he demanded and teased by turns. When his kiss turned harder, his hand tightened on her, tugging at her nipple. When his lips slid over hers, persuading and tasting, his hand gentled. The contrast melted her, making her body pliant and relaxed and open to him while need spiraled inside her.

She rocked her body into his, feeling the rush of contact, the thrill of contrast. His hand released her breast and moved down, trailing fire along her belly, making her quiver as he stroked lower until he touched her mons. She felt him bunching the fabric of her skirt to pull it up until he could reach under it and settle his hand between her legs. He cupped her sex, and Emma sighed into his mouth as she pushed into his hand, loving the pressure against her labia.

He kept her head positioned where he wanted it as he plundered her mouth while he parted her labia and thrust a finger into her tight sheath. His tongue echoed the motion, sliding between her lips as she opened for him. It felt so good to be so close to him, so much of her body in contact with his, his hand claiming her sex while his mouth claimed hers.

He added a second finger to the one buried inside her and moved them in and out in a slow, gentle rhythm, making her ready for more. "I love giving you pleasure," he said against her lips, satisfaction plain in his voice.

"I love the way you make me feel," Emma said with a sigh. "Sexy and powerful."

"You are." Gage circled her clit. "So sexy. And you've had the power to bring me to my knees with a look since you were seventeen."

"I didn't know," Emma said, shaking her head. "I thought it was luck. I never understood it."

"It's love." Gage slowly withdrew his fingers from her and settled his hand over her mons. "Although I won't say luck didn't enter into it. Luck brought you into my path and made you look at me. Once I had your eye, I did everything in my power to make you love me."

"It didn't take much," Emma confessed. She rested her cheek on his shoulder. "I fell so hard, so fast. You have no defenses at that age."

"That works both ways, you know." Gage stroked her hair. "I had no defenses against you. I would have done anything for you, and I spent the next sixteen years trying to keep you, trying to be the man you deserved."

"We didn't trust it," Emma said. "I never realized until that weekend at the hotel that deep down, because I never knew why you chose me, I was always afraid it wouldn't last. It was that fear that made me keep silent when I should have spoken up. I was afraid if I put demands on you, you'd pull further away from me and I'd lose you altogether."

Gage wrapped his arms around her and held her tight. "You weren't the only one making that mistake, Emma. You're right, neither of us trusted what we had."

"I trust it now," Emma informed him. She burrowed into him, loving the way he held her so securely, so protectively. "Because I finally trust me. I trust that I'm enough for you, that I deserve you."

Gage kissed the top of her head. "We were lucky to find each other so young, and smart enough to know a good thing when we fell into it. And thanks to some experimentation, we have a red hot sex life."

"The best gets better," Emma agreed. "I bet nobody else in this neighborhood is warming up the leather in the back of their car, steaming up the windows, and getting very, very lucky."

"My wife is a naughty nympho." Gage reached down to squeeze her ass. "She's not content with occasional missionary sex in bed with the lights off. She puts on crotchless panties and tells me to take her to the backseat of my Mercedes and knock her up."

"Are you going to get around to that?" She squirmed in his lap, feeling his erection jutting into her through his pants.

"Yes." Gage stroked the curve of her bottom. "I am going to have you, right here in this car. And if I fail to knock you up on this round, I'll do you in every room in the house, in every position we're physically capable of, again and again, until you're either pregnant or too exhausted to continue."

Emma laughed. "I don't think we could get through all the rooms and all the positions in a single night."

"I'm committed to the goal." Gage shifted her forward

on his knees and unzipped his pants. "I like to have a plan and then focus on it until I achieve success."

"I love a man with a plan," she informed him. "I also love a man with a hard cock."

"You must love me a lot." He touched her hips. "Lift up a little, I have to get my pants down. It's not proper car sex unless your ass is bare. You can lose points for not getting caught bare-assed and pumping."

Emma raised herself up and balanced while he worked his pants down to his knees. His penis stood up, hard and ready, and it tempted her to touch and taste him.

She shifted herself over onto the seat beside him and lowered her head to his lap.

"Emma."

"Hmm?" She circled the base of his thick shaft with her hand and pumped up and down before swirling her mouth over the rounded head of him.

"If you suck me off, it kind of defeats our purpose out here."

"I won't swallow," she promised, and drew him into her mouth as far as she could take him.

She felt his fingers weave into her hair, holding her close but loosely so her freedom of movement wasn't restricted. She ran her mouth up and down his length, lapped at him with her tongue, sucked, and stroked him with her hand in a uniform rhythm. He tasted salty and male, and he was so smooth and hard in her mouth. She loved the way he moved his hips in time with her, feeding her his cock and letting her play with him the way she wanted to.

She gave him one last, long, swirling lick and kissed his shaft before she raised her head. "You taste good."

"So do you. And I want some. Lie back for me, Emma."

She reclined against the rear passenger door, one leg bent on the seat, one foot resting on the floor, her legs open for him. Gage caught the hem of her skirt and pulled it up to her waist, leaving her bare except for the scrap of lace that framed her sex.

"Are you going to let me go down on you, Emma?" He folded down the front passenger seat to make more space and adjusted his position. "Are you going to spread your legs wide and let me taste you?"

"Yes." Emma grinned at him, feeling hot and shameless with her dress unbuttoned to the waist, leaving her breasts on display, her skirt hiked up, and her thighs open for him.

She felt a breath of warm air as his mouth came down to kiss her sex. He teased her with his lips and tongue, light, probing licks, soft kisses, nibbling at her, swirling his tongue inside her, and then lapping at her clit while she arched and moaned in reaction.

He slid a hand up her bare thigh to touch her while he tasted her, petting her sex while he explored her with his mouth. When he raised his head, he kept his hand over her, moving against her mons. "I want you to ride me while I fuck you, Emma. I want to make you come with my cock inside you and feel your pussy gripping and squeezing me so hard my balls explode. I want to fill my hands with your ass while I fill you with come."

She felt her belly flutter and her heart lurch. Her breathing quickened, and heat flashed through her. "Gage . . ."

"Come on, Emma." He settled back in the seat beside her and helped her straddle him, facing him again. "Come and get the ride of your life."

She lifted her hips while he positioned his cock, then slowly lowered herself as he thrust up until he was fully seated inside her. "Does that feel good, Em?"

"Yes." She leaned into him and felt his arms wrap around her. She tightened her inner muscles around his shaft and felt him react, grinding against her to make her feel the pressure deep inside. "So good." She moved on him, rocking her hips, feeling the slide of his shaft and the way her body gave way to welcome him.

"I love you, Emma." Gage kissed her forehead as he moved with her.

"I love you, too." She curled her hands into his shirt and felt a rush of emotion as the reality of what they were doing sank in. Coming together. Making love. Hoping to make new life and making their own lives new again by reaffirming the joy they found in each other.

She could imagine them twenty years in the future still celebrating the love they shared with their bodies. Love didn't fade with time, and the need for each other only deepened as the years passed.

"Are you okay?" Gage smoothed back her hair and brushed her cheek, holding her close while he took her with devastating thoroughness.

"Never better." She arched into him and loved him with all of her body and her heart while he took it all and gave her all of himself in return.

Pleasure built and burst and built again, each time gaining in intensity, until the last wave finally receded, leaving her panting and spent on his lap. His hands gripped the soft flesh of her bottom, keeping her where he wanted her while he stayed planted deep inside her.

Gage brushed a kiss across her forehead as he cuddled her in the aftermath. "Are you happy now, or am I going to have to give you another round of backseat boinking?"

Emma laughed. "I'm happy now. I just wanted to go back to where we started."

"We never leave that behind," Gage said. "It stays with us, and we add on to it." He shifted under her. "I don't mind trading cramped spaces for nice, soft beds, though."

"Beds do have a lot to offer," Emma agreed. "Do you want to take me to one now?"

"Yes." He nuzzled her cheek. "And then I plan to take you on one."

"What a wonderful plan." And one she was more than happy to go along with.

The End

Read on for a preview of Charlene Teglia's
upcoming erotic romance

Wicked Hot

Available from St. Martin's Griffin in August 2008

Cursed to roam the earth as a succubus for eternity, Edana offers men their most erotic fantasy in exchange for their immortal souls. As a demon, no human can get close enough to love her without being destroyed by her powers. But Eli Moss is a Nephilim, a descendant of a branch of angels that has begun to bind and banish demons. When Edana is sent to seduce and destroy him, she discovers that he's immune to her powers. Their epic struggle is about to get very personal . . . and WICKED HOT.

"I wasn't sure you'd come." He stood in the moonlight with his hands in his pockets, looking almost bashful. Which was laughable, considering our reason for being here.

"I'm here. Whether or not I'll come remains to be seen." I gave him a wide smile and let my trench coat fall open, showing off the black lace bra, panties, and nothing else underneath except my belly button ring winking in the moonlight.

Garrett, if that was really his name, seemed very interested in what wasn't under my coat. I let him get a good long look at ample cleavage and a sleek, bare midriff. Men are visually stimulated and the more aroused he became, the better my night would be.

The dogging event hadn't drawn too much of a crowd, just a handful of onlookers. I could easily pick out the ones who'd want to do more than watch.

Ah, dogging, how easy you've made my job, I thought.

Walking the dog was the popular euphemism for a pre-arranged meet for one purpose; having sex in a public place. A big draw for voyeurs and exhibitionists alike, dogging events were frequently broadcast on the Internet so the show could be witnessed by the broadest possible audience.

Like shooting fish in a barrel.

I shrugged off my trench coat and let it drop to the grass. I'd agreed to meet Garrett at this park after sunset, and I noted with some pleasure that the lawn offered a lot more room to maneuver than the inside of a car in a public parking lot.

Those cramped encounters so tended to discourage audience participation. The choreography required for front seat group action gives new meaning to the term "cluster-fuck."

I settled my perfect ass on the fabric of my discarded London Fog and smiled all around. "Who's first?"

A tangible rush of lust filled the air and just like that, I had them all.

Fish in a barrel.

Garrett was first, of course. I let him touch me because it was the best way to hook the ones who liked to watch. They watched his hands unfasten the black lace bra that pushed my cleavage up to heights no mortal woman could aspire to, and there was an almost audible sigh as the lace fell away and nothing but Garrett's hands covered my twin peaks.

Garrett was a little clumsy and had no idea what to do with a body like mine, but he was fully aroused and his sexual energy fed me until I was damn near orgasmic. But far from satiated. Never satiated. The more I fed, the more I hungered, and the circle of men watching us was only going to whet my appetite.

I feasted on their lust, expertly playing them, pulling them into my field and draining them and they never saw what was happening. Garrett's eyes grew glazed and a confused look came over his face as he approached the threshold.

"What—?" he asked. It was an incomplete question, but I answered him anyway.

"You're a pervert, Garrett," I informed him in a matter-of-fact, nonjudgmental voice. "And now you're a damned pervert. Thank you for your soul. Welcome to Hell."

"You've been a naughty girl, Edana." Nick's voice was deep and approving when I joined him in his office later that night. "Ten men at once. Want a spanking?"

"I'm not that kind of girl." I gave him a wide-eyed innocent look and dropped into the seat across from his desk. I was still wearing the panties and while I'd put it back on, I'd left the trench coat hanging open to provide a nice peep show effect.

I wasn't wearing anything else. I'd left my bra in the grass at the park. I like to leave souvenirs and they're not docked from my pay. Actually, since it counts as littering, and could stir impure thoughts in the mind of whoever finds my discards, I get bonuses on top of the amusement factor the habit gives me.

"You're my kind of girl." He patted his lap. "Take off the trench coat and come sit."

"You're the boss." I shrugged out of the trench and strutted around to him, then gave him a little lap dance action. I got a light spank on my ass for my trouble. I sat down then and heaved an aggrieved sigh. "Is this all the sexual harassment I get? You're not even trying."

"I want you to conserve your energies. I have a special job for you, Edana."

Nick kissed the side of my neck and toyed with my nipples as he spoke so I wouldn't feel ignored. I responded to the gesture, even though I knew I wasn't going to be favored with anything that might feed my need.

"Who?" I asked. I didn't expect an immediate answer. I knew he'd tell me the details when he was good and ready.

"What," he corrected and I felt something other than my nipples stiffen.

"Not human?"

"Partially."

I swiveled around to face him and hooked my legs over each side of the chair so I straddled his lap. "Tell me more."

He shook his head. "None of your tricks. You've fed well enough tonight." Since my thighs were spread wide, he gave me a light spank on my mound and I hissed at the mixture of arousal and denial. "I want you to seduce a Nephilim."

"A Watcher?" I quit trying to play-seduce Nick and sat up straight. The Nephilim had once been a widespread race, the half-breed results of intermarriage between human women and angels who'd abandoned both heavenly and hellish realms in favor of life on earth.

The Nephilim had been called many things. "Watcher" was one of the more innocuous terms. They'd also been known more accurately as the Terrors and the Weakeners. "I thought they were extinct. Either they killed each other off fighting or drowned in the Great Flood."

"They're strong. And persistent." Nick flicked my clit overly hard on purpose and I scowled at him.

"That wasn't necessary," I protested.

"I'm evil." He shrugged and let his finger travel up to toy with my belly button ring. "This particular Nephilim is a problem. He's giving me headaches. He conjures and binds. He banishes."

At the "b" word, I went ice-cold. "I thought you liked me," I said with a quaver in my voice. "You're sending me out to get banished?"

"I'm sending you because I have confidence in your skill and abilities, darling Edana." He leaned forward and kissed me, filling my mouth with a thrust of his forked tongue and a smoky flavor that was distinctly Nick. "Seduce him. Steal his soul. I want this troublesome Watcher in Hell."

I wasn't comforted. I may have large breasts but words like "bind" and "banish" do stick in my feather head and while flattery is always nice, I really would have preferred some kind of weapon besides supernatural sex appeal. "You suck as a motivational speaker."

"Nevertheless," he breathed the word against my lips. "You'll do as I say. Because you're mine and I send you where I will."

Well, he had me there. But that didn't mean I'd just rush off to my doom. "Come on, Nick," I wheedled. "Wouldn't you like a presidential candidate instead? A televangelist? An engineer?"

"I want him," Nick said. He placed three fingertips on my belly and when he drew them away, three little brands in the shape of his fingertips remained. The burns would heal almost instantaneously, but he'd made his point.

"Fine," I said, getting up. "I'm tired of this afterlife anyway. It's all sex energy and no actual sex."

"Fiendish, some would call that." Nick actually smiled at me when he said it, the smug, evil bastard.

"Whatever. It's like a cosmic joke that in my human life I died a virgin and after centuries as a succubus I can't ever get a human to punch my ticket because my demonic powers drain him before he can do the deed." I felt genuinely aggrieved over that, and let it show in my face. "And now, after all I've done for you, all the souls I've stolen, all the men I've led to their downfall, you're sending me out to be Watcher bait. I hate you."

"Everybody hates me. I'm the devil. It comes with the job description." Nick stood up and patted me on the head. I kicked him in the shins with the pointy toe of my strappy come-fuck-me shoes. He just laughed. "I like your style. I always have." He turned serious then. "You're capable of this, Edana. I am not setting you up to fail. I want him stopped and I want him stopped now, before I lose any more demons to him."

I blinked at that. How many had this bad-ass Nephilim tagged already? It had to be pretty bad for Nick to get personally involved. He might be the devil, but he didn't micromanage. If he wasn't leaving this matter to one of his lieutenants to handle, if he'd taken on the task of assigning me to deal with it himself, matters were serious.

It was like a bad joke. Hell had a serious problem, and *I* was the one getting sent to deal with it. Armed with my Frederick's of Hollywood wardrobe.

"Do silver bullets work on Nephilim?" I asked.

"No." He tweaked my cheek. "Arm yourself with feminine wiles. They're more powerful and much more lethal. Go shopping."

"Damn."

"That's what you are," Nick agreed in a cheerful voice. "Go damn him, too."

"Right," I said, my lack of enthusiasm palpable. I didn't even wiggle my ass at him as I left the room. I was too depressed. Instead, I peeled out of the panties, kicked off the spike heels and left the items scattered behind me as I headed for my computer terminal. Since the ambient temperature in the office was always measured on the Kelvin scale, clothes were the last thing I needed.

Hell's Internet crashed frequently and without warning, and if that didn't cause me enough aggravation the computer would blue-screen periodically. Shopping for this job could take a while. Which was fine with me. My afterlife as a succubus might not be perfect, but it beat nonexistence. I wasn't in a hurry to cease to be.

Although arguably nonexistence isn't really possible. I've heard enough theologians going on about this one to have heard all the points and counterpoints on that debate. Demons can assume physical form, but in our native state, we're energy. Energy can't be created or destroyed. So how can we cease to exist?

I don't know the answer, but I know nobody's been able to contact a banished demon to find out if they're still self-aware and if they've retained consciousness. My best guess is that energy can be used up, and the prospect of a blast from a powerful Nephilim aimed point-blank at me didn't fill me with positive thoughts.

My best hope was to strike first. Get him before he got me. Do unto others and all that.

Before I started browsing for battle armor in the form

of my chosen undress uniform, I did some research to see what I could dig up on the Nephilim. What little I knew wasn't nearly enough to help me spot possible vulnerabilities I could exploit. Still, all men had their weaknesses and I'd had a lot of experience in using those weaknesses to my advantage.

I learned they'd been known as giants among men, much taller and stronger than their purely human counterparts. Their race had also been credited with bringing the knowledge of magic to humans. The epic of Gilgamesh documented the heroic exploits of one member of this not-so-lost race. Those recorded deeds were enough to make me feel chilly despite my location. Gilgamesh had been one historic bad ass and he'd gone after the first succubus, Lilitu. She'd survived and escaped, but he'd come out the clear winner in that contest.

Great. As far as I could tell, I was going up against a sorcerous warrior giant. A powerful being with supernatural abilities and human form with far greater than human strength.

And due to the mixed nature, a soul.

The soul and the human form might make him somewhat vulnerable to me, but I didn't like the odds.

"Seduce him," I said out loud. Right. Because he wouldn't see through a succubus and know it was a trap.

Done with my depressing search through the pages of history, I switched my attention to my current files. Nick would have sent me the information on my target and I wanted to know my enemy.

His name was Eli Moss. His face . . . well, his face would have made me take notice even if I wasn't a being who subsisted on sexual energy. I can't really say he was handsome in the classical sense of the term, but he was certainly compelling. He had animal magnetism and it showed even through the computer's display.

The mixed heritage altered features in a way that would look exotic to human eyes but not abnormal. Just more rugged, harsher, more beautiful in purely a masculine way. More jaw and cheekbone than your average man, deep-set hazel eyes that seemed too aware, too knowing. He wore his black hair shoulder length with two small braids on each side, an unusual style in modern times. The hairstyle emphasized his features.

Oh, and he was really big. All over. A giant among men, indeed. I couldn't help it, I felt my nipples tingle and a distinct flare of heat in my midsection as I considered the total package.

And that was just the effect of graphical rendering. What impact would he have in the flesh?

I licked my lips and considered my mission. He was either going to be a feast for my demonic senses like no other, or my downfall. If I allowed him to distract me, guess which was more likely?

"You seem a decent fellow," I said to his image. "I hate to kill you." The line from *The Princess Bride* earned me a reprimand in the form of Barry Manilow's hit "Mandy" pouring from a hidden speaker. I scowled in the general direction of the source of the music, if you could call it that. I knew better than to complain out loud, though. I'd only get something worse.

I wouldn't actually be killing him, I thought, as I studied Eli's face. He was half angel. The loss of his human soul would mean what, exactly? I couldn't find any precedent in the records. As far as I could tell, angels and demons alike had left the Nephilim alone. I didn't even know they still existed, which meant at some point they'd passed into the collective realm of myth despite the fact that they demonstrably were still around. Why?

Whatever the reasons, the centuries-long agreement to ignore each other, to live and let live, had ended with this Eli. By binding and banishing demons, he'd forced Nick to take action.

And lucky me, I was the official response. Too bad I wasn't being sent as an ambassador for peace. I didn't think there was enough underwire in the world to distract this man from my nature. He'd see me coming and I'd be toast.

I started shopping for the perfect outfit to wear to my funeral. If I was going out, I'd go out fighting and dressed to kill.

For reasons possibly known only to him, Eli lived as close to the middle of nowhere as it was possible to get in America, in a tiny Washington town of three thousand people surrounded by Olympic National Park. Oh, and it was also the wettest spot in the continental United States, with an average of one hundred and forty inches of rain a year.

I hated rain.

Fortunately, the black leather miniskirt and matching bustier I wore would shed water, and I had a black leather trench coat to help keep me dry. My thigh-high boots would sink up to the heels in mud if I had to do any walking. I made a mental note to avoid that.

I would stand out like a sore thumb among the loggers

who made their home here. I also wouldn't pass for a visiting hiker. Tourists might come from all over the world to visit the Olympic Peninsula, but they dressed for camping and fishing, not seduction.

I wasn't trying to blend in, though. I wanted to get Eli's attention. If I couldn't arouse his sex drive, I wanted to arouse his curiosity. He would be smarter than the average human, with his mixed heritage, and while that probably meant better physical self-control, it also might mean he'd get overconfident in his ability to put mind over matter, so to speak.

None of the demons who'd fallen to this Watcher had been a succubus. It was actually a smart move on Nick's part. Send a seductress who might slip under his guard instead of a warrior whose presence could only mean a direct challenge.

Besides, he might hesitate to hit a girl. You never could tell.

That's right, think positive. I parked my jeep on the private road that led to Eli's sprawling log cabin retreat in the woods, popped the button that opened the hood and counted to one hundred. Figuring I'd timed it about right, I shrugged off my trench coat, climbed out, and went around to bend over the hood.

With any luck, Eli would be along right about now. I planted my feet shoulder-width apart and dipped my lower back to emphasize the curve of my ass and make the short skirt ride up higher. I wasn't wearing any underwear. The odds were stacked against me as it was, I didn't see the point in pulling my punches.

I heard the low growl of an engine coming up behind me. I resisted the urge to turn around and look. The motor stopped, and booted feet crunched in the gravel. A rough voice that sounded as gravelly as the drive said, "What's a nice girl like you doing in a place like this?"

I turned my head and gave him a slow, knowing smile over my shoulder. "Who said I was nice?"

Eli Moss was even bigger in person than I'd expected. He was at least seven feet tall, and built to scale. Even with towering heels, I was a shrimp next to him. I wasn't a true demon, after all. I'd started out as human and in my current form I was still human small.

He tilted his head and considered my answer. He took his time looking over the picture I made, my skirt showing off the lower curve of my ass and the soft flesh between my thighs.

"Naughty girl, are you?"

"Yep." I arched my back to give him a tantalizing display of pussy before I grasped the leather hem and pulled the skirt up higher to bare one side of my butt in invitation. "Very naughty. Want to spank me?"

"You'd like that, wouldn't you?" He smiled at me and I felt it like a punch in the gut. I actually sucked in a breath. How could he be terrifying and still make me want to get closer at the same time?

"Yes." I figured I might as well be honest. I was lust incarnate, after all. And he was something I'd never expected to encounter. My hunger stirred. He would feed me and feed me, able to last longer than any human male. Unless he destroyed me first.

Eli laughed and walked up to me. He planted the palm of one large hand on my butt cheek. "Then I'll have to find another way to punish you."

That sent a shiver of ice through my veins. There were far too many ways he could punish me for me to mistake the threat for a joke. "Wouldn't you rather spank me?" I asked. My voice dropped into a lower register.

"No." He stroked the soft skin of my butt, not lusting, just contemplating the options. His hand felt warm against my skin in contrast to the cold rain. "I think maybe I'd better bind you until I figure out what to do with you."

Oh, Hell. "If you're not sure what to do with me, I have lots of suggestions." I knew it was hopeless, but I had to try.

"I'm sure you do." He gave my bare ass an almost affectionate pat. Then Eli spoke in a language the world hadn't heard since before the time of the great flood, when all the earth's languages were one language and the Nephilim lived openly among humans. When he fell silent, I was bound.